At His Mercy

At His Mercy

A Forbidden Lovers Novel

SHELLY BELL

FOREVER

New York Boston

Copyright © 2017 by Shelly Bell
Cover design by Elizabeth Turner. Cover image © Shutterstock. Cover copyright © 2017 by Hachette Book Group, Inc.

Forever
Hachette Book Group
1290 Avenue of the Americas
New York, NY 10104
forever-romance.com
twitter.com/foreverromance

First Edition: June 2017

Forever is an imprint of Grand Central Publishing.
The Forever name and logo are trademarks of Hachette Book Group, Inc.

The publisher is not responsible for websites (or their content) that are not owned by the publisher.

The Hachette Speakers Bureau provides a wide range of authors for speaking events. To find out more, go to www.hachettespeakersbureau.com or call (866) 376-6591.

Library of Congress Cataloging-in-Publication Data
Names: Bell, Shelly, author.
Title: At his mercy / Shelly Bell.
Description: First edition. | New York : Forever, 2017. | Series: Forbidden
   lovers ; 1
Identifiers: LCCN 2017003017| ISBN 9781455595976 (softcover) | ISBN
   9781455595952 (ebook)
Subjects: | BISAC: FICTION / Romance / Adult. | FICTION / Romance / Suspense.
   | FICTION / Romance / Contemporary. | FICTION / Contemporary Women. |
   GSAFD: Romantic suspense fiction. | Erotic fiction.
Classification: LCC PS3602.E4552 A95 2017 | DDC 813/.6--dc23 LC record available at
lccn.loc.gov/2017003017

ISBNs: 978-1-4555-9597-6 (pbk.), 978-1-4555-9596-9 (ebook)

Printed in the United States of America

LSC-C

10 9 8 7 6 5 4 3 2

For Melanie
My sounding board, my buddy reader, my best friend.
You are my rock. Remember, no matter where I live,
I'm only a phone call away.

Acknowledgments

First, I have to thank my wonderful husband. We've weathered a lot of changes this year, and through it all, you've shown tremendous strength and patience. You've taught me that together, there's nothing we can't face. Thank you for continuing to encourage the voices in my head. I can't wait to spend the next sixty years with you.

To my parents, thank you for never reading my books but buying them anyway, and for being two of my greatest supporters. I hope you know how much I love you.

To Jessica Alvarez and the team at BookEnds, thank you for always going above and beyond for me. I couldn't have asked for better champions, and I'm so glad to have you all in my corner.

To Megha, who saw the potential in Tristan and Isabella, thank you for making my dreams come true. I'm thrilled to be working with such a gifted editor.

To all the bloggers, reviewers, and readers, thank you from the bottom of my heart for not only reading my books but for telling your friends to read them too. Word of mouth means everything to an author, and I'm grateful to have the most passionate readers. I couldn't do this without all your support and, more importantly, I wouldn't want to. I hope you love Tristan and Isabella as much as I do.

And last but never least, to Patty, Meghan, Heather, and Reem. Without you, there'd be no Tristan and Isabella. You're an amazing group of women, and I'm proud to call you my friends.

At His Mercy

PROLOGUE

18 months ago...

Consciousness came slowly, creeping into Isabella's mind like the first rays at dawn. A steady drum pounded in her temples, pain banding around her head as tight as a noose squeezing a neck. She tried to swallow, but her throat proved useless.

Still, she could breathe, which meant she wasn't dead.

At least not yet.

But death felt imminent, hanging over her like the blade of a guillotine.

Why couldn't she move?

Her eyes wouldn't open. No. They *couldn't* open, sealed shut by an unidentifiable glue. Her heart banged a staccato beat against her breastbone, panic surging.

There was something wrong.

Something she should remember...

"Shh, Izzy." A gentle hand patted the top of her head like her father used to do when she had a bad dream. "Don't cry. I'm here now."

She was crying?

Rather than soothe her, the voice, soft and sweet as a lullaby, sent her pulse racing into overdrive. It was as if she was stuck in that place between asleep and awake, unable to escape the violent nightmare that chased her. That voice was hauntingly familiar. At one time it had brought her such joy to hear it. Then it had brought only tears. Now, it brought something else...

Fear.

Memories of the last few weeks slammed into her.

She remembered.

She remembered everything...

Everything but how she had gotten here.

The breakup. The hundreds of calls and texts that had followed.

"Leave me alone," she said.

"I don't know how," he responded, his eyes filled with tears.

"Then pretend I died."

Words had power, didn't they? She'd known from the moment she threw those words out into the universe that they would come back to haunt her.

With every ounce of strength she had, she concentrated on getting her lids open. If she didn't do it soon, she might never get the chance again. She needed to look into the eyes of the boy she'd once loved.

The boy who decided it wasn't enough to pretend she had died.

She knew it in her bones.

He was planning on making it a reality.

Her eyes opened. The rays from the setting sun gleamed through the window, bathing her captor in light. He looked down at her with undeniable affection even as he held a butcher knife to her throat. "Hello, beautiful. I missed you while you were asleep." He leaned down and pressed his lips to hers, a long, chaste kiss that caused her stomach to revolt. "I thought maybe I gave you too much ketofol and you wouldn't wake up in time."

In time for what?

She tried to move, but it was as if her body was encased in concrete.

What had he done to her?

A whimper of fear escaped her throat.

He lifted her limp wrist. "I decided you were right. There's no way I'll ever be able to live without you. But I don't have to. I figured out a way we can be together forever."

The sun caught the blade of his knife as it arched through the dusty air.

A silent scream shrilled in her head.

Without control of her limbs or the power of voice, she couldn't escape the inevitable.

She was at his mercy.

Sharp pain exploded up her arm as her blood spilled down her wrist onto the pristine white sheets.

She didn't want to die.

But as the world spun around her and the sun began to set once more, she realized...

She didn't have a choice.

ONE

If there ever was an unassuming location for a sex party, the quaint Tudor-style house in front of her definitely fit the bill. For Pete's sake, there were children's bicycles on the neighbor's lawn.

Her cousin, Dreama, must have given her the wrong address.

Isabella Lawson rifled through her purse, cursing the starless night and wishing for the umpteenth time that someone would invent a purse that lit up when you opened it. After digging her way to the bottom, she finally located her cell.

A black screen.

Of course it was dead.

She leaned on her grandfather's old Buick and growled in frustration. Would anything go right?

Tonight's event was going to be her first sex party. And probably her last. But since Isabella couldn't call Dreama for the right address, her plans to screw were screwed.

"What are you wearing?" asked her cousin.

Startled, Isabella spun around and pressed a palm to her chest as if trying to keep her racing heart from flying out. Her cousin had scared the stuffing out of her. She glanced down at her outfit. "What I've worn all summer." Even she could admit that black stretch pants and a pink T-shirt with her family bakery's logo probably wasn't standard sex party wear.

Dreama blew a ring of smoke into the humid air, then took another puff of her cigarette. "That isn't what I meant. I'm wondering why the hell you're still wearing it."

Fanning away the smoke, Isabella fake coughed. "I came straight from work. I didn't have time to change. Not to mention, everything I own is in boxes." About to leave for her freshman year of college, she'd packed up the majority of her clothes. "And I wasn't about to ask Mom to borrow something of hers. She would've grilled me for information until I told her the truth." Isabella plucked the cigarette from her cousin's mouth, dropped it on the concrete, and ground it out with her shoe. "Would you have preferred if I'd told your aunt that you're taking me to my first sex party?"

Dreama shook her head, a little laugh escaping her lips. "That's all I need. Aunt Maria not only blaming me for corrupting her innocent daughter, but hauling my ass to church to confess my many sins." She jumped up onto the hood of Isabella's car and fished through her purse. "And I didn't bring you to a sex party. It's a play party."

Isabella raised a brow in both confusion and at the fact that her cousin had just added another dent to the car's collection. "There's a difference?"

Dangling a cigarette between her fingers and rolling her thumb over her lighter, Dreama smiled. "Yes. Intercourse isn't permitted at a play party."

"You didn't tell me that."

"Sure I did," Dreama said, bending to light her cigarette.

What was the point of being here then? She could've not had sex anywhere. The idea of coming to this thing was to experience BDSM in a relatively safe environment.

Isabella snatched the cigarette from her cousin and stomped on it. "No, I think I'd remember a detail like not getting laid at a sex party." If the party wound her up, how would she get any relief? She'd already packed away her vibrator.

"Play party," Dreama repeated, jumping off the hood of the car with a *pop*. "And don't worry. There are other ways of getting off than intercourse." Cracking up, she lewdly wiggled her fingers and stuck out her tongue.

Isabella's cheeks heated. "Oh."

Dreama placed a hand on her hip. "Maybe I shouldn't have brought you here. You're so innocent."

She ran her fingertip along the pink scar on her left forearm. She'd always thought innocence referred to the status of your virginity. How wrong she'd been. Innocence was a state of mind, and she'd lost hers the hard way. Her scars would always remind her of that. "I'm not innocent," she said quietly. "Not anymore."

As her cousin was one of the few who knew the truth about what had happened to Isabella last year, her eyes clouded over with sympathy. "No, I suppose you're not." She curled her hands around Isabella's shoulders, concern etched on her face. "Are you ready to go in and get a first-hand look, or would you rather go get a drink somewhere? I'm good either way."

"Isn't your Dom in there waiting for you?" Isabella asked.

Dreama's lips tilted up in a smile. "Master Jamie is inside, but he'll understand if I go get a drink with you. He knows you and I won't get to see each other for a while."

"I want to go inside," she said. And she did, despite her racing heart and her sweaty palms. "I need to do it. You know I do."

After surviving what she and her parents referred to as "the incident," Isabella found that she'd lost her ability to trust anyone, especially herself. As a result, instead of having gone away to college as planned, she'd allowed her parents to convince her to stay at home and work in their bakery full-time. Her life in limbo, she'd spent her days at the bakery and her nights either in therapy or at home, hiding away in her bedroom.

But everything changed the night she'd hung out at Dreama's and stumbled upon her huge collection of BDSM books.

After a long conversation with her cousin, Isabella realized she wanted to learn more about BDSM and borrowed a few of the books. Something about the lifestyle had resonated with her. Warmth permeated throughout her limbs at the idea of a man giving her structured rules to follow and at knowing there were established boundaries neither of them could cross. The sensation was so foreign, she almost didn't recognize it.

Until she realized it was peace.

The unsettling feelings she'd harbored since puberty didn't mean there was something wrong with her. Other people fantasized about being restrained and punished by a lover too. Of course, things like that weren't spoken about in her large Italian-Irish Catholic family. No, she was expected to do her duty for her husband with her legs spread and her eyes shut tight without complaint. Husbands weren't supposed to tie their wives to the bedpost and take them every way imaginable while she cried "no" and thrashed beneath him, all the while violently coming over and over.

She'd spent the following six months researching BDSM and discussing it with her therapist. At first, she hadn't understood how she could want to be dominated or why she craved a little pain with her pleasure. Shouldn't her past have turned her off to those yearnings?

For days, she'd walked around feeling both shame and guilt until she'd finally accepted that her sexual inclinations had little to do with what had happened to her. Yes, she was submissive. That didn't mean she was weak or asking to be a victim.

Now, with eight weeks of her local BDSM group's introductory class under her belt, she was ready to participate in her first real power exchange with an experienced Dominant. Dreama had assured her that she knew almost all of the Doms at the party, and with rules in place, Isabella would be perfectly safe.

In Isabella's opinion, giving up her power to a Dom tonight would help her reclaim control over her life. Tonight, she'd take back what she'd lost and become whole again. And damn it, if it went as she suspected it would, and she got off on being dominated, then she'd accept that her sexuality was different. But it was hers, and she'd own it.

Dreama released her hold on her. "Yes, I know all the reasons you need to do this, but once you get a taste, you may develop a particular palate. Life will become a lot more complicated."

Isabella shrugged. After tonight, her particular "palate" would have to wait four years for another taste. It wasn't as if she would have time for a Dom/sub relationship in college, even if she did manage to find a compatible partner in the Michigan Upper Peninsula's small college town of Edison. "I'm not worried, but thanks for the warning. I'll be sure to take that into consideration."

Scrutinizing her, Dreama pursed her lips. "Before we go in, we need to do something about your outfit."

Spoken like a true fashion maven. Dreama was wearing one of her own creations, a black bustier with metallic blue ribbons and an attached lace skirt. No one would ever guess from her clothes tonight that during business hours she was a buttoned-up, by-the-book parole officer.

But even with her cousin's skills, Isabella's outfit was hopeless.

Isabella pulled her shirt taut, showing off the logo for her family's bakery. "Unless you have something in your car, I think I'm stuck with what I'm wearing."

Dreama scanned her up and down, smiling. "We'll make it work. Slide your arms out of the sleeves." When Isabella did what she was told, Dreama folded and tucked the sleeves into the opening at her neck. "Now take off your pants."

She raised a brow. "When I thought about attending my first play party, somehow it wasn't *you* I pictured ordering me to remove my clothes." Giggling, she shimmied out of her black pants and twirled around wearing nothing but a shirt made into a dress and white cotton boy shorts. "What do you think?"

Her cousin whistled. "You look hot."

She laughed as she picked up her pants and tossed them into the backseat of her car before locking it. "I look like a stripper."

"You'll fit right in." Dreama winked and threw her arm around Isabella's shoulders, leading her to the front door. "Ready to play?"

Play. An innocuous word for such decadence. Was she ready to become part of it?

Smiling, she turned to her cousin. "Hell, yeah."

* * *

With his dungeon gear bag slung over his shoulder, Tristan Kelley sidestepped Yvette, the blonde sub headed his way, and made a beeline for the exit. There wasn't a sub here worth staying for, and while his dick hadn't seen much action lately, other than some lube and his palm, nothing had raised his interest tonight.

"Leaving already?" asked the amused voice from behind him.

Only a few feet from the door, he pivoted toward his best friend and business partner, Ryder. "I've got some stuff to do before the move upstate."

Debating whether he was making the right decision, he'd put off packing until the very last minute, but now that he had finalized his contract, there was no changing his mind.

"I call bullshit, Tristan. What's the real reason?"

He scrubbed a hand over the two-day-old stubble on his cheek. "I meet the same single women at every play party, and at one time or another, each has expressed an interest in becoming my permanent sub. Why can't I find someone who just wants a night or two of kinky fucking without expecting more?"

At twenty-eight years old, he wasn't looking for a long-term relationship, vanilla or otherwise. Every sub he'd played with this year had thought she'd be the one to tame him, but he'd done the whole commitment deal once with disastrous results. Because of his ex-wife, Morgan, he'd lost everything that had mattered to him. There was no way he would go down that road again with a woman.

"Don't look at me. I'm with you." Ryder grinned. "At least I don't have to worry about that with Maggie. Gotta love open marriages. We single men reap all the benefits while the poor married saps have to deal with all the day-to-day bullshit that goes into a relationship. Speaking of which, I'd be happy to tag team her with you. I'm sure she wouldn't mind."

Ryder had an even bigger aversion to commitment than he did, never fucking the same woman twice. Someday, Ryder would meet someone who would knock him on his ass, and when that happened, Tristan was going to make sure he had a front row seat.

Tristan shook his head. "No thanks. Not in the mood."

The ménage thing was sexy as hell, and he'd certainly participated in his fair share, but there wasn't a woman here who could make his dick stir from its slumber tonight.

Besides, it didn't matter to him that Maggie was in an open marriage. Maybe it was because of his past, but in his opinion, having sex with someone other than your spouse, even with their consent, was infidelity. But he didn't judge others, just as he didn't want someone else to judge him for his sexual preferences.

Ryder shrugged. "Suit yourself. She's waiting for me in the master bedroom."

"Thought you abided by the no-sex rules at your parties."

"It's my house. If I can't fuck here, where am I supposed to do it?" Ryder asked, his gaze glued to Yvette, who'd yet to become a notch on his bedpost. Leave it to his best friend to line up his next conquest while having a naked woman waiting for him in bed. Compared to Ryder, Tristan was a prude. "If you change your mind and stay, the other bedroom is open and available. Just like all the subs." He snagged a bottled water off the bar and winked at Yvette before returning his attention to Tristan.

"That's the problem. I just want someone for one night. Someone I'm not going to see again."

"You've certainly made that easier, considering you're moving this week."

"Not permanently. And I'll occasionally come back to the city. Lord knows I'm not going to find anyone in the life-style up there." Although with the women he'd met lately, he'd been thinking he might go vanilla for a year. It certainly couldn't be any less fulfilling.

"Maybe you should've thought about that before you agreed to the job," Ryder said, his brows knitted into a frown. "Hey, there are kinky people everywhere. And you did have your first real experience with BDSM there."

"Somehow, I think the chances of finding another Olivia in that one-horse town is slim to none." Olivia had been four years older than he was and the first to show him the ropes. Literally. "You sure you'll be okay without me?"

Ryder folded his arms across his chest. "Don't worry about leaving me to run everything. I've already got phone calls into my contacts about the expansion into the southwest."

Shit. He and Ryder had discussed that they needed testimonials for the long-term success of their products before they'd expand into other territories. "Tell me you're joking. We don't have the capital—" At Ryder's smirk, Tristan realized he'd been played. "You dick."

"Give me a little credit. I wouldn't make any major decisions without your consent." Ryder pounded him on the back hard enough to make his teeth chatter. "Have fun and don't do anything I wouldn't do."

Tristan punched him in the arm. "There isn't anything you wouldn't do."

"True that. Speaking of which, I'd better go meet Maggie before she starts without me." On a laugh, Ryder walked off with the swagger of a man who was about to get laid.

Meanwhile, Tristan had a date with his right hand.

As he inched his way through the crowd to the front door, Dreama, a sub he'd met but never played with, came in. She gave him a little smile, careful not to make eye contact, and forged a path toward the basement. She was a sweet girl, but there had never been any sparks between them, and she was now in a collared relationship.

Seeing the opportunity to sneak out before someone else stopped him, he stepped to the door.

And there she was.

Tristan's breath caught in his chest as if he'd been kicked in the ribs. She was a vision in pink, her long red hair flowing down her shoulders and pale skin that was just begging for him to mark. He could practically see his pink handprint on her ass and the way the flogger would make it appear as though her entire body blushed.

Along with several of the Doms in the room, his eyes tracked her as she entered the house with her gaze lowered, her blatant innocence calling to him . . . to all of them. She was new blood, a little lamb who had stumbled into a den of hungry wolves. It was only a matter of time before they'd be circling her, eager to get a taste.

He hesitated to leave, his curiosity roused by this angel in pink. Had she come with Dreama? Who the hell was she?

He hungered to harness that innocence for himself. To have her kneel at his feet in submission and to feel her silky skin against his rough palms. He stood rooted to his spot as she passed by him, leaving the scent of vanilla behind.

His whole body thrummed with anticipation, as if it was prepared for something momentous. The cock that had been hibernating all night suddenly blazed to life and began throbbing mercilessly against the front of his pants. He couldn't recall the last time he'd felt this way. *If* he'd ever felt this way. He'd been numb for so long, nothing exciting him beyond a momentary thrill from domination. Now it was as if every part of him was awake.

There was no reason to stay, and yet he couldn't make himself walk out the door. Not until he learned more about this mysterious beauty, and why the hell she affected him this way.

For a few minutes, he leaned against the wall and observed her. It was clear from the way she moved tentatively into the house that this wasn't her typical scene. She tugged at her hair, curling it around her finger, and repetitively pulled at the hem of her odd dress, seemingly uncomfortable in it. Hell, it was so short it barely covered her ass, but that wasn't unusual at a play party. In fact, she was still wearing more than half the women here.

Dreama stopped to put her arm around the mystery woman, whispering in her ear. She steered her over to the far side of the room, where a man in black leather waited with obvious eagerness.

Tristan crossed his arms and frowned. He didn't know the guy well, but he knew he was relatively new to the BDSM lifestyle. She should be with someone with more experienced, especially if his gut was correct and she was as innocent as she looked.

But it wasn't his business.

His redheaded angel shifted her weight from foot to foot as Dreama appeared to introduce the two of them before sauntering off and leaving her on her own. *I should go.*

By all accounts, she'd already been claimed for the night. There was no point in watching her scene with another man. Voyeurism wasn't his kink, especially when he craved to be the one doing the dominating.

His feet moved, only rather than taking him in the direction of the exit, he found himself standing just inches away from her, angling himself so that he appeared to be admiring the garish painting on the wall as he listened in on their conversation.

"I know Dreama meant well, but I have to be honest. I don't think I'm ready yet to play with someone who doesn't have any experience," the guy said, surprising Tristan with his accurate assessment.

At least now he didn't have to worry about her sceneing with someone who didn't know what he was doing. There were plenty of qualified Doms here tonight who would just love to get their hands on her.

His body tightened with tension. Why didn't that make him feel any better?

Time to go before he did something stupid...like volunteer.

"Oh. Sure. I understand," she responded, her voice as dulcet as he'd imagined.

Intending to leave, he took a step backward and began a pivot toward the door, when she crashed into his right side. So much for making a clean getaway. Not wanting to be rude, he flipped around to apologize and came face-to-face with her.

She stared up at him with clear green eyes. "I'm so sorry."

Her pale pink lips were swollen as if she'd just spent the last ten minutes with his cock between them. Jesus, were they naturally that plump? Her tongue darted out, moistening her bottom lip and leaving it glistening in an invitation to sample.

"No," he said, his voice sounding a bit grittier than usual, "I'm sorry." It was a lie. He couldn't have planned it better. He coughed to clear his throat before offering his hand. "I'm Tristan."

A cute little notch formed between her brows as she accepted, placing her palm against his. Her skin was just as soft as he'd imagined it would be.

"I'm . . ." She lowered her gaze and a beautiful blush crept down her cheeks, disappearing under her dress.

For a myriad of reasons, some people didn't want to give their real names at these parties. He wasn't sure why she was hesitant, but seeing that blush sent a jolt straight to his cock.

"Why don't I just call you Angel?"

"Angel?" she asked breathlessly, peeking up at him through her lush lashes and smiling. "I like that."

All thoughts of leaving the party fled. He couldn't go before he got a taste. She was positively edible, and he couldn't wait to sink his teeth into her.

He took a step closer to her, her hard nipples brushing against his chest. He dipped his head to her neck, inhaling. God, she made his mouth water. "You smell like vanilla."

"I'm a baker," she said, a tremor in her voice. Her hands went to his chest, fisting his shirt in her hands as if using him to keep herself upright. "I didn't have time to shower. Or change."

That explained why she was wearing only that surprisingly sexy makeshift dress. It was actually a shirt. "You smell delicious." He sucked the lobe of her ear into his mouth and nibbled. She tasted as sweet as cake, and if her pussy tasted half as delicious, he'd likely go into a diabetic coma by the time the night was over.

At her quiet moan, he whispered, "And your clothes are irrelevant. In five minutes, the only thing you'll be wearing is a smile. That is, if you consent."

Her breathing quickened. "If I say yes, what will I be consenting to, exactly?"

Images of her naked and bound flashed through his mind. There were so many dirty things he wanted to do to her, each one ending with her climaxing harder than she ever had before. And he was just the man to make that happen.

He cupped her heart-shaped face in his hands. "Paradise."

TWO

Isabella had never been so turned on. Her body was practically vibrating. She'd only been with Tony, and he'd been a boy. Tristan, on the other hand, was the definition of a man. He towered over her petite frame, and although he wasn't bulky, she could feel the hard contours of his chest under her hands. He reminded her of a lion with thick, dark blond hair framing his face and stubble lining his angular jaw. His gaze homed in on her as if she were his prey about to be devoured.

Physically, he was everything she fantasized about and more. In fact, she was fantasizing right now about plunging her fingers into his hair as he worked his mouth between her thighs. But it wasn't just his looks that had her panties growing wetter by the second.

It was as if she'd been waiting her whole life for this moment. That all the pain she'd suffered in the past had been worth it because it had led her here to this man. There was an energy between them that drew her to him like steel to a magnet, or in this case, submissive to a Dominant. She'd met several people who alleged they were Dominants, but this was the first time she hadn't needed to be told. This man exuded confidence and control. From the way his eyes seemed to demand her obedience to the way his lips tilted up in a slight grin as if he knew exactly how her body was responding to him.

A man like Tristan was exactly what she needed for tonight. Temporary and uncomplicated. If she'd been at a different point in her life, she could've given her heart along with her body. But she no longer had a whole heart to give. Hers was just barely beating. Maybe if she'd met him a few years from now after she'd graduated from college, tonight would have been a beautiful beginning rather than a brief moment in time when their paths had intersected before diverging once more.

Still, staring up at him as he cradled her face in his hands, she wasn't naive to think he felt the same connection. Not when he could have any woman in the room.

Hopefully, he wouldn't change his mind once he learned the truth. "I need a little more than your promise of paradise before I consent." She took a quick breath. "You should know...I'm new to this lifestyle."

Although his expression didn't falter, his fingers twitched against the skin of her neck. "When you say new...?"

"This is my first play party."

He removed his warm, gentle hands from her body.

A painful slash of disappointment cut through her. But what had she expected? Why would he be interested in her, someone dressed in a pink T-shirt and who smelled like a bakery when he could have someone like Dreama, a woman who wore her sexuality on her sleeve and dressed accordingly? She couldn't blame him for wanting someone more experienced.

As the fantasy of what might have been faded into blackness, she wondered why his rejection hurt so much.

With a fake smile, she gave him a polite nod and turned to go find Dreama. But before she made her first step, he grabbed her by the arm, yanking her to him so that his strong chest pressed against her back.

He licked up the length of her neck until he got to her ear. "I don't remember dismissing you, Angel. As soon as I saw you walk into the house, I knew that you hadn't done anything like this before. It doesn't bother me. I fucking love the idea of being your first."

She sucked in a breath. He'd noticed her when she'd arrived? A chill of excitement raced down her arms and across her chest.

"You want to know what I'm going to do to you if you consent to playing with me tonight?" His hot breath tickled the shell of her ear. "Anything I want." He bit down on her lobe, causing a slight sting before soothing it with his tongue. "And what I want is to turn that creamy white skin of yours pink as your T-shirt. Then, when you're wet and throbbing, and you're out of your mind with the need to come, I'll finger-fuck that pussy of yours until you see stars. How's that to start? Does it meet with your approval?"

Holy hell in a handbasket.

The image sent a flash of heat to her lower belly, rocking her off her axis and causing her to wobble, her knees suddenly weak as a newborn foal's. Between her thighs, the muscles clenched and rippled with what she swore was a mini orgasm. "Yes." She coughed, clearing the rasp of arousal that had formed in her throat. "I can honestly say I approve wholeheartedly."

His expression turned hungry as his eyes raked over her from head to toe. For a moment, she had the urge to flee just to see if he'd run after her. Pressing her hand to her chest, she shivered, the idea of it surprisingly arousing. What would he do to her when he caught her?

He didn't give her the chance to find out, snatching his black duffel bag off the floor before interlacing his fingers with hers and dragging her through the throngs of people.

She couldn't help but wonder what was in that bag of his that would turn her skin pink. "Where are you taking me?" she asked, her heart hammering wildly.

"Somewhere we can talk."

Talking was the last thing she wanted to do. Her body was hovering on the edge of the unknown, and ready to make that giant leap. "Couldn't we skip the talking?"

Tristan placed a hand on the base of her spine, directing her past the kitchen. Although the gesture probably meant nothing, it felt almost...territorial, as if he was staking his claim to her. "Safety first. This is your first time and you deserve the full experience. Besides, negotiating is part of the fun. Think of it as cerebral foreplay."

He was right. She knew nothing about him other than

his first name. To hand over her submission without at least having a conversation about safe words and limits would be foolish. But negotiation, fun? She could think of several other things she'd rather do with her mouth at that moment. "I practiced negotiating a scene in my BDSM training class. It was nothing like foreplay."

As they neared a staircase leading down to the basement, she caught sight of her cousin backed up against the wall, a man kissing her as if he were trying to steal the breath from her lungs, and his hand up her skirt, clearly touching her between her legs.

Isabella inhaled sharply, her abdominals clenching. She looked away, both equally turned on and uncomfortable at witnessing her cousin in such a public display of passion.

Tristan leaned down to speak into her ear, his warm breath heating her from the outside in. "Perhaps you weren't doing it with the right partner."

Rather than take her downstairs, he led her out a screen door onto the backyard patio. The night was silent but for the crickets' chirping, and once again, she was surprised that this kind of party occurred in middle-class suburbia. A tall wooden fence surrounded the yard, so that she could only see the roofs of the homes next door. She had to imagine that whoever owned this house would value his privacy.

She folded her arms across her chest, trying to ignore her makeshift dress riding up her legs. Of course, Tristan didn't miss it at all, his gaze dropping without apology to her bared thighs. "And I suppose you're the right partner? Awfully cocky, aren't you?"

He moved closer, invading what little space he'd permitted her, until she had to tilt her head back to look up at him. "I am and with good reason, but my being the right partner for you has nothing to do with my cockiness." Not a part of them touched, and yet she felt his heat on her skin like a brand. At some point, and she had no idea when, she'd dropped her arms to her sides, so that there was no barrier between them other than mere inches and a layer of clothing. His lips hovered over hers as a delicious scent she couldn't identify permeated from him, wrapping around her like a warm blanket on a winter's day. "I know you feel it too."

She swallowed hard. "Feel what?"

The air pulsed with excitement.

Arousal.

Danger.

She should run now, but the spell he'd woven held her in its grasp. The ease in which he dominated her equally thrilled and terrified her, her heart knocking against her breastbone and her panties dampening from his power over her. This is what she'd wanted. *What she'd craved.* And yet, she couldn't have prepared for it, the reality far more powerful than she could've ever imagined.

He glided a finger down her neck and across her collarbone, leaving a trail of goose bumps in its wake. "That energy buzzing through your body like a live current. You can't manufacture that, Angel." He dragged his finger lower, his eyes on hers as it descended between her breasts, and she held her breath, waiting to see where it would go next. "That's what makes me the right partner."

He took a step back, depriving her of his touch.

Bastard.

Like dangling bait on a hook, he'd given her a brief taste only to snatch it away before she could sink her teeth into it.

"So what happens now?" she asked, eager to feel his hands on her again.

A smile tugged at his lips. The man knew damned well what he was doing to her. "First thing's first. I need to ensure that you're capable of giving consent. You're clearly over the age of consent or your cousin wouldn't have brought you here."

Just barely, and she was clearly the youngest at this party. Searching his face for markers of his age, she found no signs of wrinkles hiding behind the light brown scruff framing his face or gray hair in that lion's mane of his. If she had to guess, she'd wager he was in his late twenties to early thirties. Would he change his mind if he knew she was only nineteen?

"How do you know I'm over the age of consent?" she asked.

"Because Dreama is an active part of the local BDSM scene and knows we take the rules about 'safe, sane, consensual' very seriously. If she knowingly broke one of those rules and brought you even though you were unable to give consent, she wouldn't be welcome back to any of the local organized play parties until she went through a thorough retraining and made amends to the community. And even then she might never be accepted."

That sounded terrible. While her cousin had a tendency to flit from one obsession to the next, it seemed she had committed herself completely to the BDSM lifestyle. Isabella would hate to ruin it for her. "So if someone makes a mistake, they're ostracized from the community forever?"

"No," he said, shaking his head. "Plenty of subs and Doms make mistakes. Let's say you're my sub, and contrary to my demand that you not wear any panties when I take you out to dinner, I discover a satin barrier when I go to finger you under the table. Not only would you lose out on an orgasm, I'd deny you one for at least twenty-four hours."

"I could go twenty-four hours without an..." *Ugh*, she couldn't help blushing as she said the word. "...orgasm. I do it all the time."

He snaked his arm around her waist and yanked her to him, causing her to gasp in surprise. "But not around me you haven't." With one hand at the small of her back and the other cradling the back of her head, he held her hostage in his grasp, allowing her to feel every hard inch of him. As if the evidence pressing against her lower abdomen wasn't enough, his voice grew husky, thick with his desire for her. "Imagine having a vibrator inside of you for hours. The remote control in my possession so that I could bring you to the brink of climax before turning down the setting and denying you that pleasure. Imagine my hands all over your body, my tongue on your nipples, on your clit. Your pussy pulses with need, only I refuse to allow you release. Then I remove the vibrator and replace it with my cock, sliding deep and using your body to give *me* the sweet release you so desperately crave."

He paused, the vivid imagery he'd been painting just hanging there, frozen in animation.

"And then what?" she asked breathlessly.

Releasing his grasp on her, he shrugged. "Then I'd go to sleep."

Her mouth fell open. "That's...that's..."

"Punishment." His victorious smile told her all she needed to know. He'd played her, showing her firsthand what it would be like to be punished by him.

"I was thinking diabolical."

He laughed. "That's BDSM. At least, my version of it. It's called edging. And it's effective." His eyes narrowed at her. "Judging by the enlargement of your pupils, I'd say it would work extremely well on you."

Yeah, well, too bad she'd never get the chance to find out. "What else do you do for punishment?"

"I don't need all the bells and whistles that some of my friends in the lifestyle prefer. It's much more intimate to use the palm of my hand on your bare skin than a flogger or paddle." He skated both hands down her spine, drawing her close. "But there's a time and place for it all, and tonight, I'm itching to make that creamy skin of yours as pink as your T-shirt. That is, if you consent."

"Yes, I consent," she said quietly, heat gathering in her core as his fingers glided over her panty-clad behind. She didn't think she could take more of his teasing. Is this what it would be like to be his? If so, she wasn't sure she could handle a man like Tristan for more than one night.

"It's your first play party. Does that mean you've never been flogged?" he asked.

"I took the intro class given by Metro Leather and tried

out a bunch of impact toys." She shuddered. "Well, not the cane or a single tail. I'm not that much of a masochist."

His eyebrows raised in question. "But you are one?"

She lifted a shoulder. "I don't think so, but I don't mind a little pain."

Leaving one hand on her butt, he buried the other in her hair and twisted it around his fingers. "So if I pull you hair like this...?" In contrast to his previous soft, teasing caresses, he yanked her hair so hard, it wrenched her head back and brought tears to her eyes. "Yes or no, Angel."

"Yes," she said automatically, surprising herself with the swiftness of her answer and the way it sent delicious tingles throughout her core.

"And if I bite you like this..." He bent his head and sunk his teeth into her neck, lighting up every nerve in her body from that small bite of pain.

Her eyes fluttered shut, hot bliss flowing through her. "Oh, yes."

"If I pinch you like this..." The hand on her butt snaked its way around her torso, coming to her breast. Tristan squeezed her nipple between his fingers, pressing harder and harder until she groaned and tried to escape it, forgetting about his hold on her hair until the pain on her scalp increased.

"*Mm*." She'd momentarily lost the ability to speak, too many sensations bombarding her at once. The tingles between her legs morphed into an almost unbearable throbbing.

"We need to talk more about consent. Can I touch your pussy?"

At this point, she'd die if he didn't. She tried to nod, but his hand in her hair wouldn't allow for it. "Yes," she said on a whimper.

Her sore nipple pulsed as he let go of it and cupped her...pussy over her panties. He ground his palm against her, his fingers easily sliding back and forth between her covered labia, the exquisite pressure not enough to make her come. She tried to shift closer, to get more friction on her clitoris, but his hold made it impossible. He was torturing her again, playing a game in which she didn't know the rules.

Removing his hand from between her legs, he made a sound low in his chest that sounded like a growl. She whimpered in protest, growing tired of his teasing, and her eyes flew open just in time to witness him bring his fingers to his nose and deeply inhale before blatantly licking her arousal off them.

So.

Damn.

Hot.

"You're so responsive," he said as if it was the best thing ever. "And you're fun to torment." He chuckled at her frown, way too happy about her suffering. "What about bondage? Do you like being restrained? Bound by rope?"

Her chest constricted, black dots swimming in her vision. Suddenly, she was back there with Tony, frozen in her body and unable to scream for help while he carved into her wrists. She'd been helpless, her life force bleeding out of her, as the sun set and plunged the cabin into black. Her only companion had been the boy who, after cutting her, had slit his own wrists and then curled up beside her like a lover, waiting for death to take them both.

She sucked in a harsh breath and forced the nightmares to retreat back into the shadows.

No, she wouldn't allow the past to ruin this for her.

Tristan gently cupped her chin, concern in his eyes. He positioned his thumb over the side of her neck. "Angel. Are you okay?"

"Yes, I'm okay." Because tonight was different. She had the power to say no. "But, restraints are a hard limit for me."

His inquiring gaze burned straight through her. "Your pulse is racing. It's more than a hard limit for you," he said softly. "Something happened."

"Yes, but I don't want to talk about it. It's in the past."

"It may be in your past, but I don't want to do anything that would cause you to panic. If I grab your wrists like this, will it trigger you?" He gently pinned her back against the brick of the home and grabbed her wrists, lifting them above her head.

She waited for the panic to set in, but with Tristan's crisp scent invading her senses and the care in which he handled her, the only thing she felt was aroused. Again. "No, I don't think so. I like it."

"Good to know." Heat flashed in his eyes as if he was planning how to use it to his advantage, and then his expression turned serious. "Have you had alcohol or done any drugs tonight?"

Would he believe that she'd never drunk or tried drugs? "No. I don't do either."

He smiled until his gaze fell upon her wrists. She tried to yank them back, but it was too late. The damage was done. "The scars on your wrists—"

"I don't want to talk about it." She hated having people make assumptions about the scars, but she also didn't feel the need to broadcast that someone else had tried to kill her. "You don't have to worry. I'm not suicidal."

She waited for him to change his mind. To turn around and walk away. Or worse, to press the matter.

His thumb stroked the pink scars. "You said you came from work. Have you eaten?"

She blinked at the change in topic and looked at the door to the house. That was it? He wasn't going to push for the details on how she'd gotten those scars? "I ate a sandwich on the way over. Why?"

"Just want to make sure you don't crash and pass out on me."

"I don't faint."

His grip on her tightened, every part of him pressing against every part of her. "That tells me you've never been properly fucked before."

As if proving him right, she wobbled, her legs a bit unsteady. Sweat trickled between her breasts. "Because I haven't fainted? Who the hell faints from sex?"

"Not sex. No one faints from sex." He relinquished his hold on one of her wrists and swept his thumb across her bottom lip. "I said properly fucked. Have you ever been properly fucked, Angel?" he asked, his voice like a caress she felt all over her body. "Has any man ever made you so crazy you thought you'd die if you didn't get his cock inside of you? If you couldn't feel his fingers digging into your thighs as he spread you open and devoured you whole? Have you ever come over and over, so hard and so many times you couldn't be sure where one ended and the other began?" His thumb plunged into her mouth, sliding over her tongue, before retreating. *"Not. Properly. Fucked."*

Her heart pounded in time with the beat between her legs. No, she'd never been properly fucked. She'd never been *fucked* at all. That was part of the reason she was here. Of course, Dreama had smashed that fantasy into a hundred jagged pieces when she'd informed her earlier that penetrative sex wasn't allowed.

She coughed to clear the arousal that clogged her throat and glanced at the door again. "Well, I ate, so don't worry, I won't faint."

He cupped her chin and forced her to look at him. "The fact that you won't look me in the eyes tells me you're hiding something. Did you really have a sandwich for dinner?"

"I did." *Sort of.* "It was a salted caramel cookie sandwich stuffed with vanilla frosting."

He didn't smile, but she could tell he wanted to, the corners of his mouth twitching and the skin around his eyes crinkling. "If I were your Dom, there would be consequences for lying...but that's not what tonight is about. This is a play party after all." He took a giant step back from her and held out his hand. "Are you ready to play?"

THREE

Tristan wanted to devour his Angel whole.

With her delicate hand in his, he led her down the stairs to the basement dungeon. Ryder had designed it for these play parties, but rarely used it. His friend enjoyed meaningless kinky sex, but didn't get into the formalities of it.

Not like Tristan did.

The negotiation with Angel had been the hottest of his life. She'd had no idea how hard she'd made him, her quiet little sighs and the blushes from his dirty talk as intoxicating as a drug. Inexperience radiated off her.

And fuck if that didn't make him want to dirty her up.

Never had he experienced such overwhelming lust. Without even knowing it, this woman had managed to challenge his tightly reined control, her innocence like waving a red flag at a bull. He wanted to strip her bare, first of her clothing and then of her defenses. He wanted to show her pleasures beyond her wildest dreams and lick her senseless until she shouted his name as she climaxed on his tongue, knowing she'd taste as sweet as she smelled.

If it weren't for that damned rule against penetrative sex, he'd teach her exactly what it was like to be *properly fucked*.

But their timing couldn't be worse.

Tomorrow, he'd leave for Edison, and he had no definite plans for returning to the city in the near future.

That meant he had only one night with her.

He'd definitely make it a night she'd never forget.

For a moment earlier, he'd almost considered calling off the negotiation, troubled by the scars on her wrists. They were classic marks of an attempted suicide with the scars faded to a dull pink, telling him the injury hadn't been recent. It wasn't unheard of for people to find solace in BDSM after enduring a mental illness like depression. While there would always be some like Ryder who indulged in bondage and the occasional spanking, some, like Tristan, practiced it for the emotional release. Sure, like Ryder, he got off on raw, dirty, and uninhibited fucking, but for him, it was so much more. The power exchange eased his tension and made him whole, completing a puzzle with a piece he hadn't known was missing. Perhaps it was the same for Angel. He only hoped that whatever had haunted her in the past had been laid to rest, because now that he knew she was out there, he couldn't imagine living in a world where she didn't exist.

He pulled Angel toward a small cove to the right of the staircase and tucked her against his chest, resting his chin on top of her head and facing her toward the room. The erotic scents of leather and sandalwood mixed with her vanilla one to create an aphrodisiac that went straight to his cock. With his arms encircling her waist, he tried to see the room through her eyes, as if he were experiencing it all for the first time.

And in a way he was, because he'd never experienced this with *her*.

Sex had always been an enjoyable act, but the rush he got from dominating his partner elevated it to another level—like comparing a spring shower to a hurricane. He had a feeling that dominating Angel would make those hurricanes seem like plain old thunderstorms.

She'd told him she'd attended the training workshops, so he'd wager she was familiar with most of the room's implements. Ryder had bought a few basic pieces from a local artist who'd hand carved the spanking benches, bondage tables, and Saint Andrew's crosses herself. No one outside of the lifestyle would ever guess that the famous woman who painted bucolic scenes of farmhouses and horses had a kinky side.

Light chatter mixed with intermittent soft cries and moans of those in ecstasy sent sparks racing down his spine. Any other time, he would've already had a submissive under his whip, but for some reason, he hesitated with Angel. While he definitely had an exhibitionist streak, a huge part of him wanted to shield her from the others' eyes. He could tell himself it was to protect her, this being her first real experience with BDSM.

But he'd be lying.

With several scenes of light bondage and impact play occurring in the room, Isabella turned her head toward the submissive lying spread eagle on a table, her arms and legs shackled by chains, whose Dom dripped glossy white candle wax over her breasts. Angel licked her lips, as if she was attempting to taste the passion and pain from the air. At the crack of a paddle on bare flesh, she jerked back into him, emitting a small gasp, her body trembling.

Screw it. She obviously couldn't handle public play. He'd take her upstairs and they'd spend the rest of the evening getting to know one another. "Are you sure you want to do a scene tonight? If you're not ready—"

"I'm ready. I want this." She covered his hands with hers. "With you. I know as the submissive, I don't have the right to ask, but I was wondering if you'd... flog me."

He slowly rotated her around and was shocked by her flushed cheeks and saucer-sized pupils.

She wasn't frightened.

She was *aroused*.

His cock thickened in response. "You always have the right to ask for what you want, and don't let anyone tell you otherwise," he said. "Your Dom won't always agree, but I have no objections to using my flogger to turn that gorgeous pale skin of yours pink. In fact, I've been thinking about nothing else since you stumbled through that door."

Right now, he was thinking of doing a lot more to that body of hers. Things involving his tongue, lips, hands, teeth, and cock between her sweet thighs. But he'd start with a flogging if that's what she desired.

Planting a possessive palm on her lower back, he directed her safely around the active scenes to the back of the room, where he dropped his bag on the floor in front of an available Saint Andrew's cross. Normally, for a flogging, he'd restrain a submissive to the X-shaped piece, but after observing her reaction to the suggestion of bondage, he'd refrain from it tonight. Rubbing the ends of her silky hair between his fingers, he stood in front of her to block out everything and everyone else. His heart pounded furiously. Jesus, he was actually nervous. When was the last time that had happened?

"Unless you have a safe word you'd prefer to use, I like the traffic light method," he said. "'Red' stops the scene immediately, 'yellow' is a warning for me to proceed with caution, and 'green' means good to go." He collared her throat with his hand, feeling her pulse race underneath his fingertips. "What color are you at, Angel?"

She glanced at the cross, then smiled at him. "I'm one hundred percent green, Tristan."

Leaning toward her, he picked an errant piece of hair off her cheek and tucked it behind her ear. "I'm going to start by taking off your clothes, Angel." He buried his nose in her hair, whispering in her ear. "If you want, you can keep your panties and bra on."

She slowly lifted her arms to give him the ability to remove her makeshift dress. "I'm not shy."

Needing to see . . . to touch . . . to savor what she hid underneath her clothes, he put his impatient hands on her hips and bunched the thin cotton in his hands before quickly whipping the shirt over her head, leaving her naked except for her white boy shorts and bra. No satin or lace for his Angel.

Never had simple cotton been so seductive.

On high perfect breasts, her nipples puckered from exposure to the air, tightening into hard buds.

The rest of her body was just as perfect. Toned and curvy, with creamy skin and enough padding that he wouldn't have to worry about cutting himself on sharp hip bones, she nervously nibbled on her bottom lip as she stood before him like a woman who had no idea she was actually a goddess.

It was time to rectify that.

The moment his palms made contact with the softness of her freckled shoulders, the room's temperature shot up ten degrees. She sucked in a short breath just as he exhaled one, the electricity between them as charged as lightning. There wasn't enough time to explore her the way he wanted to, but he would do his best with the time he did have. Like savoring the unwrapping of a present, he slipped his thumbs underneath her bra straps and peeled them down over the silky flesh of her biceps. Despite her earlier bravado, she trembled as he unhooked the bra and removed the fabric from her chest.

"Fuck, you're beautiful, Angel." She was even more beautiful than he could have imagined, her cotton candy nipples capping small mounds of freckled flesh. His mouth actually watered at the thought of getting his lips around them.

Her lids lowered as he swept his fingers down her neck...her sternum...her soft belly, watching the entire way as he made his descent. Reaching the band of her panties, he stopped, giving her a moment to change her mind. At her nod of consent, he slid two fingers over the middle of the damp cotton, eliciting a hum from her. "Beautiful and wet."

He crouched in front of her and dragged her panties

down her legs, revealing the tight curls between her thighs. Her spicy scent intoxicated him, increasing the hunger he felt for her tenfold and threatening his control. *Later.* Later, he'd get his mouth on her, but now, as her Dom, he had a job to do.

Standing, he bunched the panties in his hand and placed them in the pocket of his jeans. Spinning her around, he pressed her back to his front and slid a finger between the lips of her pussy, groaning as he accumulated her arousal and swirled it around her clit. "You're on fire. You must like what you see in this room. What turns you on the most?"

She rested her head against his chest, his fingers thrumming her clitoris. "You, Tristan."

Reluctantly, he removed his hand. "Likewise, Angel." He slid an arm around her waist and brought her closer to the Saint Andrew's cross. "Let's see if you feel the same way after your flogging."

Her green eyes went glassy, almost as though she were drugged. If he didn't know better, he'd think she was already slipping into subspace, the altered state of consciousness where a submissive fully surrendered to her Dominant. But to do so before they even began the scene would be incredibly rare. *Rare, but not impossible.* The idea that she trusted him so completely gave him a high he'd never felt, like a million bees were buzzing through his veins.

He wanted to mark her. Brand her. Make her feel his presence on her skin for days.

"Spread your legs wide and get as close as you can to the cross," he ordered, his voice low and commanding. When she complied, he grabbed her wrists and raised her arms over her head. "Hold on to both sides of the frame, and don't let go or I'll stop." Normally he'd strap her down, but they'd have to improvise because of her bondage hard limit. "What's your safe word?" he asked, reminding her that she also had the power to stop the scene.

"Red."

He brushed his knuckles over her cheek. "Use it if you need it." On those words, he moved away, positioning himself a few feet away from her back. She peered over her shoulder as he rifled through his equipment bag and pulled out two of his favorite floggers. "I'll start light, Angel. Face front and keep still."

He didn't keep her waiting long.

Choosing his softest deerskin flogger, he struck, the tails hitting the rounded flesh of her right butt cheek in a dull thud. Immediately, he fell into a steady rhythm, working the strikes around her body in a circular motion from her thighs to her upper back.

Like a massage, he used the flogger to warm up her skin and lull her into a relaxed state. As the minutes passed, her shoulders dropped, indicating he'd been successful. "What color are you at, Angel?" he asked, checking in with her.

"Green," she said automatically. "Is that it?"

He chuckled. "I told you I was going to start light. Now that you're warmed up, I'm going to switch floggers."

Picking up the leather one with the thin falls, he got into position behind her and rotated his wrist. His cock twitched in response to the resounding crack of the leather hitting her skin and thickened as the pink evidence of his mark appeared. Showing her no mercy, his stinging strikes forced her body forward, her hard nipples brushing the wood of the cross. In no time at all, her entire backside turned a beautiful, fiery red. Just from flogging her, he flew into a Dom space like he'd never experienced before, her submission like a drug coursing through his veins.

She moaned, her fingers tightening on the wood, and her entire body shook with tension. "Tristan, I need..."

He dropped his flogger to the floor as he rushed to her side. "What do you need? Do you need to stop?" he asked, stroking his hand through her hair.

Her dark pupils engulfed her green irises. "I need to...come." With a hand on her shoulder and another one on her hip, he slowly turned her toward him, the spicy scent of her arousal as strong as if he were nose deep inside of her. She slid her fingers into the hair at the base of his neck. "Touch me. I'm burning up inside."

He ached equally as bad, his cock currently trying to punch its way out of his jeans and make its way inside her slick heat. A possessiveness he'd never known bubbled up inside of him. He could use his fingers or his tongue or even the handle of his flogger to get her off. But he wouldn't. Not in front of an audience. No one else would watch her come apart. Her orgasms were for him alone to witness.

"Me too, Angel." He pulled her to his chest and tucked her head under his chin, holding her naked body tight against his clothed one so that she could feel his torment. "I've never wanted to fuck anyone more in my life."

"Do you always follow the rules?" she asked, her words muffled by his shirt.

Yes. Rules had kept him sane since his freshman year at college.

And yet where had those rules gotten him?

Divorced by his early twenties. Almost penniless. His credit destroyed to the point he couldn't even get approval from the bank for a conventional business loan unless he made a steady salary for more than six months.

What was the worst that could happen if, for one night, he threw caution to the wind and did what he wanted rather than what was expected?

"Upstairs. There's a bedroom." He tipped up her chin, feeling a bit like the Big Bad Wolf seducing Little Red. "Feel like breaking the rules with me tonight?"

FOUR

Leading her upstairs from the dungeon, Tristan replayed the memory of the sweetest word in the English language falling from Angel's lips.

Yes.

For one night only, they'd break all the rules.

He'd never experienced such a perfect connection with any submissive before. It was as if she were made for him. He wanted to get under her skin and brand his essence into her so that every other man would know he'd staked his claim to her. Wanted her to picture his face every time she closed her eyes at night. Wanted her to imagine her fingers were his cock every time she masturbated. Wanted his name on her lips every time she climaxed.

He wanted to become her Master.

Own her body and soul.

And that thought terrified the shit out of him, because the timing couldn't be worse. He had nothing more than dominance and a few orgasms to give her. She was so damned innocent, and he no longer remembered what it was like to believe in permanence. If she was the forbidden apple in the Garden of Eden, he was the snake. But he was too selfish to walk away. He wouldn't give up the opportunity to slide inside her perfect heat and feel her clench in abandon around him.

Ignoring the puzzled looks of the others, he pushed open the door to Ryder's extra bedroom and yanked her inside before slamming the door. Using the switch, he dimmed the lighting.

There wasn't a spot on Angel's body that he didn't want to see, touch, and taste. Fucking her in the dark would deprive him of what he craved, and deprivation was the last thing on the menu. Tonight was all about indulgence.

His hunger for her growing stronger by the second, he stalked toward her, loving the way her eyes widened and her chest rapidly rose and fell. He slammed her back against the door, his mouth coming down on hers with brutal intensity. She tasted just as she smelled—like a vanilla cupcake with buttercream frosting. He'd never smell vanilla again without his dick getting hard. His tongue met hers in an erotic dance of domination and submission in which he led and she followed. He was starving for her.

Little gasps and moans flew from her lips, her body growing soft and compliant under him. He twisted the lock on the door and palmed her thighs, lifting her off the ground to take her to the bed. She wrapped her legs around his waist as he carried her to the bed and laid her down, his body falling on hers.

Checking in, he nipped her ear and whispered, "What color?"

"Green." Her tongue darted out as if searching for his. "Now fuck me," she demanded, a beautiful blush staining her cheeks and neck. No matter how confident she purported herself to be, her innocence cut through her facade.

Holding back a laugh, he smiled against her cheek. Even though she was trying to top from the bottom, he loved her eagerness. Bucking up her hips, she attempted to grind against him, no doubt to get pressure on that swollen clit of hers. "So what does a girl have to do to get you to properly fuck her?"

Unconsciously, she was testing his dominance and engaging him in a power struggle. The submissive inside her required a firm hand, and it was just her luck that he had one.

"Who's in charge here?" he asked, dropping the timbre of his voice in censure.

She lowered her lashes. "You are."

"Exactly. I'll fuck you when I'm ready." His cock was demanding entry into her heat, but he wanted to savor the short time he had with her. He slid down her body, settling between her thighs and going up on his knees. "Which I'm not." Those breasts of hers were begging to be marked first.

He lowered his head to her breast and sucked a nipple into his mouth, enjoying the shiver that wracked her body. He wanted to give her something she'd never forget. Teach her more about the pleasure that could be found in pain. He released her nipple and gently bit the creamy flesh of her breast.

"Ow!" she cried. "You bit me."

"Nothing gets by you." She probably wasn't aware of it, but when he'd bit down, she'd arched her body up toward him, rather than trying to retreat. The way she'd responded to the flogging had all the indications that she was a bit of a masochist. He soothed the bruising skin with his tongue, laving it with careful attention.

He brushed his thumb over her nipple, loving those breathless little gasps she made with every pass. "Don't fight the pain. Surrender to it. Every time you change your clothes for the next few days, you'll see these bruises and think of me."

Her tongue darted out, moistening her lips until they glistened. She reached up and laid her hand on his cheek. "Like I'd ever forget you."

Fuck, she undid him.

He kissed her palm, then returned to his mission. Over and over, he bit and sucked the flesh of her breasts, leaving behind bruises as tiny souvenirs. Her breathing accelerated as she writhed beneath him. Seeing his marks on her sent a sense of satisfaction through him that he hadn't felt in years, making his balls ache with the need for release.

But still he wasn't ready, the driving desire to taste her pussy outweighing his own need to come.

He slid down her torso until he was up close and personal with the red curls between her legs. His fingers combed through them, becoming sticky with her arousal, and his eyes almost rolled back into his head. She was drenched, wetness coating the top of her inner thighs. Using two of his fingers, he separated her labia, exposing her pink folds and the swollen bundle of nerves at the apex of her pussy.

Fucking gorgeous.

"Hold on, Angel." Driven by his insane hunger for her, he bathed his tongue inside of her, lapping up her sweetness.

Her thighs tightened around his ears as her hands plunged into his hair, her fingers digging into his scalp. "Oh my God. That's..." The rest of her words were cut off by her moan.

If he didn't know better, he'd almost think no one had ever done this to her before. Either way, he'd leave her with a memory she'd never forget. Working her clit with the flat of his tongue, he slowly inserted a finger. Holy shit, she was tight, her walls gripping him like a hot, wet glove. Sweat beaded on his forehead and his cock throbbed, his restraint nearing its breaking point. Pressing down on her belly with one hand, he slipped a second digit into her soaked channel and crooked them, finding the sensitive spot that would light her up from the inside and rubbing.

Her legs trembled as her pussy clenched around his fingers. "What are you doing to me?" she asked, her head whipping back and forth on the pillow. On a long, keening cry, she climaxed, her body growing rigid as her delicious pussy clenched and released, over and over again, and her ecstasy spilled around his fingers. He eagerly drank her up like a man who'd been lost in the desert, the spice of her orgasm bursting on his tongue. When her body softened and her legs collapsed on the mattress, he withdrew his fingers and lifted his head.

There were so many things he wanted to do to the body laid out before him, but he couldn't wait another moment without sinking into her. He stripped off his shirt and jumped from the bed, taking off his boxer-briefs along with his pants and retrieving a condom from his wallet. It was his only one, but he had no doubt his friend stored plenty more, as well as other sexual aids, in the nightstand beside the bed.

Sprawled out on the bed, with her red hair fanned out on the pillow and her legs slightly spread, Angel glowed in satisfaction. She watched him through hooded eyes.

He rolled the latex down his length and climbed onto the mattress, seizing her by the ankles with the intention of flipping her over and taking her from behind, as was his usual way when his submissive wasn't restrained. But something stopped him, a silent voice that whispered she deserved more—and so did he.

"Eyes on mine, Angel," he demanded as he moved between her thighs and notched his cock to her opening. "You close them and I stop." He inched his way in slowly, letting her grow accustomed to his size. "And trust me, you do not want me to stop." Her lids began to shut, but at his threat, they flew open. Dominance wasn't about whips and chains or fancy sex toys; it was about assertion of power. Angel had tried her hardest to test it, possibly to even usurp it, but right now, with her soft body underneath his, she yielded to him completely.

Fully seating himself inside her without any resistance, he realized he'd aptly named her Angel because he had truly found heaven in her pussy. Heat traveled from the tip of his cock to his balls as he slid his length back and forth, pumping shallowly. "Wrap those gorgeous legs around my waist and hold on, Angel. I'm about to take you on the ride of your life."

She clung to him as if he were her life raft, her thighs squeezing his hips as she planted the heels of her dainty feet above his tailbone, and her fingertips gripping his shoulder blades. She surrounded him, every part of her touching him, inside and out. He wanted to bury himself deep and take her hard, slam against her over and over again until they both exploded and collapsed in a sweaty heap of tangled limbs. Instead, he fought against his urges, slowly and steadily rocking into her as if they had all the time in the world.

In between her gasps caused by his pelvic bone brushing against her clitoris, Angel's brows crinkled in confusion. "I thought you were going to take me on a ride."

"I am," he said, continuing to fuck her at a leisurely pace that would drive them both out of their minds. "Fast and hard will get us both off, but where's the fun in that? Some rides are meant to be savored." He wasn't in the mood for a quick fuck. Not with her. He kissed her lips with tenderness, mirroring their lovemaking. "Submit to me, Angel, and let go."

She nodded, her lashes fluttering as she fought to keep her eyes open, and her nails digging into the skin of his back. Little by little, he was stoking the fire, letting the pressure build, and careful not to let it burn out of control.

When her gaze skittered away, he forced his hips to stop moving, an action much harder on him than her. But she'd broken his demand to look into his eyes. As her Dom, it was his role to set and enforce the rules or she'd never submit to him. Bracing his weight on one arm, he grabbed her chin and coaxed her eyes back to his. "It's not supposed to be easy. Nothing worthwhile ever is. But the reward..." He swiveled his pelvis and drove his needy cock inside her. "The reward will be worth it."

He took her hands in his, lacing their fingers, and brought them above her head. They stared into one another's eyes as he moved inside her, their bodies intertwined, turning two into one. Seduced by the unguarded sensuality reflected in her emerald irises, he lost himself in her innocence.

It was as if she was an endless well and he was falling into her.

He'd gladly drown.

Her moans floated in the air like a symphony in a room filled with rock music, unique and lovely. Her inner walls tightened around him and her legs trembled.

"Tristan?" she half asked, half cried, her limbs tensing.

"Fall, Angel," he whispered. "I promise to catch you."

She repeated his name, but this time, she shouted it. Moans spilled from her lips and tears slid from her eyes as her pussy clenched and released around him, over and over. Through it all, his little submissive's eyes never left his. Not once.

It was too much for him. As much as he wanted to remain buried inside her for hours, he'd reached his limit.

Electric sparks skated down his spine and wrapped around his balls. Heat blasted through him, tearing away his control. He came and came hard, harder than he'd ever come before. And still he couldn't stop himself from slowly pumping himself into her, not nearly ready to leave the oasis of Angel's body. Not yet. Maybe not ever.

But as her Dom for the night, he knew it was time to attend to her needs. A slight gasp escaped her as he gripped the condom and carefully removed himself from her slick heat.

"Stay put," he whispered, planting a chaste kiss on her forehead. She didn't move, sleepiness evident in her half-lidded eyes. He disposed of the condom, then quickly collected a wet washcloth and a tube of arnica cream from the adjoining bathroom. When he returned to her not a minute later, he wasn't a bit surprised to find her already dozing.

For her being a newbie to BDSM, he'd worked her over pretty hard. He probably should've taken it easier on her tonight, but he didn't regret his decision to show her what it could be like between them. In the years since he'd lost everything, he'd become convinced that a true connection between a Dom and sub was a fictional tale better suited for an erotic romance story. But Angel had him reconsidering.

Her eyes fluttered as he gently cleaned between her legs. "What are you doing?" she asked groggily.

He smiled at her. "Aftercare."

She closed her eyes again and sighed. "It's nice. Thank you."

It was nice. Damned nice. Not that he minded doing it, but he'd always considered aftercare as a requirement. This was different. He wanted to take care of Angel. As she flitted in and out of sleep, he massaged her arms and legs and applied arnica cream to reduce the swelling from the flogging. Then he helped her under the covers and did the one thing he hadn't done in years.

He slid into bed beside her.

He didn't do sleepovers with subs because it gave them expectations of the possibility of more. And he just wasn't capable of it.

Until now.

Until her.

Although he swore to himself he'd let her rest, he woke her up twice during the night to fuck her again. He promised himself that, in the morning, he'd make his breakfast out of her pussy before asking to see her again.

But when he opened his eyes to the sun streaming in through the window, his arms were empty. She had left, the only trace of her the scent of vanilla and sex lingering in the air.

If he wanted to, he could track her down through her cousin, Dreama, but they'd agreed to one night, and despite having changed his mind, he'd honor her wishes. After all, with his new job, he'd have little time to devote to a relationship.

He rolled out of bed and got dressed. There were a dozen things to do before he left for Edison University.

Perhaps someday, when the timing was right, he and Angel would meet again.

He stuck his hand in his pocket, his palm closing over soft cotton.

Until then... he was keeping her panties as a souvenir.

FIVE

Carrying a heavy backpack filled to capacity with gently used textbooks, Isabella breathed in the fresh air and took in the beauty of the campus. She really loved the small-town feel and the way it was tucked away in the sparsely populated Upper Peninsula of Michigan. Twelve hours north of home and a more temperate climate, it wouldn't be long before the forest surrounding the campus turned from a deep dark green to a mass of vibrant orange, yellow, and red. There wasn't a cloud in the blue sky, and the sun shone on the entire campus, making it look like one of those photos on the front of the school brochures used to lure potential students. Before this morning, Isabella would've thought the pictures were Photoshopped, but clearly, Edison University didn't require it.

She couldn't believe she was finally here. After the incident, there was a time she thought she'd never leave her parents' home for college. But she didn't want the life of her parents or her siblings, one tied to the family business. While she loved to bake, she wanted to do something...*more*. That's why she'd fought so hard to regain her power through countless sessions of therapy and experimenting with BDSM. She couldn't give up her dreams of having her own business someday. She wasn't sure if it meant her own bakery or if she'd find another passion. But Edison was the first step in making her dream a reality.

As she crossed a short cobblestone bridge that arched over the Edison River, a smile tugged at her lips. Halfway across, she stopped and looked over the wooden edge, watching the ducks floating down the gentle stream and diving their heads into the water for tiny fish darting in between the rocks.

She hadn't been able to get the hours she spent with Tristan off her mind. He'd given her so much more than he knew. More than memories that made her heart race and her thighs clench. He'd given her confidence. Confidence in herself. Confidence in her sexuality. Confidence that some men could be trusted. If she ever saw him again, she'd tell him how much that night last week had meant to her.

She hadn't been prepared for the lingering effects Tristan would have on her. He invaded her thoughts several times a day, often at the most inopportune times, like at her going-away dinner with the entire family, when her toddler cousin proudly stated green was for go and red was for stop. While everyone else had clapped, Isabella had grown hot, blushing from head to toe as her mind flew back to Tristan asking her what color she was at as he flogged her to the strongest orgasm she'd ever had. Well, at least until he'd blown that one out of the water later that night.

She shivered, the warm late summer air unable to prevent the goose bumps from forming, and the latent desire left-over from last week made yet another appearance. At least this time there was no one around to witness the way her body reacted to her memories.

Continuing on the path back to her dorm, she wondered if her roommate, Chloe, would be there when she returned. Her half of the dorm room had already been set up by the time Isabella had arrived late that morning, but Chloe was conspicuously absent. Isabella had unpacked without inter-ruption, listening to the squeals of happiness coming from the other rooms. Maybe she should have left her own door open and met the women who would share her floor, but after years without any close friends, she'd grown uncom-fortable around groups of people. Besides, she wasn't here to socialize. College was her opportunity to make something of herself, and she wouldn't allow anything to interfere with goal.

Not even the memories of Tristan gazing into her eyes as he made love to her. And that's what it had been. Making love. The words *sex* and *fucking* couldn't come close to ex-plaining what had transpired between them. After her flog-ging, she'd expected he'd want to do something kinky like blindfold her. Instead, Tristan had proven his dominance over her with nothing more than his voice and his eyes. He'd surprised her with his soft caresses and sweet whispers. The intensity of their lovemaking had thrown her for a loop she'd yet to recover from. She never would've guessed a man like him would be capable of such tenderness. As he'd moved inside her, she'd never felt more connected to another person. Not even Tony, the boy she had supposedly loved at one time. And she realized, if given the chance, she could've fallen in love with Tristan.

But her time at the play party hadn't been about love. All she'd wanted was one night of submission to tide her over for four years. Yet, it had done so much more than she ever could have anticipated. After plodding through life like the living dead for a year, she felt as though she'd awoken from a deep slumber and had gone from dreaming in black and white to living in a vibrant, colorful world. Her cupcakes tasted sweeter. The music playing in the background in the bakery sounded clearer. She appreciated her brother's gentle ribbing and her parents' hugs more.

Everything had changed, and she wasn't quite sure what was responsible for it. Was it the confirmation of her submission? A by-product of the amazing orgasms? The empowerment from taking charge of her sexuality? Or did it have to do with the man who'd breathed life into her again?

After waking up in Tristan's arms in the early morning, she'd debated whether to go back to sleep or leave with her pride still intact. In the end, she'd chosen to flee like a coward, too afraid everything they had shared would somehow disappear in the morning light. By leaving before he'd awoken, she'd avoided the inevitable awkward brush-off. That way, she'd been able to maintain the fantasy that the night had meant as much to him as it had to her.

She rubbed the scar on her right wrist as she crossed the grassy courtyard in the middle of the four freshman dorms.

She'd always be grateful to Tristan for what he'd given her. Maybe someday after she graduated and returned to the city their paths would cross again.

Opening the door of her building, she practically moaned at the blast of cool air that hit her face. She didn't have to look in a mirror to know her face was red and that her hair was plastered to it. Walking back from the book-store with those heavy textbooks on her back had turned her into a sweaty mess, and she couldn't imagine it would get much better once she finished climbing the four flights of stairs to her floor. If luck was on her side, she'd have time to take a shower and change before finally meeting Chloe.

After emailing each other all summer, Isabella felt as if she already knew her. They'd connected on the university's roommate search Facebook page when Chloe responded to Isabella's post looking for another business major. Chloe was majoring in music, but responded anyway, and they'd bonded over their love of everything Chris Pine.

But of course, the door of her room was wide open, meaning Chloe was inside. Wonderful first impression she'd be giving her.

Even though the room was half hers, she knocked, giving her roommate a heads-up before she took a step inside. "Hello?"

The unmistakable sound of high heels clacked on the linoleum floor. "Isabella?"

Taller than her by at least four inches, with a tiny waist and straight brown hair with not a strand out of place,

Chloe smiled widely, showing off a set of perfect white teeth just before barreling into Isabella and hugging her tightly. "I can't believe I finally get to meet you."

Isabella laughed as she hugged her back. How long had it been since she'd had a friend that wasn't related to her? "Me too."

Chloe stepped back and waved her French-manicured hand. "Come in. I'm sorry I wasn't here when you arrived. I met up with some of the guys on the third floor for lunch. I'll introduce you to them later tonight."

"Tonight?" Isabella removed her backpack and temporarily set it by their door, the weight of it starting to hurt her shoulders.

"Our floor is hosting a progressive party, and we lucked out because our room is tequila."

Isabella couldn't begin to guess why tequila was lucky. From everything she'd witnessed of Dreama drinking too many margaritas, tequila came with one hell of a hangover. "I'm sorry. What's a progressive party?"

Chloe's arched brow rose as she gave her another bright smile. "Oh, so every room offers a different kind of alcohol. We're tequila." She pointed to the left. "Julia and Sophia next door are vodka. Across the hall, Tracy and Lindy are light beer. People go from room to room for a drink and to meet each other. You know, as an icebreaker. Too bad you missed the last few nights. The parties have been wicked fun."

Needing to rest her feet, Isabella sat on the end of their blue-and-white-striped college-supplied couch, not surprised to feel springs digging into her upper thigh. Hopefully, her twin mattress would be in better condition. "Won't we get in trouble with the RA for drinking?"

Chloe sat beside her. "Who do you think is buying it all? Madison, she's at the room by the stairs on our side of the hall, is really cool. You should see her at beer pong. She's, like, the dorm champ. Anyway, I already covered your share, so you owe me twenty bucks. If you don't have the money, don't worry about it. I'm loaded. Well, at least my mother is rich, and since I'm an only child, she spoils me rotten."

Twenty dollars? That was her food and drink budget for the entire week. "Uh, Chloe. I don't drink."

Chloe's gaze fell upon one of Isabella's scars. Her roommate's eyes widened. "Oh. I'm sorry. I shouldn't have assumed you'd want to participate. I just thought you might want to meet everyone in the dorm, especially since you've missed the last few days of move-in week. But honestly, I'm good with keeping our door shut and staying in with you tonight. You can meet the guys another time."

Ugh, if there was one thing she despised, it was pity. She knew people had misconceptions about her scars. After all, when they saw long, jagged scars on both wrists, their minds typically assumed a suicide attempt. She didn't blame them for their assumptions. But it placed her in the predicament of either letting them believe it or having to explain how she really got them.

Not Tristan though. He'd accepted her answer at face value and hadn't pressed her for details. Maybe a day would come when she'd trust Chloe enough to tell her the truth about her scars, but it wasn't today. Isabella would have to suck down her pride and allow Chloe to believe she'd once tried to end her own life. But that didn't mean she would have to accept her pity.

She'd considered telling Chloe about the incident, but the moment had never seemed right. Besides, college was the time for a fresh start.

Isabella rummaged through her pocket and came up with a twenty she'd stuck in there in case she needed it on her trip to the bookstore, and handed it to Chloe. "No. That's fine. Don't worry about it. We can be the tequila room."

Chloe hesitated for a moment before accepting the money. "Thanks. I'll make sure I ask you next time. It's an only-child thing. I'm not used to having to live with anyone else, but I promise to be more thoughtful of you in the future."

Isabella lifted one shoulder. "I know I'm not what you expected."

"You don't have to drink for me to like you. I already do." She bumped Isabella's knee with hers, then snatched her cell from the oak coffee table in front of them. "I'm going to call my mom to check in. If I don't return her call within a couple hours, she'll worry that I've been kidnapped." Standing, she gave a little laugh and pointed to a small pile of mail lying on the table. "Oh, I forgot. That's all yours."

As Chloe walked down the hall toward her bedroom, Isabella grabbed her mail, grateful for the privacy. Most of the dorm rooms on campus were one big room with two beds and two desks, but hers was divided into three different rooms, a wall between two bedrooms and a sitting area.

It was the luck of the draw, and for once, she'd gotten lucky. With a big family, she was used to the lack of privacy, but since the incident, she'd come to need it more and more. Thank goodness the night terrors had stopped or she would have never been able to have a roommate. Since she couldn't afford a single, she would've been forced to remain living at home and to commute to the local university. And as much as it would've made financial sense, she was ready to spread her wings. If she'd stayed with her family where everyone still treated her like a victim, she would've continued living like one.

Mail in hand, she went to her bedroom and pulled closed the curtain to give herself at least the pretense of privacy, trying to block out Chloe's animated voice from the other side of the wall.

Sitting cross-legged on her twin bed with her back up against the wall, she tore open the first envelope, knowing exactly who'd sent it once she caught sight of the photo of a half-naked fireman on the front of the card. When she went to read the inside, a twenty-dollar bill fluttered to her lap. Her cousin could barely afford it on her parole officer salary, which made Isabella appreciate it all the more. She stuck it in her pocket and giggled over Dreama's well wishes for a "kick-ass freshman year" and her recommendation to "get laid as often as possible."

The next piece of mail was a receipt from the university showing that her tuition and board had been paid in full for the term. Not needing another reminder of her debt, she crumpled the paper into a ball and threw it across the room, just narrowly missing the wastebasket. She picked up the final envelope, noting its unusual thickness and lack of return address before tearing it open. Growing curious, she realized it was a letter, several pages long, if the thickness was any indication.

A feeling of dread wrapped around her torso and squeezed until it stole her breath from her lungs. Hands shaking, she unfolded the letter and choked back the rising bile at the sight of the familiar handwriting.

How had he found her address here at school? It wasn't as if it was listed anywhere.

Her stomach cramped as she read page after page after page of Tony's ramblings of his undying devotion and love. Even after all this time, he still thought they were meant to be together.

There were no threats against her life.

No mention of his kidnapping of her or apology for his attempt to end her life.

It was as if he'd erased that day from his memories.

Looking at the reminders on her wrists, she wished she could do the same. Even if she had plastic surgery to remove the scars—maybe someday, when she had the money to pay for it—she'd never forget the helplessness of waking up as a prisoner in her own body, frozen and unable to save herself from death. From that point on, she knew firsthand that monsters not only hid under the bed, they were often masked with the faces of those who purported to love her.

Damn it.

Tears slid down her cheeks and dropped onto the page.

She wiped her face, refusing to allow Tony the power to suck her back into the deep hole of depression she'd found herself in a year ago.

He had no right to try to victimize her all over again.

She wouldn't let him.

He no longer had that power.

Clearly, the time he'd spent in the hospital hadn't helped stabilize him.

Maybe she should have pressured the prosecution to proceed with a trial. Instead, she'd agreed to a plea deal in which Tony would receive no less than a year of inpatient hospitalization and wouldn't be released until the doctors believed he was no longer a threat to himself or others.

Erin, the state attorney assigned to her case, had explained that Tony's attorneys had hired some of the best psychiatrists in Michigan to testify that he suffered from mental illness and that at the time of the crime, could not determine right from wrong. Tony would have gone free if a jury had found him *not guilty by reason of insanity*. Isabella hadn't wanted to take that risk. Besides, she'd just wanted to put it behind her and know that Tony couldn't get to her.

Now it was eighteen months later, and if this letter was any indication, he was as disturbed as he'd been when he'd gone into the hospital. Either the doctors hadn't effectively treated his mental illness or he'd played them from the start. She didn't know. And at that second, she didn't care. Mental illness or not, Tony had been ordered by the court not to contact Isabella or her family. So how had he been able to mail her this letter?

The old Isabella might have ignored the warning signs, but the new and improved Isabella wouldn't tolerate it.

She immediately called Erin. Since the prosecutor spent most of her time in court, Isabella wasn't surprised to get her voice mail. She left a detailed message and informed her she'd fax her a copy of the letter tomorrow.

After shoving the note back into the envelope, she tossed it onto the coffee table as if it were just another piece of junk mail. She wouldn't let Tony ruin her first night at college. Grabbing both her bathroom caddy and robe, she strode toward the community shower. Tomorrow, she'd follow up with Erin. Tonight...

She was in the tequila room.

SIX

Tristan sat at his desk, staring at the empty bookshelves and wondering how the hell this had become his life. He'd never given a single thought to becoming a teacher. Even when he was a student, he'd had a difficult time sitting still and concentrating. He needed to be constantly in motion, negotiating deals and selling the unsellable.

Teaching two classes a day, four days a week, wasn't exactly where he'd thought he'd wind up at his age. By now, he was supposed to have made his first million and proven to his son-of-a-bitch father that he didn't need him or his money.

Not that he believed money bought happiness. Money hadn't kept his father from abandoning Tristan's mother when she'd been six months pregnant with him. Ten years ago, money hadn't saved her life when she got pancreatic cancer. As for his own marriage, he had no doubt Morgan had married and divorced him precisely for the money he'd inherited upon his mother's death. When it came to the Kelley family, money brought nothing but misery.

But while money didn't buy happiness, it did buy respect. He'd watched from afar as his father was lauded by the president of the United States for his biotech company's generous donations to children's charities and named Man of the Year by *Time* magazine for his contributions to the scientific community in the treatment of childhood leukemia. All the while, his father never acknowledged the son he'd left behind when he'd married his second wife and created a whole new family.

No, money didn't buy happiness, but it sure had bought his mother's silence.

A shrink would probably theorize that Tristan's drive to succeed in business was his desire to get his father's attention. But honestly, he didn't give a shit if his father ever found out about Novateur. Unlike his father, he wasn't looking for public accolades or adoration.

No, money didn't buy happiness, but it could buy him the peace of mind that he'd never have to depend on anyone else. Because if there was one thing he'd learned, it was that the people he loved would inevitably leave him.

As it had several times, his mind wandered to his Angel. What was she doing right now? He pictured her as she'd been that night, wearing that ridiculous pink shirt as a dress with all that red hair flowing over her shoulders, only instead of being at Ryder's, he imagined her working at a bakery, her hands in a bowl, squeezing and kneading some dough between her hands as if it were his cock.

He opened his middle desk drawer and retrieved the black satin bag he'd recently purchased on a whim. Reaching inside, his hand folded over the cotton contents. He pulled it from the bag and brought the panties to his nose and inhaled. Her scent still lingered days later, a combination of vanilla, salt, and sugar.

At the firm three knocks on his door, Tristan quickly shoved her panties into the bag and threw it back into his desk drawer. "Come in."

All he needed was someone to catch him sniffing panties in his office. He might be a pervert, but he didn't need that fact broadcast across campus.

The door opened and Dean Isaac Lancaster, the man responsible for Tristan's current position at Edison University, strolled into his office. Isaac looked as though he had aged twenty years in the ten years Tristan had known him. If that's what university life would do to Tristan, he wanted no part of it. He was here for one year and then it was back to the real world, where he didn't have to worry about lesson plans and taking attendance.

At fifty-five years old, Isaac was now bald, no sign of the graying hair he'd sported a decade ago. He'd lost weight too, the extra pounds he'd carried gone from his frame. His skin had wrinkled around his eyes and mouth, giving him the appearance of constantly smiling, which Tristan knew wasn't the case.

Over drinks a few years ago, the inebriated Isaac had admitted the job as dean of the business school had caused him plenty of sleepless nights and problems in his marriage to his wife, Cassandra. But as the great-grandson of the founder of the university, and the son of the man for whom the Lancaster Business School was named, he had a legacy to protect. Tristan had no doubt that if Isaac and Cassandra had been blessed with a child, he or she would have been expected to follow in the family's footsteps.

"Your office is looking a little sparse," Isaac said as he crossed the short distance to Tristan's desk. "Most professors complain there isn't enough room for all of their possessions."

Tristan stood and shook Isaac's hand, surprised by his firm grasp. While his mentor may look frail, he certainly hadn't lost any of his strength. "I don't think that's going to be a problem for me."

Rather than giving Tristan Professor Crawford's office, Isaac had assigned Tristan to his own. It came furnished with two oak desks, one situated by the door for his assistant. His desk was placed in front of the window. Other than the empty bookcase to his left and a filing cabinet to his right, there wasn't much space in the dusty room. But then again, he didn't have much. Unlike the other professors, he didn't have to worry about things like tenure or getting published in business journals. As an adjunct professor, he received a quarter of the pay that full professors made, but none of the headaches—unless he counted dealing with the occasional argument from a self-entitled little shit over his failing grade. That couldn't be avoided.

Isaac took a seat, his eyes weary. "I received a phone call this morning from a distressed Morgan."

Tristan swore under his breath. How the hell had his ex-wife already found out about his working there? Did she have some kind of LoJack on him? Or was there a simpler explanation? Had Isaac or Cassandra told her? "I doubt she called to have you pass along her well wishes."

His friend's lips parted momentarily, then pressed together in a severe line as if he was holding back what he really wanted to say. Isaac didn't have to tell him a word. Whatever she had called about, it hadn't been good. "No well wishes. Only more unfounded accusations."

He snorted, rolling his eyes. Morgan should have become an author since she had such a gift for making up stories. "What's she accusing me of this time? I haven't seen her in over six months." Not since she'd come crawling back to him with an apology and a promise that she had changed. She had begged for another chance and had given him pitiful excuses as to why she'd betrayed him. But he'd refused to listen and slammed the door on her. Both literally and figuratively.

For good.

"Oh, more of the same," Isaac said, waving his hand. "You're a pervert with uncontrollable sexual urges and can't be trusted around a bunch of coeds. But that wasn't what worried me. She asked me a lot of questions about Novateur."

Not surprisingly, that meant her apology six months ago had been a lie. She seemed determined to prove to him that a leopard couldn't change her spots. The only thing that mattered to Morgan was Morgan. How she'd blown through his millions in just a few years was beyond him.

A while ago, he'd heard rumors she'd hooked up with a rich businessman from Detroit, but Tristan hadn't cared enough to get the poor bastard's name. Must not have lasted long, since it was shortly after that she'd come begging him to take her back.

Things hadn't been all bad with Morgan. When they'd met, they spent hours talking both in bed and outside of it. He'd told her about his parents, and how he'd give all the money in the world to have his mother alive again. She shared that she'd grown up with a drug-addicted mother and had spent years being shuffled between a filthy trailer and temporary foster homes.

He'd been looking for someone to love, and she'd been looking for security.

It was he who'd confused it with more, never imagining she'd marry him for his money.

But why was she asking questions about Novateur? Their divorce had been finalized years ago, and when she'd taken his entire fortune, she'd relinquished any right to alimony.

She had no claim on his current earnings.

"I hope you told her it was none of her fucking business," Tristan said drily.

"Of course, but I have the feeling she's up to something."

Isaac had stood up for Tristan in his wedding to Morgan. Standing in for Tristan's father, Isaac had counseled him before the marriage, pleading for Tristan to reconsider their quick nuptials and to instead have a lengthy engagement to get to know Morgan better. When Tristan refused, Isaac had kept his mouth shut and treated Morgan as if she were his own daughter. Cassandra and Morgan had developed a friendship that had survived even after she had shattered Tristan's world with her lies and deceit.

Tristan didn't understand it, but he often thought Morgan was the daughter Cassandra never had. Maybe that's why Tristan had pulled away from the Lancasters after his divorce. It was too difficult to admit that Isaac had been right about Morgan, and with his ex-wife remaining a part of their lives, he'd felt a bit resentful.

But when Tristan had needed a job, Isaac came through for him.

"Don't worry about it," Tristan said. "Morgan's always up to something. It wasn't enough that she blackmailed me in our divorce and took everything I had, she has to constantly remind me of the mistake I made in marrying her."

"You couldn't have known. She had everyone fooled."

Tristan picked up one of his most prized possessions off his desk, a baseball signed by Detroit Tiger Justin Verlander, and tossed it to Isaac. "Not everyone. You and Ryder never liked her."

His friend caught it with the ease of a younger man and returned it to its spot on the desk. "Just be careful. I don't think she's done with you."

He had a feeling he'd never completely get her sharp talons out of him. Not until he died—or she did.

For the first time, he was grateful that Edison University was in the middle of nowhere. Morgan absolutely despised the small town. "I'm living twelve hours away from her. What's she going to do? Besides, I'm broke. I've got nothing she wants."

Isaac rubbed his temples as if he had a headache. "You should have never allowed her to get away with blackmailing you. You had plenty of friends who would have taken your back at a trial."

"My innocence would have been irrelevant. All people would remember is that I liked to spank and tie up my wife." Not to mention the numerous other things he didn't want to discuss with his mentor. "No one would care that it had been consensual."

"I still can't believe she threatened to bring abuse charges against you," Isaac said with disdain.

It was one of the darkest times of his life, second only to the months following his mother's death. But he'd learned from his mistake and hadn't fully trusted another woman since. At least not until Angel. He didn't know what it was about that girl—perhaps it was her innocence—but he wanted to believe she was different. It was a shame rotten timing had gotten in the way of finding out if he was right.

Tristan folded his arms over his chest and sat back in his chair. "To get what she wants, there's no length that woman wouldn't go to. But it's over. Our divorce has been final for a long time, and I've got nothing left to give her. Her call was just a fishing expedition. Ignore her. I do."

"She still calls you?"

"About once or twice a month. I let her go to voice mail and delete the messages without listening to them." He swatted the air. "She's like a fly buzzing around my head. A nuisance but completely harmless."

"For your sake, I hope that's true." Isaac paused for a moment, crossing his legs. "Now, onto more important matters. I have a monthly get-together at my home for the professors of the business school. First one is tonight. I'll expect to see you there."

Tristan grimaced. He'd prefer to get a root canal than socialize with a bunch of teachers. "We both know I'm not really a professor," he said, hoping that fact might get him out of it.

Isaac smiled, knowing full well what Tristan was trying to do. "Adjunct professors may not be full members of the faculty, but I'd like you there just the same. It will be good for you to meet the others."

"Not trying to play matchmaker, are you?"

"Of course not. I realize it's unlikely you'd meet someone..." His friend squirmed in his chair, seemingly at a loss for words. "Suitable...for you. But it will be good for you to make some connections here."

As much as he owed Isaac, Tristan had a life to get back to. He had big plans, and teaching wasn't part of them. By this time next year, he and Ryder would have secured their loan and would be in the process of making Novateur a global competitor in restaurant automation. "You're hoping I'll like it enough to stay. I told you, two semesters and then I'm moving back to the city, Isaac." He ran his finger over the outside of the drawer that housed his Angel's panties. "And there's nothing here in Edison that will change my mind."

SEVEN

Head pounding from the lack of sleep, Isabella rubbed her temples, and her gym shoes smacked the path's pavement as she rushed to the business school. A class at eight in the morning hadn't seemed too early when she'd signed up for it several months ago, but she hadn't expected to have people partying on her floor until three in the morning.

At midnight, Chloe had ushered everyone out of their room so that they could get some sleep, but the noise had carried from down the hall, keeping Isabella awake until three, when she'd finally succumbed to exhaustion. She hoped the noise wouldn't become the norm for her floor. Between classes, homework, and work-study, she needed her sleep. At least she'd gotten the opportunity to meet some of the other students in her dorm and, even better, staying occupied had kept her from obsessing about Tony's letter. Hopefully, she'd hear back from Erin sometime this morning. For now, she had to put it out of her mind because in ten minutes, she'd attend her first class at Edison University.

Anticipation buzzed through her as she reached the Lancaster Business School, where she would be spending most of her time this year. The brick building with ivy climbing its walls was one of the oldest on campus, at over one hundred years old.

Edison didn't hire its business professors based on their academic papers or publications; every professor in the school claimed tremendous success in the business world. Some owned companies, while others worked within an established corporation, but all of them had invaluable knowledge, which they then brought to the students. The program's uniqueness made the business school one of the best in the country. Alumni included the CEO of one of the Big Three auto companies and several congressmen. Students from all over the country battled for a spot in the prestigious school.

Although the university offered general business courses for students, only a select few were chosen each year into the bachelor of business administration program. Once she finished her freshman year, she'd be eligible to apply, competing against hundreds of applicants for fifty spots. That's why it was important that she not only get straight As, but that she go above and beyond to prove herself worthy of one of those spots.

The school had a reputation for turning out the brightest and best.

And she planned on being one of them.

She stopped inside the entrance, savoring the moment. Students bustled in and out of the doors, their footsteps clomping on the hard gray-tiled floor. A staircase bisected the space in front of her, and to her left was an elevator for those who required it. The building boasted three floors, including two for classrooms and one for the administrators' and professors' offices.

After Intro to Business class, she would finally meet Professor Crawford, the teacher she would be assisting all semester. They'd spoken a few times over the phone, but he hadn't returned any of her calls for nearly a month. She worried he'd changed his mind, but her financial statements listed her work-study as paying for a huge chunk of her tuition. Now, she just had to worry about earning some money to cover incidentals.

A heavy backpack bumped into her as a student raced past, the force knocking her into a wall of flyers. He threw a mumbled apology over his shoulder before hurrying to the stairs.

One flyer caught her eye. Getting an idea, she yanked it off the wall and stuck it in her purse. A frat party would be a perfect opportunity for her to introduce her bakery side business to the students. She needed to start making money, and her idea to make cake pops would be the easiest method.

Baking from the common kitchen in her dorm would be difficult, but thanks to modern technology, not impossible. What she needed was an angle, and she had just the right one for a bunch of college students. She'd go to the parties, wait until the munchies hit everyone, and then *bam*, she'd rake in a fortune.

There was nothing she enjoyed more than creating the perfect cake for someone's special event. That's why she'd surprised everyone by deciding to go to Edison rather than working full-time in the bakery. In four years, she'd be the first in her family to graduate from college.

Baking was in her blood. Her siblings all worked for the family bakery, and it was expected that Isabella would follow in their footsteps. She'd been working there since she was a little girl, first helping in the storefront before apprenticing as a baker throughout high school.

Although she loved her family and the bakery, that life wasn't the right one for her. She wanted more for herself. She wanted to explore the world and experience life, something her family, and especially Tony, never understood.

Ready for her first college class, she headed down the hallway until she found the right room. She stood just inside the door, scanning the stadium-style classroom for a seat. Spotting a few, she took a breath and made her way to the front of the room, where she settled into a seat on the aisle. As she reached inside her backpack for her notebook and pen, a familiar voice came from the back of the room.

"Good morning, everyone."

Bent over, she froze. Her body broke out in goose bumps and her heart thumped erratically.

It wasn't possible. Her mind must be playing tricks on her. There was no way that the man who had dominated her last week could be there right now, twelve hours north of the city where they'd met. She racked her brain, trying to remember if he'd mentioned anything about his personal life, but she came up completely empty. There had been plenty of innuendo and dirty talk during that night, but he'd never revealed anything about himself other than his first name.

How could he be a professor at his age? Weren't they supposed to be... old?

But as the man behind the voice passed her on his way to the front of the room, she caught his scent, a scent she'd fantasized about for days, and sat up tall. Her gaze latched onto the back of him, raking over his lean form, and her chest tightened as though all the oxygen had been sucked out of the room.

Just a few days ago, that form had been between her thighs.

When he reached the podium at the front of the room, he turned to the class. "I'm Professor Kelley, and I'll be teaching Intro to Business this semester in Professor Crawford's place."

Her fingers curled around the arm of the chair, gripping it as if it could save her from the horror of the situation.

She couldn't move.

Couldn't breathe.

Memories of that night swirled through her mind, lighting her on fire. Him caging her against the wall as they negotiated underneath the stars. Him biting her breasts and sucking her nipples until she writhed in ecstasy. Him intertwining their hands and looking into her eyes as he slowly brought her to an explosive climax. Him waking her up twice more that night, one time with his mouth between her legs.

Oh my God.

It was him.

Tristan.

She had fucked her professor.

Properly.

Hell, the bruises from that night still marred her skin. Whenever she changed her clothes, she'd made a point of checking to see if they were still there. They were reminders of how easily he'd commanded her body and the ways he'd brought her pleasure through pain.

She thought she'd never see him again, but now he was here, standing in front of her wearing a white button-down shirt with his sleeves rolled up, showing off those muscular forearms of his, and all she could think about was how he'd used those muscles to hold himself over her as he thrust inside her.

"What happened to Professor Crawford?" a girl asked from the back.

Right. Professor Crawford. The man she was supposed to assist all year for her work-study. The one who held the future of her college education in his hands.

Tristan—no—*Professor Kelley* directed his attention to the girl sitting only a few rows behind Isabella, causing her heart to go from a gallop to a full-on sprint. Would he recognize her when he saw her? Or was she already forgotten as just one more interchangeable girl in a long line of submissives he'd fucked? She didn't know which was worse.

"Unfortunately, Professor Crawford had a stroke a couple of weeks ago," he said, only a handful of feet away from her.

Why did she have to sit in the front row? "Dean Lancaster has asked me to take over his classes for the year."

For a second, she lost the ability to breathe. Professor Crawford didn't hold the future of her college education in his hands...

Professor Kelley did.

She was at his mercy.

Not only would she have to sit in his class three times a week, she would be working for him every afternoon.

Her fight and flight responses warred with one another. Attending Edison and graduating from the Lancaster Business School was her dream. If she quit work-study, she'd lose her financing for school. Even if there was a chance she could find a different position, assisting a professor in the business school would bolster her résumé when she applied to the business administration program. She needed this job.

But could she handle working side by side with a man she knew intimately?

"We'll roughly follow the same syllabus as the one Professor Crawford posted online, with a few notable exceptions." As Professor Kelley—God, would she ever get used to thinking of him that way?—provided an overview of the class, he rotated his head slightly, his gaze bouncing over her. Before she could decide whether she felt relief or disappointment, his gaze snapped back. He stopped speaking as his eyes widened.

Guess he recognized me.

Just like when they'd made love, they locked gazes.

Her body froze while her brain ran through hundreds

of scenarios, beginning with the one where he passionately ripped off her clothes, hoisted her onto the podium, and made lunch out of her pussy. Inconveniently timed moisture pooled in her panties. He took a couple of steps toward her before he stopped. He ground his jaw and turned away from her, breaking the spell.

Realizing she had been holding her breath, she exhaled and pressed a hand over her wildly beating heart.

How the hell was she supposed to concentrate when her body was primed and ready to be ravaged by him, and her mind was being bombarded by images of the ravishment? She needed to calm down and get her head out of the gutter, or she'd never be able to make it through class.

Casually standing behind the podium, not a sign of tension in his muscles or on his face, Tristan began his lecture. Wasn't he as rocked by this turn of events as she was? Had the other night meant nothing to him?

She had to get a grip. Wrapping her fingers around the pen, she flipped open her notebook and went to work, diligently taking notes just like she would if she hadn't had the professor's naked body thrusting into hers only a few days ago.

Somehow, the next two hours of class flew by in a blur, although she couldn't recall one thing she'd written down. As the other students left the room, she gathered her things, and her stomach clenched in apprehension. She had to talk to him. Figure out how they'd proceed. Rather than merge into the stream of people headed toward the exit, she swallowed down the thick knot of fear lodged in her throat and forced herself to approach him.

He knew her as Angel, a woman with more self-assurance in her pinkie than Isabella had in her whole body.

What would he do when he realized Angel was nothing more than a mirage?

* * *

Tristan shuffled his papers, refusing to let himself look for her. His Angel was here. Acting like she didn't know him, she'd sat in the front row and took copious notes as he droned on about the basics of business.

But she did know him. Was he supposed to believe it just a coincidence that the girl he couldn't get off his mind had turned up in his class a twelve-hour drive from where they had met? Maybe before Morgan had screwed him both literally and figuratively, he might have believed it was fate.

Could Angel be spying on him for Morgan?

The papers crumpled in his hands. No, Morgan didn't get to tarnish his memories of Angel. That night had been real. More fucking real than anything he'd ever experienced. She couldn't have faked her body's response to his touch. Besides, Dreama wouldn't risk being ostracized from the BDSM community if she'd brought her cousin to a play party under dubious circumstances.

So, she was a student in his class. As long as he avoided looking at her, he'd be fine. Of course, that was easier said than done. No matter how hard he'd tried to keep from glancing her way, he couldn't help himself. And he couldn't handle spending another two-hour lecture glued to his spot behind the podium in order to hide his damned erection. He'd simply get her to drop the class.

A gentle cough came from the other side of the podium. He raised his head, and there she was, standing in front of him with one hand on her hip and her backpack slung over her shoulder. She stared at him intently.

His hands clenched into fists, and he battled his urge to grab her and kiss that mouth senseless.

When the last student cleared the room, he moved out from behind the podium. "You left without saying good-bye."

Her cheeks flushed, proving she wasn't as brave as she portrayed. "I didn't think it was required for a one-night stand."

Typically it wasn't, but what they'd shared wasn't typical. "Perhaps not, but still. Why'd you do it?"

She shrugged. "You were sleeping. I wanted to avoid the whole awkward 'thanks for the fuck' speech."

An unexpected and unreasonable surge of anger rose in him at the thought of her with other men. He'd thought she was so innocent. Had he been played again? "Do that a lot, do you?"

She swallowed hard and fidgeted with the strap of her backpack. "That's really none of your business, Professor Kelley. After all, you're my teacher. I think the subject of my sex life has been officially taken off the table."

There was the girl he remembered. Sassy and strong willed with a hint of shyness.

As he'd done that night, he saw straight through her bravado. This was as difficult for her as it was for him.

He stepped around the podium, moving closer to her, and inhaled the scent of vanilla. *God, she smells good.* He wanted to bury his nose in the crook of her neck and take a bite of her. "This is fucking uncomfortable as hell. At least tell me you're a senior and taking this class as a filler."

She bit her lip. "I'm a freshman."

He knew she was young, but a freshman? "Please tell me you're over eighteen."

"Don't worry. The age of consent in Michigan is sixteen."

"Fuck me." He was going to be sick.

She laughed and wrapped her hand around his bicep. "I'm screwing with you. I'm nineteen. How old are you?"

Thank God.

The heat of her hand soaked through his shirt. "Twenty-eight," he said, his voice coming out raspier than he would've preferred. He reluctantly removed her hand. "Old enough to know this is a complicated situation."

"What's complicated about it?" She glanced over her shoulder and then looked him straight in the eye. "We fucked. It was good, but it's over, and at the time you weren't my teacher. No one needs to know about it, and it won't happen again."

He stalked closer to her, loving how her pupils dilated in response. "Good? It was better than good and you know it." She might pretend otherwise, but she was just as affected. "But you're right. It won't happen again. You can drop the class—"

"It's not that simple." She shook her head, her red locks falling onto her face. "I'm your—I mean—I was supposed to be Professor Crawford's office assistant this semester."

She was Isabella, the assistant he'd been told to expect? Somehow, the name suited her just as beautifully as Angel. "Clearly, that won't work, *Isabella*."

Bad enough to see her sitting in his classroom all semester, but working with her one-on-one and not being able to touch her would be like walking through the desert without shoes. Pure torture. *Damn it.* He may only be an adjunct professor, but he was bound by the same rules of ethics as a full-time professor.

She was off-limits.

Her lower lip quivered as if she was holding back tears. "It has to," she said. "It's my work-study. Without it, I won't be able to afford school."

He wouldn't be responsible for her losing her college education, but there had to be another option. "I'll find another professor for you to work under."

"It's not that easy to find a placement, and even if you could, I need one in the business school to help me get into the business administration program." The strap of her backpack tugged her shirt down her shoulder, revealing a small bruise in the shape of his fingerprint on her upper arm. He inwardly preened to see his mark on her. "Besides, what will you say is the reason? 'Sorry, I can't have her as my assistant since I flogged her and then fucked her to three orgasms'?"

His dick twitched as he recalled each and every time her body trembled when she came for him. "Four. Don't forget when I..." He stopped, witnessing the blush staining her cheeks. "But you're right. I'll just tell them I don't need an assistant."

"But you do," she said. "In fact, you probably need one more than any other professor here since you have no idea what you're doing."

She was right. Isaac had promised him an assistant, assuring him he wouldn't have to worry about administrative tasks. That was one of the many enticements he'd dangled in front of him to accept this job. "Do you always say what's on your mind?"

"No." She smiled. "I'm the quiet one in my family."

"You certainly weren't quiet with me last week."

Her eyebrows rose. "Really? We're gonna go there again?"

He grew somber. Whatever lingering fantasies he may have harbored about her quickly faded away. "No. From this moment on, we're nothing but teacher and student-slash-assistant." He went behind the podium to his laptop and clicked open his calendar. "Did you and Professor Crawford agree to your hours and duties?"

"Monday through Friday from one until four. In addition to general office responsibilities, I was supposed to help him with his research for a journal article."

"I'll find something for you to work on. Let me get you my contact information in case anything comes up." He handed her his business card, then typed her hours into his schedule and shut his computer. She stayed, her eyes tracking his every move, and he knew right then it was going to be as difficult for her to put that night behind them as it would be for him.

It was up to him as the authority figure to maintain a professional distance.

* * *

Dazed, Isabella stumbled out of the business school, thankful for the blast of fresh air that cooled her heated skin. She'd done her best to convince Tristan that she could handle being his assistant, but honestly, it wasn't going to be easy.

How could fate be so cruel?

That night with Tristan had helped set her on the path toward the rest of her life. Everything was supposed to be in her past once she got to Edison. But now, past and present had collided to become one giant fucked-up mess.

If only she could pretend she didn't know the feel of his lips against hers or the flavor of his skin.

But she did.

And she wanted more of it.

More of him.

And if his words were any indication, he wanted her too.

She'd told him she'd sneaked out of the room to avoid an unpleasant scene. Truth was, she'd known that one night with him hadn't been enough, and if he'd asked to see her again, she wouldn't have declined, despite her fervent promise to herself to remain single for the next four years of school.

Nothing had changed in a week's time.

She hadn't made the promise lightly. After discussing the issue at length with her therapist, who had suggested she keep her options open to the possibility of dating again, Isabella had come to the decision she didn't want anything to keep her from her goals. She was going to get into the business administration program, and nothing was going to get in her way.

Not even her less-than-professional feelings for Professor Kelley.

Settling on a bench in front of the building, she pulled her cell out of her pocket to call Dreama and saw she had missed two calls, one from Erin and the other listed as an unknown number. She drummed her fingers on the armrest of the bench as she listened to her voice mail from Erin.

"Hi, Isabella," Erin said a bit breathlessly, giving Isabella the image of her power walking to another courthouse. "Immediately after getting your phone message this morning, I called to speak with Tony's doctor. He was extremely dismayed to hear that Tony was somehow able to mail a letter to you and assured me that the matter will be fully investigated. He also promised that it would not happen again and that Tony will temporarily have his mail privileges revoked."

That was it? A figurative slap on the wrist for violating the restraining order against her?

Erin continued. "The doctor did indicate he was surprised to hear that Tony had broken a rule. According to him, Tony has been a model patient who has responded well to both his medication and group therapy sessions." Her voice dropped to a whisper. "Based on our conversation, I got the feeling they're thinking of releasing Tony soon, but I don't want you to worry..."

Isabella didn't hear the rest. Her heart was thumping much too loudly.

It wasn't even lunchtime on her first day of college, and her past had already reared its head twice. Would the past ever let her go?

And in Tristan's case, did she want it to?

The next message played and loud static crackled in her ear. Rolling her eyes, she waited a moment for the inevitable solicitor's message that would tell her to call for her preapproved credit card. Instead, she swore she heard someone repeatedly whispering her name underneath the crackling.

The wind blew across the grassy courtyard as clouds blocked the sun's rays, and the scars on her wrists itched as if the wounds were recent.

Tony's letter was making her paranoid. This had nothing to do with him.

She replayed the message, this time closing her eyes in concentration. Frowning, she couldn't decipher whether the voice was male or female.

It was probably nothing, but she didn't erase the message. If she got another one, she'd forward them both to Erin.

In the meantime, she really needed to talk to Dreama. As a probation officer, she might have some insight into what factors the judge would consider for Tony's potential release from the mental hospital. When Isabella had asked Erin, the attorney had told her not to worry until it was time. But Dreama would give it to her straight.

And just wait until Isabella told her the news about Tristan. Her cousin would definitely have some advice for her on that.

Whether she listened to her was another matter.

With only twenty minutes to get to her next class, she stood from the bench. Across the way, a man with a cell phone glued to his ear paced back and forth on the steps of the business school. She recognized him immediately from the school's website. It was Isaac Lancaster, dean of the business school. Judging by the tone of his voice, he was not a happy camper at the moment.

Dean Lancaster ceased his pacing and pinched the bridge of his nose. "If you can't deliver the cakes tonight, I'll come by and get... What do you mean you didn't bake anything? I've had a standing order with you for five years. First day of school followed by the first Friday of every month, like clockwork." He paused, his face turning red. "Yes, I understand you're in the hospital and I'm very sorry that you're sick, but I can't serve prepackaged desserts." He heaved a sigh. "Very well then. We'll speak when you recover. Good luck on your operation."

Was it possible that fate was finally throwing her a bone?

With her head held high, she strode straight up to Dean Lancaster. "Dean Lancaster?" She extended her hand. "My name is Isabella Lawson and I believe I can help you."

EIGHT

Someone kill him and put him out of his misery.

Would he really have to suffer through one of these department nightmares every month? So far, Tristan had met half of the business school's professors, and each had a personality to rival tepid bathwater.

How was it possible he was as bored by them as he'd been sitting in the back row of their classrooms as a college student?

He'd convinced himself it was the subject matter, the ability to make microeconomics exciting a challenge when simply reciting passages from the textbook. But the men and women he'd been introduced to tonight made textbooks seem like pornography when compared to their dry conversation.

If he stayed on as a professor here, would he too stand as though he had a wooden stick up his ass?

He took another sip of the champagne, wishing he'd had the foresight to have a couple of drinks before the event. Maybe then he'd have something to add to the current conversation about the sustainable price of oil instead of nodding his head and laughing along with everyone else when he'd missed what was funny.

At least the food was good. He popped another bite-sized cannoli into his mouth and let the pastry melt on his tongue, the sweet, creamy filling reminding him of the last time he'd eaten something that sweet. He'd been between Isabella's thighs, licking the moisture from her glistening pink flesh as her cries rang in his ears. She'd tasted like honey, her climax even more intoxicating than the combination of champagne and cannoli. Tonight's desserts were a distant second compared to Isabella, but he'd take what he could get. And since he would never be getting Isabella again, he'd settle for pastries.

Shit, he needed to purge her from his thoughts. This was the wrong place to be fantasizing about a student.

Not that there was a *right* place.

But certainly the parlor of his friend, mentor, and boss wasn't it.

No matter how many times Tristan had been there, Isaac and Cassandra's home never ceased to amaze him. Built in 1895 by Isaac's grandfather after being inspired by his stay at a French château, the three-story, redbrick Victorian contained most of its original furnishings. Although Cassandra had updated the home with new appliances and modern-day conveniences, it had retained enough to make Tristan feel as if he stepped back in time whenever he visited.

"Having a good time, Tristan?" Isaac asked, slapping him lightly on the back and interrupting his companions' debate about . . . hell, he didn't even know.

"Let's just say it's given me an appreciation for what you do," Tristan said, snagging a mini cupcake from a passing waiter's tray. He was about to toss it in his mouth, but halfway to his lips, he stopped, admiring it instead. He'd never seen such a work of art on a dessert outside of those television shows about pastry chefs. A rose decorated the top of the cupcake, its delicate petals reminding him of the pink folds of Isabella's pussy.

He nearly groaned out loud. Fuck, he had Isabella on the brain tonight. What was wrong with him? He shouldn't be thinking about her at all, much less at a department dinner with the dean of the business school next to him.

He puffed out a breath, willing himself to think of anything else. The principles of microeconomics. Math equations. The sustainable price of oil.

Isaac lifted his brows in mockery, knowing full well Tristan was miserable here at tonight's event. Thank goodness the man couldn't read his mind, or he'd find himself out of a job. And he couldn't allow that to happen. There was nothing more important than Novateur. He had to remember that whenever the thought of Isabella's creamy thighs crept into his mind.

If he was this obsessed after a single night, what would he be like if he ever took another sip? He'd lose his job, his chances to get that loan, and even worse, he'd lose his self-respect.

"You'll get used to it," Isaac said. "I did."

Tristan's heart jumped into his throat until he realized Isaac wasn't talking about suppressing his desire for Isabella. "I doubt I'll be here long enough for that."

"We'll see. Teaching has a way of getting under your skin. Speaking of which, how did it go today?"

Other than running into Isabella, his day had been rather uneventful. "Let's just say I'm not that impressed with today's youth. I can't tell you how many times I lost a student's attention to an incoming message on his damned cell phone."

"It's not a professor's job to simply teach the day's lesson." His friend's habit of imparting bits of wisdom into their conversations had always reminded him of Dumbledore.

"What is that supposed to mean?" Tristan asked.

"It's your classroom. It's your role to make the rules and teach them that there are consequences if those rules are broken. As I recall, you enjoy disciplining those who've broken your rules," Isaac said with a grin, causing Tristan to choke on his champagne. He did not want to talk about sex with his mentor.

A professor he'd met earlier in the evening, Dr. Nanci Weaver, stopped beside Isaac, a cupcake in her hand. "Are you using a new bakery this year? The desserts are quite an improvement over the usual dry cookies and brownies."

Isaac nodded. "Our usual caterer lost our order, and for a moment, I thought I'd have to serve cookies out of a box, but a young lady—a student—overheard my phone conversation with the caterer and offered her services."

Nanci tipped her head to the side, her glasses slipping down her nose. "Really? A student? Is she part of the hospitality program?"

"No, believe it or not, she's studying business. A freshman," Isaac explained. "She did all the shopping and used my kitchen to prepare everything in less than four hours."

The back of Tristan's neck heated, his heart thumping wildly.

A freshman business student who baked?

"Well, you must give me her card so I can have her do my anniversary party," Nanci said to Isaac.

"I can do one step better. She's still here finishing up in the kitchen. I'll bring her out and introduce her." Isaac excused himself from the parlor and left through the door that led to the kitchen.

Waiting for his return, Tristan stood rooted to his spot. Luckily, Nanci didn't try to engage him in conversation because at that moment, his mouth was so dry, he didn't think he'd be capable of speech.

Before last week he'd never seen her, and now it was as if she was haunting him.

A man had only so much strength before he snapped like an overstretched rubber band.

Just as he'd expected, Isabella came through the kitchen door. Her beauty took his breath away, replacing it with an unfamiliar buoyancy that made him feel as though his feet were hovering above the ground. She was wearing the same pink T-shirt she'd worn when they met, only this time, she wore it over a pair of blue jeans, and had a dusting of white powder along the side of her neck. He wasn't sure if it was flour or powdered sugar.

He wanted to lick her skin and find out.

Trying to appear nonchalant, he stood off to the side of

Nanci. With a hand on her lower back that spoke of familiarity, Isaac led Isabella to them. Tristan's eyes locked onto the sight, and he clenched his jaw so hard he could've cracked a tooth. His reaction shocked the hell out of him. Isaac was old enough to be her grandfather and there was nothing sexual about the way he was touching her. And yet he couldn't deny the hot, gnawing sensation in his gut that felt a lot like jealousy. Isabella didn't belong to him, but apparently, his gut hadn't gotten the memo.

And judging by what was going on behind the fly of his pants, neither had his dick.

Thankfully unaware of Tristan's discomfort, Isaac introduced her to Nanci. "This is Isabella Lawson, the student responsible for baking everything tonight. Isabella, please meet Professor Weaver. And of course, you probably know Professor Kelley."

She tucked a strand of her hair behind her ear. "Yes, sir. We've met." A blush crept up her cheeks and her eyes widened. "I mean, we met this morning in class."

Difficult as it was, Tristan kept his expression bland and willed his dick to stand down. "As it turns out, Isa—Ms. Lawson—is also my assistant this year."

"Do you have any cards?" Nanci asked Isabella. "I'm having an anniversary party and I'd love to have you cater the desserts."

"I'm sorry, I don't have cards yet," Isabella said.

Nanci whipped a business card out from her clutch. "Call Anita, my assistant, and give her your contact information. We'll talk and see if we can make this work. The party isn't until December, so we have plenty of time to work out all the details."

Isabella nodded. "I will."

Isaac's hand left its place on Isabella's back, relocating to her shoulder. "How would you like the job as my permanent caterer? The first Friday of every month I host a department party at my home."

Tristan suppressed the irrational growl that threatened to erupt from him at seeing another man's hands on his Angel.

"I'd like that," Isabella said to Isaac with a smile. "Thank you, sir."

"No, thank you." With a squeeze to her shoulder, Isaac's hand finally went back to his side where it belonged. "You don't need to stay to clean. I've got a service to do that. If you wait a few minutes, Cassandra will give you a ride back to campus."

"That's okay," Isabella said. "I'll walk. It's not far."

"No," Tristan said a little too forcefully. "I mean, I walked here as well. You're on the way. I'll walk you home." No woman should ever walk across campus alone at night. There were far too many dangers hiding in the darkness waiting to prey on an innocent like Isabella.

In a move he now recognized as her nervous habit, Isabella tucked some of her hair behind her ear again. "You don't have to—"

"I insist."

NINE

The air must have dropped at least twenty degrees since Cassandra had picked Isabella up from the nearby market that afternoon, but she couldn't feel it because her body was still on fire from being alone with Tristan. (She couldn't think of him as Professor Kelley no matter how hard she tried.) She'd dated Tony for years and had crushed on boys before that, but she'd never experienced anything like the strange buzzing she felt every time Tristan was near.

Tristan, on the other hand, seemed quite relaxed as he walked her across campus to her dorm.

Earlier when Dean Lancaster had requested she come into the parlor to meet some of the business school staff, she'd wanted to bolt from the house, her pulse racing from knowing that Tristan was likely in that room. At the same time, it was a chance to separate herself from the mass of students who would sit anonymously in the classroom, so that when the time came for her to apply to the business administration program, the professors would be familiar with her. Of course, she would've preferred they not remember her as the hired help, but she figured it was better than nothing.

She'd been thrilled to finally meet Professor Weaver. Like the other teachers in the business school, Professor Weaver had experienced great success in the business world, but when Isabella had read her online bio, she'd related to her both as a woman and because they'd both worked with their families. The impressive woman had gone from a humble beginning of a salesperson at her family's car dealership to buying her own dealership in only five years' time and then in ten more years, boasting the largest car dealership franchise in North America. Deciding to slow down, she sold her business and now gave back to the students of Edison, teaching entrepreneurial enterprise and negotiation skills.

Isabella sneaked a glance at Tristan. She had no idea what he did other than work at the university as an adjunct professor.

What lessons could he teach her?

Her mind went to a vision of her on her knees in front of him as he instructed her on how he preferred his blow jobs. She nibbled on her lip. Did he enjoy a little tease with licks and kisses or did he like it hard, deep, and wet? She shivered, picturing her hair twisted around his wrist as he pushed her mouth down onto his cock and ordered her to take it all.

At that image, the buzzing in her veins spread to that sensitive spot between her legs. Off balance, she stumbled, but was quickly righted when Tristan caught her. Their eyes locked and time stood still.

Did it remind him of the last time he caught her after she'd tripped too?

Stealing the chance, she allowed herself to burrow in his heat and luxuriate in the safety of his strong arms. The wool sleeve of his business suit rubbed against the outside of her bicep. She inhaled deeply, taking his scent deep into her lungs.

Then before she knew it, she was standing on her own two feet again and grieving from the loss of those precious moments.

Pretending she didn't still want him was going to be harder than she first thought.

Why had he volunteered to walk her home rather than try to convince her to get a ride from Cassandra? He hadn't spoken a word since they'd left Dean Lancaster's house. Except for his overreaction at her assertion of walking herself home, he hadn't shown an ounce of emotion the entire evening. Not even when he'd looked straight in her eyes just as they had done when they'd made love.

It was as if that night between them had never happened for him.

"You really didn't need to walk me," she said, breaking the silence. "It's not that far."

As they stepped into the darkness of the night, she shivered and reluctantly admitted to herself she was grateful to have him with her. Tony's letter and that weird phone message hung heavily in her mind.

His expression remained bland. "It doesn't matter how far; you shouldn't walk alone at night on campus. Although the campus boasts the lowest crime rate in the state for a university, dangerous things still can happen." He didn't have to warn her. She could confirm dangerous things could happen anywhere.

On a narrower path, their bodies adjusted to the reduced space and moved closer to each other. Tristan's fingers briefly brushed hers.

Her heart galloped from what was most likely an accidental touch. "You're right," she said, tucking her hair behind her ear to keep herself from doing something stupid like holding his hand. "Thank you for walking with me."

Under the illumination of the lampposts, they followed the path along the Edison River, passing by the university's hundred foot bell tower. Ivy climbed the sprawling redbrick walls. During the day, the bells rang at the top of every hour, the chiming music audible across the entire three-mile-long campus.

"Do you know the legend about the bell tower?" Tristan asked, jutting his chin toward the structure.

She stopped walking and looked up at it. "Uh, no. Tell me it has nothing to do with jumping from the top."

He laughed, finally showing some emotion. "No. There's an old legend that says if two people kiss up there, they're destined to marry. According to Isaac, the story originated with his grandparents, but there are several others who have sworn the legend came true for them. Once a year, they hold a mass wedding ceremony here for couples who've kissed on top of that tower."

She rubbed the scar on her wrist. Before her life had gone

to hell, she'd believed in love and destiny. From the moment her parents had met at twelve years old, they'd been inseparable. Her mother had said it was love at first sight. They'd gotten married straight out of high school and had their first child two years later. Six kids, eight grandkids, and thirty years later, she claimed their love had never wavered.

As the youngest of the bunch, Isabella had watched with envy as her sisters had settled down with their high school sweethearts shortly after their graduations. At the beginning of high school, she'd wanted to follow in their footsteps. Tony had been the son of her parents' best friends. He'd always been a part of her life. One of her closest friends.

When he'd asked her out on a date, she'd romanticized it into destiny.

When, a year into their relationship, Tony had suddenly gotten angry at her for spending time with her friends, she'd told herself he was possessive because he loved her.

When Tony had started calling and texting her dozens of times a day to check up on her, she'd convinced herself it was because he was worried for her safety.

When Tony had gone from telling her she was the most beautiful girl in the world to telling her he only found her beautiful because he loved her, she thought she was ugly and was grateful to him for believing otherwise.

When he'd grown paranoid that the teachers were all "out to get him," she consoled him.

When he'd had trouble sleeping and woke her by knocking on her window in the middle of the night, she let him in her bedroom, losing precious hours of sleep as a result.

When he no longer cared about showering or brushing his teeth, she'd pretended it didn't bother her.

From sophomore to senior year, she'd ignored the warning signs of his abuse and later his descent into psychosis, all because she believed he was her destiny. Like many abuse victims, she'd only focused on the good moments between them. It had taken months of therapy to stop blaming herself for not ending the relationship sooner and for not getting help from her family.

"Do you believe the legend's true?" she asked.

He turned his head and stared intently at her, the heat from his gaze burning straight through her. "I believe that people make their own destiny."

What was her destiny?

Because at that second, all signs pointed to him.

Tearing her gaze away, she resumed walking and changed the subject. "Enjoy the dinner party?"

"As much as watching bread turn into toast," he said drily as he fell into step beside her.

"Not your scene, huh?"

"No. Definitely not my scene. But the dean insisted I attend." His hand brushed hers, and this time, she wasn't sure if it was an accident. "And it wasn't all dull."

There was no mistaking the inference of his words.

He hadn't been as immune to her as she'd believed.

"So how are you liking Edison so far?" he asked, changing the subject before she could decide how to feel about it.

"It's...different."

"Different, how?"

"I'm used to having more privacy." At least, her own room. There was always family around her house, but they gave her the quiet time she'd needed since the incident. "I don't think I'm going to fit in."

"It's only the beginning of the semester. You haven't had time to make that assumption."

"I'm not here to socialize." She stopped him with a hand before he could interrupt. "I know, it's college and I'm supposed to have that whole college experience, but that's not on my agenda. I'm here to work hard, not see how many shots I can do before passing out."

"I don't think you can generalize the college experience," he said slowly, as if gauging his words. "There are plenty of other students who are like you and here to get a good education. You just need to find those people."

She chuckled sarcastically. "Well, I don't think any of them live in my dorm. I've never seen so much alcohol in my life."

"It's against the rules to drink in the dorms, even if you're over twenty-one. Which I happen to know you aren't."

"I don't drink, but I seem to be in the minority." She ribbed him. "I bet you drank at college."

"I did, but that doesn't make it the right thing to do. Don't let anyone dictate how you live your life."

"Big words from a Dominant." Her cheeks heated. It was too easy to forget he wasn't Tristan, but instead, Professor Kelley. She shook her head. "Sorry, I shouldn't have brought that up."

He frowned. "No, but since you did, I'm going to clear up your misconception. I can't speak for all Dom/sub relationships, but a Dominant doesn't control his submissive's life. He simply provides guidance."

"Is that what you're doing now? Guiding me?"

She watched as he swallowed hard. "As your teacher."

"And elder?"

He stopped walking and turned to her. "I'm not that..." At her smile, he folded his arms across his chest. "You're teasing me."

"I am," she said, laughing. "But only because you made such a big deal about my age."

He cocked his head. "When have I done that?"

"Let's see." Pretending to mull it over, she tapped her cheek with her finger. "Earlier today after class when you asked how old I was."

"You said you were sixteen," he pointed out. "I think you get a thrill out of teasing me."

She did.

She liked it even better when *he* teased *her*. The memory of him pushing her against the brick wall of his friend's house last week flashed in her mind, and her body immediately reacted, as if reliving it. Heat permeated low in her belly, and a subtle tingling began between her thighs.

"You turned as white as the statue of David," she said, trying to ignore her arousal. "Even after you learned I was nineteen, your coloring didn't return to normal."

The lamppost's light flickered, casting three long shadows along the path. Her throat constricted, making it difficult to swallow.

What or who was making that third shadow?

Her eyes searched for the source, but she didn't see any-thing obvious. When her gaze returned to the shadows, the third one had disappeared. Probably just a squirrel.

"I thought you were older... that night," Tristan said on a sigh. He scowled, his nostrils flaring and his jaw clenching with tension. A sharp pain lanced her chest. She was such an idiot. While she was struggling with her attraction to him, he appeared to regret their time together.

"Sorry to disappoint you," she said curtly, turning to walk away.

He gently grabbed her arm. "I'm not disappointed. Just surprised. You seemed older. More mature."

Flooded with relief that she'd misread his body language, she let out a breath. But she was confused. If he didn't regret their night together, why had he scowled? "Maturity has nothing to do with age." She felt as though she'd aged a thousand years after the incident. "Sometimes a bad experi-ence can make you feel far older."

His gaze fell to the scars on her wrists. "Do you want to talk—?"

"No," she said much louder than she'd meant to. Prob-ably because she *did* want to talk to him about it. But revealing her secrets implied an intimacy they were trying to avoid. "It's in the past and that's where it's going to stay." Far, far away, where it would never touch her again.

He didn't admonish her for raising her voice.

He didn't need to.

His eyes spoke volumes. His pupils dilated and fixed on her. *This man.*

She recognized him.

The Dominant.

She hung her head as a wave of shame washed over her. But along with the shame came a blast of excitement she hadn't expected.

The arousal that had been on simmer went to a full-on boil. Her breathing accelerated and her heart increased in tempo, a tempo she also felt deep in her pussy. With a single look, Tristan was able to elicit the submissive within her.

Did he even realize it?

"I'm sorry," she said softly, peering up at him. "I didn't mean to snap at you."

He inhaled sharply, his nostrils flaring, and although she didn't think it possible, his eyes darkened even further. Then, as if coming out of a fog, he blinked repeatedly and pasted on a smile. "It's okay." He smiled and playfully tugged on the ends of her hair, his knuckles grazing the exposed skin of her collarbone. "If you can't snap at your professor, Angel, who can you snap at?" She gasped and shivered at the contact.

He'd called her Angel.

The smile melted from his face, and as he moved closer, he swallowed convulsively.

She wasn't the only one fighting the attraction.

With a long buzz and one final flicker, the lamppost's light died, blanketing them in the darkness.

A soft breeze curled around them. Neither one of them moved. Her pulse went haywire as she felt that electric current between them growing stronger and stronger.

Under the pitch-black cover of night, she found the

courage to admit the truth. "We both know you're more than my professor," she whispered.

He brought his hand to her cheek, cradling it in his palm and his thumb caressing the skin near her lips. "What happened between us last week was more than fucking for me," Tristan said gruffly. "I haven't been able to get you off my mind since that morning. When I saw you sitting there in my classroom, I thought it was my imagination. It took me a moment to process that you were really there."

Her heart was beating so loudly, she wondered if he could hear it. "I know the feeling."

Hot breath fanned her face, and although she could barely see anything, she shut her eyes as his mouth gently pressed against hers. She sighed, surrendering to it, knowing the moment would end too soon, and threw her arms around his neck, her fingers delving into his thick hair.

It was as if her actions had flicked a switch within him. Hand on her lower back, he pushed her closer, growling into her mouth and kissing her more aggressively. His tongue darted inside and stroked hers in a wicked dance in which he led and she followed.

He tasted like one of her desserts, sweet with a tinge of spicy underneath.

But there was nothing sweet about this kiss or what his hand was doing to her breast. He squeezed it hard, giving her that bite of pain he knew she liked, while he brushed his thumb back and forth over her nipple.

This was crazy, kissing out here in the open when it was forbidden. The danger of being caught somehow made it even hotter. During their night together, he'd shown she could trust him, and she trusted him just as much now. Maybe even more because he was no longer a stranger, her one-night stand.

What were the odds that they'd meet at a party twelve hours away and end up here at Edison University where she'd be his student and assistant? That had to mean something, right?

Something like . . . destiny.

Tension coiled low in her belly. Her insides clenched, achy and needy, and she whimpered deep in her throat.

Lifting his mouth from hers, he murmured against her ear. "You greedy for me like I am for you, Angel?"

Bending at his knees, he dropped his hand to her ass and pushed her against his erection, giving her proof. At the glorious pressure of him grinding on her clit, a loud moan tore from her lips.

"Yeah, you're greedy for me," he said huskily. "If I slipped my hand into your panties right now, I bet I'd find you soaking, wouldn't I?"

Yes, yes, yes.

She nodded, desperate for his touch.

He yanked her head back by her hair. "I asked you a question, Angel."

Her scalp stinging, she blinked through the fog of her arousal. Inside and out, her body was on fire.

And he actually expected an answer?

"Yes," she managed to say, clutching his shirt in both hands. Holding on to him as if her life depended on it. "I'm so wet for you."

His tongue caressed the outer shell of her ear. "You think about me when you touch yourself at night?"

She hesitated again, this time because she was self-conscious over the personal nature of his question. Reminding her of his power, he twisted her hair around his wrist and tugged on it harder than before.

The sweet bite of pain sent heat straight to her clit. "Yes, Tristan."

"What do you imagine I'm doing to you when your fingers are playing with that delicious pussy of yours?"

She trembled. Judging by that low, commanding voice he used—the one from the play party—he wouldn't tolerate a lie.

She swallowed down her embarrassment. "Spanking me."

He let out a rough moan as he released his grip on her. "Fuck, Angel." His hands went to the button of her pants. "I need to touch you. Taste you."

Liquid heat coursed through her as all thoughts of propriety flew out the window.

A familiar melody by her favorite band singing about signs and sins blared, stilling his nimble hands and crashing through the reverie.

Her cell's ringtone.

Breathless, they quickly broke apart and took a step backward, leaving a socially acceptable distance between them. Tristan clasped his hands behind his head and exhaled. "Shit. Shit. Shit."

Her stomach plummeted to the ground. She glanced at her phone, seeing she had missed a call from Chloe, and then looked back to Tristan. Based on his reaction, it wasn't hard to figure out he regretted the last few minutes.

"I'm sorry, Isabella," he said, confirming her suspicion. "I'll always treasure the night we spent together and tonight's...kiss." He took a deep breath, his shoulders rising practically to his ears before they dropped on his long exhale. "But it was a mistake and it can't happen again."

Disappointment flooded her, her stomach twisting, and she bit the inside of her cheek hard, the pain keeping her from saying what she really wanted.

We can make it work. Keep it a secret. It's destiny. But why bother if he didn't want her as much as she wanted him? If he didn't think she was worth the risk? If he thought it was a *mistake*?

She was such an idiot.

How many times would it take before she learned that there was no such thing as destiny?

TEN

Tristan took the long way home, his mind as cluttered as his new apartment and his cock as hard as steel.

After tonight, one thing was clear.

Keeping his hands off Isabella would prove to be the greatest challenge of his life.

Not ten minutes alone with her had passed before he'd practically mauled her like a starving bear eating his first meal after hibernation. Her taste had been as sweet and rich as honey on his tongue.

Just being with her was tempting enough to drive him mad. But when she'd bowed her head and apologized for raising her voice, she'd sealed her fate. Until that moment, he hadn't even realized that sometime between Isaac's home and the broken streetlamp, he'd stopped thinking of her as his student and had started thinking of her as his Angel.

Treating her like his Angel.

And she'd responded to his dominance, resuming her position as his submissive as if it were a role she'd been born to play.

If the phone hadn't interrupted them, who knows how far they would've gone?

He'd been two seconds from fucking her against the nearest tree.

He'd done the right thing by telling her it couldn't happen again.

Maybe if they both denied their attraction for long enough, they would start to believe it.

She was too young to understand that one wrong decision could alter the entire course of her life—and not necessarily for the better. At her age, he had almost lost himself to grief after his mother passed. He'd indulged in drugs and alcohol-fueled sex with nameless girls, oftentimes waking up in strange beds to faces he couldn't remember.

If it hadn't been for Isaac and Ryder, he would've ended up either dead or in prison. When he'd stopped attending classes, he should have been thrown out of school. But Isaac had refused to give up on him and, along with Ryder, had pulled him from the brink of disaster. They had dragged him to classes, kept him sober, and showed him that he wasn't alone in the world. Isaac had arranged for a grad student in the business department to tutor Tristan in order to catch him up with his class assignments.

It hadn't been long before she tutored him in more than school. As his Domme, she'd taught him self-discipline and patience, and for two glorious semesters, his body and mind were hers to command. It was when his need to control outweighed his pleasure in submitting that she'd taken him to his first play party and shadowed him as he'd topped his first submissive.

He often wondered if Isaac had arranged his tutoring with the knowledge that she would indoctrinate him in the BDSM lifestyle, but talking about sex with his mentor had never rated high on his list of things to do. To Tristan, it was like talking about sex with his father. Bad enough to have to sit through the basic birds-and-the-bees talk, but his penchant for tying women up and spanking them was better left unsaid.

If he and Isabella succumbed again to their attraction, they'd be playing with fire. No matter how much he wanted her, he couldn't be responsible for ruining her dreams.

After an hour of walking, he finally gave up and turned down the street to his apartment complex. Off campus and on the border of the next town over, it wasn't the nicest part of the area—but it was the cheapest. The tenants in his building were mostly those who worked in service positions at the university or at the shops around the campus. Thankfully, the property manager housed students on the opposite side of the complex. No one wanted to run into their professor after school hours.

He climbed the stairs to the second level, stepping over the broken beer bottles and cigarette butts. Sometimes it was hard to believe he'd gone from living in a penthouse loft, complete with a security guard manning the front desk and panoramic views of downtown Detroit, to this. Not that he'd ever felt at home in the loft. It was cold and sterile, decorated by some famous designer that Morgan had hired. Why he'd paid thousands on furniture they couldn't use or sit on was beyond him. Everything was white and light gray, and so damned clean, he'd worried about touching anything.

While he'd given in to Morgan's demand for city living, the perpetually single Ryder had bought the house in the suburbs that Tristan had eyed. Ryder had told him when the time came, he'd sell it to him at market rate. Tristan had laughed, knowing full well Morgan would never move. As it turned out, Ryder had never expected them to last. Too bad when the time came that their marriage was over, Tristan could no longer afford to buy the house from his friend.

A long shadow fell across his feet. He looked up and saw the devil herself standing by his apartment door.

First the phone call to Isaac and now a visit? His mentor had been right. Morgan was definitely up to something.

On the outside, she was just as beautiful as ever—petite and toned with thick hair that fell down her back in golden waves—and yet, all he saw was the ugliness she hid underneath all her flawless skin.

He strode past her as if she wasn't there and stuck his key into the door's lock. Maybe if he ignored her, she'd go away.

With a hand on her hip, she turned toward him. "Nice place. I mean, it's not as nice as the loft, but I can tell by the smell of the Dumpster, this apartment complex has real class."

Bad enough that she'd taken everything from him, but she had to constantly remind him of that fact.

Not about to invite the devil inside for a tour, he sighed

and leaned his shoulder against the door. "Morgan. What the hell are you doing here?"

"Visiting old friends," she purred. Reeking of that ridiculously expensive floral perfume she always wore, she reached up and began fussing with the collar of his shirt. He grabbed her wrists and pushed her off of him. "Well, don't you look handsome, Professor Kelley. Coming home from a date?" She laughed. "No, if that were the case, you'd be wearing your leathers. It's not easy to beat up poor, innocent women while wearing a suit, right?"

He took a deep breath, counting to ten before speaking. If he lost his cool, he'd be playing right into her greedy hands. "You know damned well I've never beaten up a woman."

"I doubt a court would agree once I showed them the photographs," she said, smiling in victory. "But let's not waste time rehashing the past, darling. I'm simply exhausted from all the fresh air I've gotten."

She'd always hated it in the Michigan Upper Peninsula. The closest she preferred to get to nature was sunbathing nude on a yacht off the coast of the Bahamas.

"So I take it you were already on your way here when you called Isaac?" he asked, wishing she would just get to the heart of the matter. Talking to Morgan always exhausted him, and he had another long day of teaching tomorrow.

Her eyebrows shot up in a perfect arch. "Is that what he told you? I didn't call Isaac. I shared a meal with him this morning at this charming little restaurant at a bed-and-breakfast off campus." She paused, pretending to consider. "I wonder why he would lie to you."

"I don't believe you." Isaac would have mentioned it. This was just another one of her games, and he was done playing. Didn't she have anything better to do than drive twelve hours just to gloat over his circumstances? It wasn't as if she could get more money from him. It would be like trying to bleed a rock.

"Why would I lie?"

"Because it's your nature."

She blinked, and if he didn't know any better, he would've sworn he saw hurt flash in her brown eyes. "You always did see the best in Isaac. But the man isn't exactly the saint you think he is."

He knew everything he needed to know about his friend. "This is just another one of your manipulations. I'm over it, Morgan, and I'm over you. Ruining my life was a game to you, and now that the game's over, you're bored, so you're trying to start another one. Get this through your head. I'm. Not. Playing."

She pursed her lips. "You couldn't be more wrong, Tris. I'm not the one playing a game. You think you know everything, but you're still in the dark, and it's not up to me to show you the light. You'll have to find that out on your own. And whether you choose to believe I'm telling the truth about Isaac is up to you."

"What do you want from me?"

A knot of dread lodged in his chest at her confident smile.

"I want what you promised me in your wedding vows," she said, her eyes as dark as her cold, black heart. "I want it all. And I'm not going away until I get it."

ELEVEN

Lips still tingling from Tristan's kiss and her heart bruised, Isabella let herself inside her dorm room. After the long day on little sleep, she wanted nothing more than to go to bed. But the moment she spotted Chloe crying on the couch, all thoughts of sleep disappeared.

"How did it go at Dean Lancaster's?" Chloe asked, wiping underneath her eyes with her finger.

"Good, but forget about me. Are you okay?" Isabella hovered by the door, not sure of the etiquette in this situation. Should she give her some privacy? A hug?

Chloe waved her hand and sniffed. "Not really. Do you ever feel as if no matter how hard you try, you'll never be good enough?"

All the time. Throughout their relationship, Tony systematically destroyed her self-esteem. She hadn't felt pretty enough. Smart enough. Good enough.

Maybe that was why she was so driven to make something of herself now.

She sat on the couch and put her arm around Chloe. "What happened?

"I had my first practice audition today in vocal music class." She picked up a half-eaten chocolate bar off her lap and took a bite. "I thought it went really well. But my professor tore into my performance." She sighed and gave a little smile through her tears. "I know it was the first day of school, but it was just disappointing, you know? So I called my mom..." Her bottom lip quivered. "She told me I should switch majors now because I'll never make it as a singer."

How could a mother say that? Wasn't it her job as the parent to support her child?

Isabella rubbed Chloe's back reassuringly. "I'm sure she didn't mean it."

Her roommate shrugged. "No, she did. My mom...let's just say she's not the nicest woman in the world. At least to me. Unless she's single"—she rolled her red-rimmed eyes—"which rarely happens, she doesn't pay a lot of attention to me."

"I'm sorry," Isabella said. It was hard for her to imagine, especially since her own family tended to be the opposite. Always in her face. *She* was the one who'd pushed them away.

"That's probably why I got into a lot of trouble in high school. My therapist told me it was my way of getting her attention. A cry for help." She paused, her gaze flicking back and forth to Isabella's wrists. "When it didn't work, I tried to kill myself."

While her first instinct was to correct Chloe's misconception that she had also attempted suicide, she was more concerned that her friend had tried. "Chloe—"

Her roommate put her hand up. "I'm fine now. You don't have to worry you're going to come home from class and find me dead on the floor." She patted Isabella's knee as if *she* were the one needing comfort. "I've had hours of therapy and I'm in a much better place now. Enough that my psychologist thought going away to college would be good for me. A fresh start." She let out a shuddered breath. "The problem is even though I intellectually know I'll never get my mom's acceptance, I still crave it. Singing has always made me feel special, but today's class really shook my confidence. Add in the conversation with my mom, and I just lost it."

It suddenly struck Isabella how similar they were. Both of them had gone through a rough time in high school and had come to college for a new beginning.

Isabella plucked the candy from Chloe's hand. "Will you sing for me?"

Chloe's eyes widened. "Now?"

"Yeah."

"Okay," she said almost shyly. "But be honest. Better I know the truth than waste four years of schooling." She popped up from the couch and stood a few feet in front of Isabella. "I'll do a bit of my audition piece." She bowed her head, and when she lifted it, she began to sing.

The first note sent shivers down Isabella's spine.

Chloe had a voice like she'd expect to hear from a Broadway star: Powerful, rich, and dulcet. Singing about unrequited love, she made Isabella feel every word, bringing thoughts of Tristan.

Would that be her this year? Longing for a man who didn't want her?

Isabella's eyes burned with unshed tears—tears she refused to cry. Eventually, she'd get over her feelings for Tristan, right?

When Chloe finished, Isabella stood up and clapped. "Your professor must be insane because that was amazing. Seriously, I got shivers."

A huge smile broke out on Chloe's face. "So you don't think I should listen to my mom and change majors?"

"I think it would be a crime to throw away a talent like yours, and if music makes you happy, you should pursue it. Don't let anyone else tell you how to live your life." If Isabella had listened to her family, she'd be working at their bakery and living at home until the day she got married. But business school was *her* dream, and unlike Chloe's mom, they supported it. A stray thought entered her mind. "Unless of course your mom refuses to pay for college if you remain a music major."

Chloe snorted. "No. She couldn't care less what I do. That's why her statement bothered me so much. She only said it to hurt my feelings," she said nonchalantly.

Isabella's heart broke for Chloe. "I'm sorry she's like that. What about your dad?"

Her friend shrugged. "He's not in the picture."

"Oh." *Way to stick your foot in your mouth, Isabella.*

"Well, according to Mom, he's not someone I'd want in

my life. And considering the losers she dates, he must really have been bad." She looked Isabella straight in the eyes and arched a brow. "As long as they have deep pockets, she tends to overlook their other faults," she said bitterly.

There was no mistaking her words were filled with hidden meaning. What horrible things had those men done? Abuse her mom? Had they hurt Chloe? Chloe took back the candy bar from Isabella and returned to her spot on the couch. "Are you close with your mom?"

She'd obviously changed the subject on purpose. If she didn't want to elaborate on her statement, Isabella would have to respect that. There were things she wanted to remain private too. After all, Chloe didn't need to know about Tristan or that she was a submissive.

"I used to be." Before she'd gotten lost in her relationship with Tony, she'd told her mother everything. She'd always carry around a slice of regret in her heart for not repairing her relationship with her mom before she left for college. "It was my fault. She's great. Busy, but she always made time for me."

After Chloe had revealed so much, she felt almost obligated to confide in her about her own past, but even more surprising was that she wanted to tell her. "I pushed my mom, my friends, everyone, away for a guy." She held out her arms and turned over her wrists, displaying the pink jagged lines. "These scars...I didn't do this to myself. Senior year of high school, my boyfriend tried to kill me by slicing my wrists open."

Chloe's face blanched and her hand flew to her chest. "Oh

my God. How scary." She took Isabella's hand and brought her to the couch. "I hope he's in prison."

"No, a mental hospital. His official diagnosis is schizo-affective disorder, which is like schizophrenia and bipolar all rolled into one." She clenched her hands into fists. Just thinking about it flooded her with anger and fear. "I don't know. I don't care. All I know is he's not supposed to be able to contact me in any manner, but yesterday, I got a letter from him in the mail. I don't know how he got my address here because I made sure it was unlisted on the school's directory."

"Um." Chloe winced. "There is one way he could've gotten around it. I have you listed as my roommate, and my address is published. I'll make sure to go on the directory and change it."

Isabella shook her head. "If that is how he found me, then it's too late."

He would've had to spend hours combing through the thousands of names.

He was still obsessed with her. And yet, according to Erin's message, the doctors thought he'd improved.

What if they let him out, and he came after her?

A restraining order wouldn't stop him.

"We could change rooms," Chloe suggested.

She briefly considered it. "No. I'm not going to let him dictate my life anymore. His doctor assured my contact at the prosecutor's office that it wouldn't happen again. If they can prove he contacted me, they'll throw him in jail for violating the restraining order I have against him."

She trembled, chilled to the bone at the thought of seeing him again. She just hoped he'd remain in the hospital for a long, long time.

"I'm really sorry you have to deal with that." Chloe took her hand. "I hope you know, you can tell me anything. I'd never betray your trust."

"Thank you. Same here."

"Now I understand why you have no interest in guys right now." Chloe waggled her eyebrows. "If I were you, I'd probably give up men all together and become a lesbian."

Isabella giggled. *If only it were that easy.* "Tony didn't ruin me on men." But Tristan might have. How would anyone ever measure up to him? One touch and her body went haywire. Hell, her panties were still wet from earlier. "I've actually been with someone else since Tony."

Chloe smiled. "Must have been good if you're blushing just from thinking about him."

Crap. If she was that transparent, she wasn't sure how she'd be able to face him tomorrow. He'd take one look at her and know what she was thinking.

Which was why she could no longer think about it.

She pressed her fingers to her swollen lips, almost feeling his warm, demanding mouth on hers. They had a chemistry that would be hard to deny, but in the end, he'd been right to stop it before it went any further. This morning she'd been resolute to keep the past in the past—and that included Tristan.

From this point forward, Tristan was only someone that she used to know.

TWELVE

Between lectures and office hours for Tristan's job as professor and sales calls for Novateur, the month flew by in a blur.

At his desk reviewing his lesson plans, Tristan realized he truly hadn't anticipated just how much he would enjoy teaching.

Growing up, he hadn't been a good student, more often than not cutting classes to hook up with some girl. His mom and teachers had begged him to take school seriously, but he was one of those kids who would rather experience life than read about it, even if it got him into trouble.

That's why it shocked him how easily he'd adjusted to the daily grind of an educator, especially on the small-town campus. He'd even started to fill his bookshelves with biographies about some of his favorite entrepreneurs.

Most of the students in his Introduction to Business classes were freshmen and sophomores who had no intention of pursuing business as their major. They slumped in their seats, staring with blank looks as he explained the theory of consumer choice and the utility-maximizing rule. But others sat up a bit straighter, raised their hands, and participated. Those were the ones that made it all worth it.

One in particular had caught his interest...

Like she had every afternoon since school began, Isabella sat dutifully at her small desk in the corner of his office, reading her textbook for European History class. It hadn't escaped his attention that she hadn't turned the page in the thirty minutes since she'd gotten there.

Nothing she did escaped his attention.

Not in the classroom, where she still sat in the front row, and not for a single moment of the five weeks they'd breathed the same air in his hundred-and-eighty-square-foot office.

How many times had he excused himself this month to go to the men's room to jack off? With the amount of time he spent in there, she probably thought he had some kind of stomach issue. But what other choice did he have? She'd bend to get a file, her lush ass sticking up in the air, and all he could think about was pushing her face down on his desk and fucking her into tomorrow.

Growing warm, he took a swig from his water bottle.

Since their walk back to her dorm, they hadn't spoken about what had happened that night or what might have happened if her phone hadn't interrupted them. For him, the memory of it remained fresh in his mind, but she'd given him no sign of any lingering affection.

What had he expected when he'd been the one so adamant about it not happening again?

With a huff of exasperation, Isabella slammed her book shut and swiveled in her chair to face him, likely catching him staring at her. "Are you ever going to give me work to do, or should I just plan on doing homework every day?"

He clenched his teeth and screwed the cap back onto the water bottle, rather than doing what he wanted.

Yank down her pants, turn her over his knee, and spank her for that disrespectful outburst.

Yeah, that would go over well.

Unfortunately, there wasn't much for her to do since she wasn't permitted to grade papers or create lesson plans. Isabella's tasks were limited to answering his phone, scheduling appointments, and collating copies of handouts. She'd mentioned she was supposed to help Professor Crawford with his journal article, but as an adjunct professor, Tristan didn't need to publish. Still, it didn't make sense not to use her when she was so readily available. Maybe he could utilize her skills for Novateur to get a fresh set of eyes on it.

"You really want to help?" he asked.

"Yes, I really want to help." She rolled her chair over to his desk. "That's what I'm here for. So what do you need?"

"I own a company called Novateur that invents, designs, and installs state-of-the-art smart kitchens for restaurants. Would you be interested in helping me design a system for a bakery? I need to create a few demos for my partner, Ryder."

"Ryder. The owner of the house where we...met?" A blush stained her cheeks.

God, he loved to make her blush.

"The same one." He slid a brochure across the desk to her.

"Restaurants, bars...we can design it so you can run almost everything with your voice."

"Who does the sales?" she asked, a groove forming between her brows as she studied the brochure.

"Me." He shifted in his chair, her question touching on a sore point. "Or it was until I took this job. Now he's doing most of that work."

"Does he mind that you left?"

Ryder hadn't wanted Tristan to move for a job, insisting they'd find an alternative means of capital to expand Novateur, but neither of them wanted to lose control over the business that meant the world to them. The only other option to qualify for financing had been for Ryder to buy out Tristan's share in the company. They'd tossed the idea around for a couple days, but ultimately, Ryder had been the one to reject that option, insisting that together they'd "fly high or die trying."

"We've been friends since college, when we were roommates and bonded over cheap beer, bad porn, and late-night revelations about how much we despised our fathers." *Despise* was too soft of a word for how they felt. "Ryder understands better than anyone that I owed Dean Lancaster."

Isabella stilled, her voice quiet. "Why do you owe him?"

He paused, drumming his fingers on the desk. "I lost my mother during my freshman year."

"I'm sorry." Her green eyes softened.

"I went off the deep end. Instead of flunking me, he helped me get my shit together and gave me a second chance. So when he called over this summer asking if I would teach Professor Crawford's classes, I didn't even think to say no."

He left out the part that Isaac had likely only offered him the job because he knew Tristan needed it.

Isabella didn't need to know about his failures.

For so long, he'd been crawling out of the muddy hole that was his life. Here at Edison, he was just Professor Kelley. Not the son of the billionaire Winston Kelley. Not the ex-husband of Morgan Kelley. Not the man whose ruined credit was keeping his best friend's dream from becoming a reality.

Maybe it made him a selfish asshole, but he wanted to keep his inadequacies a secret from Isabella as long as possible. He liked the way she looked at him without any judgment in her eyes.

She leaned across her desk and took his hand. "I'm glad you had him. Forgive me if I'm overstepping, but what about the rest of your family?"

Warmth permeated in his chest. Her skin was soft, but there was a strength to her grip. The touch awoke memories of the night they met, and how beautifully she'd taken the flogging. And that wasn't the only thing her touch had awoken. If she leaned over the desk any further, she'd see his cock trying to punch its way out of his trousers and would quickly learn why he spent so much time in the bathroom.

He had to remember she'd only offered her hand in sympathy. It didn't mean anything more. Because if it did, despite his intention to keep things professional, he wasn't sure he could stop himself from putting her hand where he really needed her touch.

He should give her hand a little squeeze to let her know he appreciated it and then move away.

But he didn't.

"I don't have any other family," he answered. "My father left us when I was a baby."

She didn't need to hear his sob story. His mother had been all he needed.

"Anyway, what do you think?" he asked, changing the subject. "Is helping me with Novateur something you might be interested in working on this semester?"

A brilliant smile graced her face. "Yeah. I'd like that." Her gaze fell upon their clasped hands, and her smile slid away. She swallowed hard and her tongue darted out, moistening her lips. "After all, I am here to serve you."

She had no idea what those words did to him.

Like a siren's song, they called to the Dom in him. She made him want to master her, to teach her not about business and economics, but about pleasure and pain, domination and submission. His cock twitched at the thought of her spread out on his desk, her pussy glistening, ripe and ready to be eaten.

He coughed and shifted, his hardening cock becoming a distraction from their conversation.

All from a fucking touch and an offer to please him.

And she hadn't even meant it. Not really. She was just offering to do her job.

For all he knew, she was already over him and onto someone new.

How many girls had he nailed by the end of his freshman

year? At least a different girl every weekend, if not two, and some at the same time. College was, after all, a time to experiment.

Why should Isabella be any different? She had the world at her feet, a clean slate.

She couldn't be oblivious to the appreciative stares of the guys whenever she walked into the room.

Hell, he certainly hadn't missed it.

There was no question Tristan wanted her in his bed.

On his desk.

Under his desk.

And everywhere in between.

But he wanted more than her pussy.

He wanted her submission, needed it like fire needed oxygen to burn. He'd always said he didn't want more than one night with a sub.

Now he realized it was because he hadn't met Isabella Lawson.

When his Angel had gifted him with her submission, it had left a mark on him just as real as the ones he'd made on her skin that night. He'd gotten a taste of what it would be like to own her body and soul, and he hungered to taste it again.

His heart lurched almost violently against his chest. He felt the beating of it everywhere. In his neck. His ears. Even his damned cock.

"Tristan." Her whisper broke through his thoughts and brought him back to reality.

His gaze fell to their joined hands. As if it were as natural to do as rain in spring, he was lazily sweeping his thumb back and forth across her freckled skin. His mouth watered at the thought of running his tongue along the soft arc between her thumb and forefinger.

He craved to taste the salt of her skin.

To bite and suck and lick it.

To hear her moan.

He looked up and found her staring at him with round, dilated eyes. Her chest rose and fell with quick, shallow breaths.

Her hand trembled and the pulse in her wrist raced beneath his thumb.

But she didn't pull away.

She still wanted him.

As if drawn by an invisible force, they both rose from their chairs.

Awareness heated the air, and the tension between them grew tauter with each passing second, systematically erasing all the reasons why they were a terrible idea.

The bright afternoon sun streamed through the window, the beams hitting Isabella in just a way that it almost seemed as if she glowed. His office melted away from his vision, taking everything with it, everything but his Angel.

He burned to feel her softness against his rougher skin and to taste her on his lips.

A heady warmth suffused him, and his heart banged a staccato beat against his breastbone. He ached to plunge his fingers into her red hair and hold her head steady as he devoured her mouth.

Her fevered breath caressed his face as he leaned across the desk to claim her.

A knock on the door came only a second before it creaked open. "Isabella?"

The tension snapped and they recoiled from one another.

"Chloe." Isabella's cheeks turned a fiery red as she swirled around to face the door.

He stood tall and stepped out from behind the desk, grateful he'd worn a looser pair of trousers that would hide his hard-on.

A pretty girl with brown hair strode through the door. "I thought you were going to meet me in front of the business school."

Isabella went into action, grabbing her backpack from next to her desk. "I'm sorry. I must have lost track of the time."

"Don't worry. My audition isn't for another two hours," Chloe said, waving her hand and then turning to him. "You must be Professor Kelley." She extended her hand. "I'm Chloe Donahue, Isabella's roommate. It's nice to finally meet you. I've heard a lot about you."

He stiffened. What had Isabella said about him? "All good I hope."

Chloe smiled and nodded. "Of course. Thanks for letting Isabella leave a little early today. I have an audition tonight for Maria in *West Side Story*, and Isabella offered to help me prepare."

Isabella couldn't get out of there fast enough. She grabbed Chloe by the arm and ushered her toward the door. "Have a good weekend, Tris—Professor Kelley."

She was gone before he could return the sentiment.

What the hell had just happened? He'd been ten seconds from ravaging her. Almost lost control.

Dangerous territory for a Dominant.

The last time he'd done that, he'd screwed up his entire life, and he was still recovering from the fallout of it.

He glanced at the clock on the wall. If he left soon, he could get to the city by morning. He hadn't fucked anyone in weeks. Since Ryder's party, he'd only had his hand and the memories of Angel's tight heat. But jacking off did nothing to alleviate the constant ache permeating his balls. It was as if now that his cock had gotten a taste of Angel's pussy, it would settle for nothing less.

Still, a few sweaty hours of fucking a well-disciplined submissive might be just what the sexual doctor ordered.

Who cared that the thought of being with anyone other than Isabella left a bitter taste in his mouth?

He'd get over it once he had a naked woman tied up in his bed.

He had to.

THIRTEEN

So, Maria, huh? She's the lead, right?" Isabella asked as she and Chloe walked across the grass in front of the music building.

Her pulse was still speeding like a runaway train. Chloe had almost caught her and Tristan...

What exactly?

About to kiss?

About to fuck?

It had certainly felt like that to Isabella. She hadn't meant to take his hand, but when he told her about losing his mom and having no other family, she couldn't help herself from wanting to console him. Sex had been the furthest thing from her thoughts. But the moment her palm covered the sinewy skin of his hand, images of his mouth on hers, his cock inside of her, had distracted her from her original purpose. All month, she'd fought against her feelings for him, locking them away during the daylight hours and pretending he was nothing more than her professor. But at night, when she was alone in the dorm room and underneath her sheets, she fantasized about the Dominant.

"Yeah," Chloe said, jolting her back into the present. "I'm sure I won't get it, but because of you, I thought I'd give it a try."

"Because of me?"

"Just knowing I have your support gives me the courage to try. I've never had that before. My old friends...let's just say there's a reason I don't speak to them anymore. They were more interested in the drugs my money could buy than helping me prepare for an audition."

That support went both ways. Since the night Tristan had kissed her, her roommate had unknowingly been instrumental in keeping Isabella's mind off Tristan. She was always there for her, whether it was for a meal, a study session, or just a late-night talk. And she always had a stash of chocolate on hand, a best-friend requirement, in Isabella's opinion.

Isabella hadn't received another letter from Tony, but every day, when she looked through the pile of mail, her stomach clenched and her heart thumped just a little bit faster. Chloe somehow sensed Isabella's fear without her even having to voice it, always by her side whenever they checked the mail and holding her breath until she saw the relief on Isabella's face.

A few minutes into their walk, Isabella realized they had passed the music building. "Where are we going?"

Practically skipping with giddiness, Chloe pointed at the structure in front of them and smiled. "The Edison Tower."

Her throat tightened at the memory of Tristan telling

her the history of the tower. She'd found the legend romantic, and for a brief moment, had allowed herself to imagine she and Tristan up there. Of course, her fantasy was complicated by the fact that she had a fear of heights. In the end, it hadn't mattered. She and Tristan would never kiss on top of the Edison Tower.

Chloe sprinted the last few feet to the steel door at the foot of the brick structure.

Isabella didn't hurry, her curiosity of the legend trumped by churning nausea. "Are you sure we should be doing this?"

"Come on," Chloe called, waving her over. "It's one of the only places on campus to get any privacy." She pulled a curled wire from her pocket and straightened it. "A girl in my vocal class told me the acoustics are great up here." Chewing on her lip in concentration, she slid the wire into gap between the door and the wall, moving it up and down near the handle.

"Doesn't the music building have practice rooms?"

"Yeah, but they have to be reserved in advance and it's almost impossible to find one available." At a loud click, Chloe turned the handle and the door popped open. She put a hand on her hip and ushered Isabella inside. "See? If they wanted to keep us from the top, they'd make sure they had a better lock."

Isabella roamed past the frame of the door and stared up at the curved staircase that would lead her more than one hundred feet up. "I guess."

Light filtered in through narrow windows, illuminating

the dust floating in the air. She wrinkled her nose. It smelled like old gym socks in there.

And people found it romantic?

With a bang, the door slammed behind her. She startled, her muscles tensing.

Obviously noticing her discomfort, Chloe patted her back and nudged her toward the stairs. "Don't forget to breathe."

"I'm not the biggest fan of heights," she admitted, trudging up the steps.

"Then don't look down. What's the worst that could happen?"

"I trip and fall over the side, plummeting one hundred feet to my death?"

"I promise, I won't let that happen," Chloe said, her hand on Isabella's lower back. "So... what was going on with you and Professor Kelley when I walked in?"

Crap. Had she seen us leaning toward each other? Isabella concentrated on keeping her voice nonchalant. "Why? What do you mean?"

"I swear I could've cut the tension with a knife."

"Nope. No tension," Isabella said quickly.

"You didn't tell me how hot he is. And how young. He can't be more than thirty-five."

"He's twenty-eight."

She was being tortured. Climbing up seventy-five steps in the dark, out of breath and anxious, and now Chloe was grilling her about Tristan. Could it get any worse?

"Tell me the truth," Chloe said as Isabella reached the top and walked into the room housing the carillon, a keyboard composed of carillon bells. "You've got a crush on him, don't you? I know I would."

Panting, Isabella leaned over and put her hands on her knees. If she denied the crush, would it make Chloe more suspicious? After all, she couldn't conceptualize a single heterosexual woman who wouldn't find Tristan attractive. "Maybe a little bit. But he's my professor. Nothing could happen even if I wanted it to."

Chloe turned in a circle, looking at every corner of the space. Unlike Isabella, she was breathing normally, unaffected by their trudge up the stairs.

"I had sex with my music teacher in tenth grade," Chloe said so softly, Isabella could barely hear her. "It started innocently. She'd ask me to stay after school for extra vocal lessons and paid me a lot of attention. Attention I craved."

Oh, Chloe. Isabella straightened, her stomach churning for a different reason now. She had a feeling this story wasn't going to end well.

Chloe stopped her twirling and hung her head to her chest. "I was flattered by it, you know? She'd hug me a lot. Find reasons to touch me. And then one day she kissed me. I was afraid that if I stopped her, she wouldn't give me the lessons anymore. And...I liked her. She was beautiful and talented, and out of all the students in the school, she wanted me."

If anyone understood what that was like, it was Isabella. She'd felt the same way when Tony and she had started dating.

Her friend heaved a sigh and headed out the door to

the narrow platform that wrapped around the entire top of tower.

"Did you tell anyone?" Isabella asked, following her outside.

"No." Chloe shook her head, her eyes glistening. "But someone saw me leaving her house on a Sunday morning and reported it. The school administration wanted to keep the scandal quiet, but everyone found out anyway. She was fired. I haven't spoken to her since." She turned around and put her hands on the metal handrail. "I tried to kill myself not long after. I was confused to say the least. I thought I was in love with her."

Isabella's heart broke for her friend. She came up behind Chloe and rubbed her back, letting her know she was safe to continue. She wouldn't judge her.

"My therapist showed me that my teacher had taken advantage of me," Chloe said, her voice stronger now. "That even though part of me had enjoyed the attention and the sex, I wasn't in the position of giving consent." She looked over her shoulder at Isabella, her gaze searching and just a bit knowing. "I'm not telling you this so that you feel bad for me. I'm telling you this because I don't want to see you get hurt. Sleeping with a professor, even a hot one like Professor Kelley, won't end well."

Her friend's advice shook Isabella to her core. Did she really suspect something was going on between her and Tristan, or was it just a friendly warning? A huge part of her wanted to tell Chloe about Tristan. After all, she would understand. But something held her back.

She squeezed Chloe's shoulder. "No, I imagine it wouldn't. I am sorry that happened to you, but I can assure you, Professor Kelley isn't taking advantage of me."

Chloe gave a single nod and flipped around to face the campus. "Wow, what a view. You can see the entire campus from up here. Come closer, silly, and look."

From her spot, she could see the tops of the trees. Any closer and she'd see how far she could fall. "No, I'm good from here."

Chloe snorted and grabbed her by the arm, pulling her the couple of inches to the railing. "I promise I won't let anything happen to you. The wall is high enough that even if you did trip, the worst that would happen is you might bang your head against it."

She was right. The top of the brick reached her chest, and there was another foot of railing on top of it. No one could accidentally fall over the railing, unless they climbed the ledge.

Still, she didn't look down at the ground. Instead, she kept her gaze level, which gave her a perfect view of Edison University's campus. Now she understood why couples sneaked up there to kiss. Thinking of Tristan, she located Dean Lancaster's house and tracked the path that they'd taken together.

She smiled at Chloe. "It's beautiful up here. I'm glad you brought me."

Chloe nibbled on her lower lip. "Isabella, there's—"

Her phone blared from her pocket. "Hold on." She held up one finger and checked her cell's screen, expecting to send the caller to voice mail. Her stomach flip-flopped at the familiar number and she quickly answered. "Hello?"

"Hi, Isabella," prosecuting attorney Erin said, in that same breathless voice she'd used the last time she'd called. "I'm sorry to bother you on a Friday night, but I promised to call you if there was any news. I just got a phone call from Tony's psychiatrist. He's not going to extend the petition for the continuing order of involuntary health treatment. There's a hearing next Friday at one in the court. Tony is going to be released from inpatient care."

A crushing weight on her chest made it difficult to breathe. She'd known his release was imminent, but now that the moment was here, it had knocked her sideways.

"What does that mean?" she asked. "He just walks free?"

Days. That's all she had left. Then Tony's freedom meant the loss of hers. Because no matter where she went, she'd walk in fear.

"No, he'll still be required to attend daily outpatient treatment," Erin said, as if that would reassure her. "I know you're scared, but you have the restraining order. If he violates it, he'll go to jail this time, not the hospital. I wish I had better news, but you knew when we made this deal with the defense that the day would come when Tony would get out of the hospital."

Warmth enveloped her. In her panic, she hadn't even realized that Chloe had put her arm around her. "I just didn't think it would be so soon."

"You're twelve hours away. You're safe in Edison. But if he does contact you, you let me know and I'll make sure he goes away for much longer than eighteen months."

The attorney meant well, but she didn't understand.

Life isn't fair.

How many times had Isabella heard that phrase?

Too many to count.

But until she'd dealt with the legal system, she hadn't really comprehended it. She'd thought the law was created to protect victims like her, but she'd learned the hard way that she was wrong.

It protected the accused.

The guilty.

"Isabella? Talk to me," Chloe said, worry etched on her face.

Isabella glared at her phone. She couldn't even remember hanging up with Erin. "He's getting out," she whispered. "Tony's getting out of the hospital."

"What?" Chloe threw her arms up in the air. "They can't do that."

"Apparently they can."

Her friend grabbed her and pulled her into a tight hug. "I'm so sorry. I'm here for you, okay? You're not alone. Not anymore."

Tony would be loose in the world, and she had only a piece of paper to protect her.

That piece of paper wouldn't help her sleep.

It wouldn't help her concentrate in class.

And it wouldn't keep her from wondering when or how he'd try to kill her again.

FOURTEEN

Tristan had gotten as far as leaving Edison's city limits before he turned his car around and went back to his apartment.

He just couldn't do it.

He'd imagined himself at a play party with a faceless, naked sub bent over a spanking bench who was waiting for his hand. When that face had morphed into his Angel's, he'd known he was fucked.

Because he didn't want a faceless sub.

He only wanted his Angel.

And it wouldn't have been fair to use another woman as a substitute for her.

Especially since it wouldn't have worked.

Instead, he'd spent a couple of hours at the university's gym, lifting weights and running on the treadmill. Freshly showered, he was still too keyed up to return to the confining space of his apartment.

After grabbing a sub sandwich, he decided to walk around campus. On the weekends, most students preferred to hang off campus at the bars and clubs on Main Street, which meant the campus itself was pretty dead, so long as he stayed away from the dorms and the sports arena.

The sun began dipping below the pink and purple horizon. The air smelled crisp, like burnt leaves and pine. Fall had always been his favorite season, but for the last several years, he'd forgotten to enjoy it. As a kid, he'd played in the leaves, raking them into piles before jumping into them. He and his mother would take hayrides at the nearby orchards, where'd they pick their own apples off the trees and find the biggest pumpkins in the patch. At Edison, it meant bonfires, tailgating, and football. And only a few hours away, he'd usher in the season with a walk through the most awe-inspiring forest in the state.

But when he'd moved back to the city after college, he'd been too busy to celebrate autumn. Morgan wouldn't be caught dead on a hayride or picking her own fruit. The fall months were no different than any other time of the year. Returning to Edison was a reminder to slow down. To enjoy every day as if it were his last. He'd missed this.

He strolled down the path, unconsciously taking himself to the spot where he'd last had his lips on Isabella's—the Edison Tower.

What was it about this woman that made him nearly lose control?

It wasn't about sex, although he couldn't deny he wanted to fuck her.

Hard, often, and in every way possible.

But he wanted so much more from her.

Her thoughts...her feelings...her fears...her dreams.
Her submission.

She was a lit match and he was gasoline. Together they would burn hot and bright. But what would their flames destroy as a result?

He ran his hand down his cheek when a streak of red on top of the tower caught his attention. He squinted, sure his eyes were playing tricks on him. But the image didn't disappear.

It was Isabella.

What the hell was she doing on top of the Edison Tower? Was she up there with another man?

Had he imagined their connection earlier?

He paced back and forth in the shadow of the tower.

He had no right to be jealous. She was free to date. It was better this way. If she was taken, then he couldn't touch her. Couldn't taste her. Couldn't dominate her.

Fuck that.

Before he could think about the consequences, he'd burst through the door and bolted up the stairs to the top. With all the crazy things he'd done in college, he'd never broken into the tower and come up there.

Like she was a beacon, he spotted her immediately. The wind blew her hair in all directions as she stood as still as a statue at the railing. She was still wearing the same light long-sleeved blue shirt and jeans as earlier. No jacket. Even from several feet away, he could see her shivering.

The sadist in him itched to spank her for not taking better care of herself and wearing a coat.

The Dom in him needed to wrap her in his arms to warm her.

But the man in him...just wanted her.

Not wanting to scare her by his sudden presence, he made sure to make noise as he came outside, stomping his feet on the concrete floor.

She whirled around, her hand over her chest. A blush crawled up her neck. "What are you doing up here?"

"I was out walking and saw you up here. Came to see if..." He stopped as he took her in. Her skin was paler than usual, and her eyes were red rimmed. "You've been crying."

She lowered her gaze and rubbed her thumb over her wrist. "It's nothing."

He strode to her and tipped up her chin. "It's not nothing. Was it me? Did I upset you?"

"No," she whispered. "You've done nothing wrong."

She looked so fragile. Like a porcelain doll. Small and breakable.

Her eyes were haunted. He'd seen that in her only one other time. During their negotiations when he'd mentioned bondage.

He lifted her hand and turned it palm up, exposing her wrist. "Does it have something to do with your scars?"

She tried jerking her hand back, but he refused to let go. He'd dropped the subject that first night because she was a stranger. She wasn't a stranger anymore.

She might not tell her professor.

But she sure as hell was going to tell her Dom.

"Tell me, Angel," he demanded.

She froze, her pupils dilating in response to his order. Still shivering, she exhaled a shuddered breath and fixed her stare on his chest. "It's not easy for me to talk about it. God, I don't even know where to start."

"Try the beginning." He took off his coat and offered it to her.

She didn't hesitate to accept, slipping her arms into it and pulling it closed. A long pause followed as she turned away from him and stared out over the railing. He'd just about given up hope, when the words spilled from her lips. "Tony was the boy next door and my very best friend up until our freshman year of high school, when our friendship bloomed into something more. I thought I loved him. Which was why I didn't notice the changes."

"Changes?"

"The summer before our sophomore year, he started getting jealous of the time I spent with my girlfriends. It was so gradual, I didn't realize that by the time school started up again, I hadn't seen my friends in weeks. As the months went by, he became more and more possessive."

He brushed a piece of hair off her face and tucked it behind her ear. "None of your friends confronted you about it?"

She studied her shoes as if they were the most interesting items in the world. "Maybe in the beginning, but Tony said they were just jealous of us because we were so lucky to have found each other so young." Her shoulders dropped on a breath and, finally, she met his gaze. "Dreama figured out something wasn't right. I had become withdrawn. Quiet. Anxious. She had an intervention with me at her apartment and made me see that Tony didn't need to physically hurt me for it to be abuse. It was one of the hardest things I ever did, but I broke up with him."

"I'm guessing he didn't take it well?"

She shook her head. "At first, he was completely understanding. He told me we'd always remain friends and apologized for hurting me." Pausing and taking a deep breath, she bit her lip hard enough that he was surprised she hadn't drawn blood. "But a few days later, it all changed. It was as if he refused to acknowledge we'd broken up. He was constantly calling and texting me. Showing up at my house for dinner. So, I told him that I needed my space. I was so angry, so tired of having to deal with it. It just...slipped out." She looked him in the eyes. "I told him to pretend I was dead."

Tristan's stomach clenched at her anguish. He brushed a tear away with his knuckle.

He wanted to make it all better for her. Make it so she never cried again.

She took another ragged breath before continuing. "A week later, he caught me in an empty parking lot as I was getting into my car at the mall. I didn't see him behind me until it was too late."

"What did he do to you?" Tristan asked, his voice cracking.

"He knocked me out with an injection of ketofol he'd stolen from his father's vet practice and brought me to his family's summer cabin." Her voice had grown quiet as she seemed lost in the memory. "When I woke up, I couldn't move a muscle. The drugs he gave me kept me immobile. He had a knife."

Her scars.

She didn't have to say any more. Tristan grabbed both of her hands and brushed his thumbs over the raised pink lines on her wrists.

The son of a bitch could've killed her.

Had tried to kill her.

The idea that he could've gone through life not knowing she existed made his soul hurt.

He laced their fingers together, connecting them. Never wanting to let go. "How did you get away?"

"Dreama. We were supposed to have dinner, and when I didn't show, she got worried. Turns out she'd put some GPS app on my phone that linked to her cell. My parents recognized the location and called the police. They got there before I..."

Died.

The unspoken word hung in the air like a storm cloud.

She shook her head. "Doctors said he wasn't sane at the time of the incident. There was a chance the jury would find him not guilty by reason of insanity. And I just wanted it to be over. I agreed to a deal. Involuntary commitment to a mental hospital and a restraining order. There's a hearing next Friday. They're going to release him." Tears streamed freely down her cheeks now.

"Oh, Angel." He took her in his arms, holding her tight. "Let me help you."

"I can handle it myself. It's not your fight," she insisted, her chin raised in defiance.

There was his beautiful, strong-willed Angel. It was time to prove to her just how much power she had.

"Isabella, don't you get it?" He placed his hands on her cold cheeks. "Your fight is my fight."

* * *

Isabella hated feeling powerless.

Her fate was in the hands of the court. In this case, there'd be no jury or testimony. Tony would have an attorney representing him, but Isabella would not. If the judge permitted Erin to speak, she could raise the evidence of the letter, but it was unlikely the court would intervene. If Tony's physicians attested that he was no longer a danger to himself or others and would willingly participate in therapy, the judge would release him.

Chloe had vowed to stand by her side and help her through this. She hadn't even wanted to go to her audition, but Isabella had forced her. Nothing would happen until Monday. For now, she was safe.

The minute Chloe left, Isabella had broken down, her body wracked with sobs. She wasn't sure how much time passed before the tears dried and the resignation set in. One minute the sun had been high above campus, and the next minute it was twilight.

She hadn't expected Tristan.

But that's who had burst through the tower door.

Wearing jeans that molded to his thighs and a casual blue Henley, he didn't look much older than the students he taught.

Then again, tonight Professor Kelley was nowhere to be found. The man holding her, comforting her, demanding her to talk...that was all Tristan. Funny how she'd come to distinguish between his two personas. Both demanded respect and attention. But only Tristan used that deep and silky tone that made her toes curl and her heart race. Only Tristan had that gleam in his eyes, the one that promised a world of pleasure and pain and everything in between. Only Tristan called her Angel.

He wanted to help her? She had to give up her power in order to claim it. That's the only way she'd find the strength to fight.

She took a step back from him, breaking out of his arms. "There is something you can do for me."

"Anything."

She hoped he meant that.

"Dominate me."

The color of Tristan's eyes changed, the blue in them darkening to the color of a stormy night. Blond stubble lined the sharp angle of his jaw. Memories swamped her, memories of how his stubble felt rubbing the skin of her thighs as his tongue had circled the bud of her clitoris.

Her panties dampened and the only sound she could hear was the pounding of her heart. Time seemed to freeze as that magnetic pull between them strengthened, leaving her helpless to its lure.

He curled his fingers around her nape and eddied her

away from the railing. "Be sure, Angel. Because once we do this, there's no turning back."

"I'm sure. You're the one who said we 'wouldn't' do this again," she said, reminding him of his words from the sidewalk.

A smile tugged at his lips as he twirled her around and pushed her against the tower's brick wall. "If I remember correctly, I said we 'couldn't' do this again, not that we 'wouldn't.'"

Swaying on her feet, she planted her palms on his chest. "If this happens, I need to know you're in this for the long haul. That you're not going to change your mind again."

"A day hasn't gone by that I haven't thought about kissing you," he said hoarsely. "Fucking you." He took a deep breath, his eyes growing hooded. "Dominating you."

A long moment passed as they stared into each other's eyes.

She licked her parched lips, moistening them, preparing them. "You could lose your job."

"You could be expelled."

"It's unethical."

"Dangerous."

His mouth hovered only millimeters over hers. "We doing this?"

She hooked her arms around his neck. "God yes."

And then his mouth slammed onto hers, stealing the air from her lungs. His lips, hot and rough, didn't ask for permission or search for consent, but instead took and demanded. He plunged his hands into her hair, cradling her skull as though she'd bolt if he let go, and tilted her head, feasting on her mouth.

Oh lord. Was the world spinning?

He tore his lips away and pulled her toward the door. "Let's go."

Her heart banged against her sternum, and suddenly, she was no longer cold. "Go where?"

His smile was full of wicked promises. "Somewhere you can feel free to scream."

FIFTEEN

It took less than ten minutes for them to walk to his apartment.

Well, *walked* may have not been the right word.

More like sprinted.

In order to keep anyone from seeing them together, she'd stayed on the opposite side of the road from him. Only when they got to his building did they finally come together.

The inside lobby was a bit run-down and smelled like garlic. With the key dangling from his hand, Tristan hustled them up the stairs to the second floor, and thirty seconds later, he ushered Isabella inside his apartment. She took off his coat and swept her gaze around the room, taking in the living room's dark leather sofa and coffee table, and the dining area's four-seat kitchen table. It was simple, comfortable, and best of all, didn't smell like garlic.

The door slammed behind her. She twirled around, just in time to see Tristan coming toward her, his strides long and sure, and his eyes dark and focused solely on her. His mouth crushed against hers, stealing her breath as well as her sanity. She reveled in it, giving back as much as he gave, their tongues dueling and teeth clashing.

Growling low in his throat, he yanked her closer and lifted her, giving her no other option but to wrap her legs around his waist. From her pebbled nipples to her swollen clit, every part of her ached for him.

He carried her down a short hallway to his bedroom and placed her on the edge of his bed. "Don't move," he ordered in a deep, guttural voice that warned her there'd be consequences if she disobeyed.

Heat suffused her, and the inner walls of her pussy fluttered.

What would he do if she violated his command?

Did she want to find out?

She smiled.

Hell, yeah.

At the sound of a drawer opening, she turned her head and watched him palm what looked to be a dark piece of fabric. She bit her lip as she tried to figure out what he had in his hand. A tie to use as a blindfold, maybe?

When he lifted his head, he caught her staring.

Uh-oh.

He frowned, his brows wrinkled in disapproval, but the corners of his mouth lifted just a bit. "I thought I told you not to move," he said in censure. Dark and dangerous as a lion, he prowled to her and dangled a pair of panties in front of her face.

He kept women's panties in his drawer?

Recognition dawned. "Hey, those are mine!" She reached

out to snatch them, but he quickly balled them in his fist. "Pervert."

He grinned. "You ain't seen nothing yet, Angel. I had them in my desk at work, but I worried someone might find them, so I brought them home with me." Fisting her hair, he tilted her head back. "Now open your mouth."

It was deviant.

Filthy.

Sexy.

Her pussy clenched in anticipation of being gagged by her own underwear. Apparently, he wasn't the only pervert.

"I thought you said we were going somewhere I could scream," she said, in no mood to be compliant. If he wanted her submission, he'd have to work for it.

His lip curled and mischief danced in his eyes. "Oh, feel free to scream as loud as you want. No one will hear you."

"And if I refuse?"

He snapped her head back until it almost reached the mattress. "Then you don't get my mouth on your pussy."

Said pussy dripped with anticipation. She dropped her jaw, opening wide, and he immediately stuffed her mouth with the panties.

"Good girl." His hands skimmed down her sides. "You need to stop, you take out those panties and say 'red.' Otherwise, they stay in that mouth of yours."

He bunched her shirt up over her head and dropped it onto the floor. "If I remember correctly, you get loud when you come. Don't need anyone to hear you through the walls. I'll have to train you to be quiet." His thumbs brushed over her nipples, lighting her nerves on fire. "White lace. Pretty. But I want my tongue on the pretty underneath."

He unclasped her bra, freeing her breasts, and with a hand on her stomach, pushed her onto her back. Goose bumps covered her arms, and her nipples tightened even further as the air wafted over them. Bending over her, Tristan sucked a nipple into his mouth and swirled his tongue over the tip. Ribbons of heat connected her nipple to her clit. Every pass of his tongue made her pussy contract.

The gag effectively muffled her moan.

He lifted his head from her breast and instructed her to remove his shirt before taking her other nipple between his teeth.

She hurriedly slipped the buttons out of the holes, eager to feel his skin on hers. Tristan alternated between biting and sucking the sensitive bud into his mouth, making her feel restless and needy for him. Her hands skated up his bare chest, the heat of it nearly singeing her palms.

With one last wicked nibble, he stood tall and peeled the shirt down his arms, letting it float to the floor. She barely had a moment to drink in the sight of him before he dropped from view.

Like a kinky version of Prince Charming, Tristan knelt in front of her and removed her shoes and socks. She shivered, the sensation of his hands on the arch of her foot intensely erotic. He spread her thighs and settled between them. "Look at me," he said gruffly.

She picked her head off his bed, watching as he unbuttoned her pants and slowly drew down her zipper.

"Lift," he ordered, patting the side of her thigh. Once she complied, he hooked his fingers inside the waistband of her pants and dragged them and her lacy panties down her legs, leaving her completely bare. "I was a fucking moron for thinking I could ever walk away from this pretty pussy." He pressed a gentle kiss on her mound and ran a finger up her wet labia. "Mine," he whispered reverently as his head descended.

Sparks danced along her spine as his tongue flicked her clitoris, and a muffled scream tore from her throat.

He gripped her thighs tightly, his fingers digging into her flesh, but she barely registered it, her focus narrowed to one spot. With expert precision, he lashed her tiny bud, creating a storm inside her that raged out of control.

Her body bucked up, and her eyelids closed, the intensity of the pleasure too strong for them to remain open. She shook, her toes pointed and her fingers curling as he mercilessly stroked her to an explosive climax. Ripples of scorching bliss poured over her, liquefying her bones and boiling her blood.

When she found the energy to open her eyes a half minute later, Tristan stood before her, completely naked, his condom-covered cock jutting out from the nest of curls at its base. "Ready for your punishment?"

As if she hadn't just orgasmed, the storm in her pussy flared back to life, and her heart banged a staccato beat against her breastbone.

His mouth glistening with her arousal, Tristan grinned wickedly and took two giant steps toward her. Before she knew it, he'd somehow flipped her onto her stomach.

"You still get off thinking about my hand smacking that perfect ass of yours?" he asked, squeezing her cheeks. "Let's see if the reality is as good as your fantasy. I'm giving you five spankings. This first one is for your failure to follow directions." He placed a hand on the middle of her back.

Thwack!

Fire erupted on her backside.

That fucking hurt. But the fire quickly died and was followed by a pleasant tingle.

Okay, maybe this won't be so bad.

"And this is for speaking to me in a disrespectful tone at the office earlier today."

Wait, what? When did she do that?

Thwack!

She squirmed, the sting of his hand resonating outward.

Damn him. He shouldn't punish her for something she did before they got together.

"Stay still," he ordered quietly but firmly. "The third one is for making me so crazy, I had to jack off in the office bathroom every day."

He did? That's what he was doing in there while she was sitting at her desk, completely oblivious?

God, she would love to see him make himself come.

Thwack!

This time, the blistering pain registered, but along with the sting on her ass came a deep, toe-curling pulsation in her pussy. The air seemed to thicken and heat around her, enveloping her in a cocoon of warmth.

"And this is for making me think you were over me."

Over him? How could he have believed that? Not a single day had gone by that she hadn't craved him. If it weren't for spending all her free time with Chloe, she would've completely lost it this past month.

Thwack!

She sighed. That last smack had been harder than the others, but the quick flare of pain was worth the pleasure that followed. Her entire body throbbed.

"Punishment is all done, Angel. I'm proud of you for taking it so well." He lightly caressed her fiery skin with his fingertips. "You should see how pretty your ass looks right now, all red from my hands. Another day, I'll take a picture of it to show you." His voice sounded like he'd swallowed sandpaper, thick and rough, and full of desire for her.

She loved that spanking her had turned him on.

"I went easy on you this time, Angel," he added. "Was the spanking as good as you fantasized?"

Yes and no. It had definitely hurt more than she'd anticipated, but what she hadn't expected was how satisfying it would be to please him. Of course, with her panties in her mouth, she couldn't say any of that to him.

He cupped her pussy, penetrating her with what felt like more than one finger. Groaning, she clenched her muscles around him. "Soaked. Yeah, you liked your punishment, my dirty Angel."

His body rolled over hers, his chest on her back and his arms caging her in as if he were a wild animal and she was his captive prey. She sucked in a breath through her nose as he notched his cock to her opening.

"Take me," he growled. "Take all of me."

In one hard thrust, he filled her with his hard length.

Her heart fluttered wildly, the beat of it drumming in her ears.

He slowly withdrew, almost to the tip, and then slammed back into her, knocking the breath from her chest and lighting up all the nerves inside her channel. Time stood still as he took her hard and furiously. He grabbed her waist, hauling her onto his cock each time he slammed into her. "You feel good around my dick, Angel."

With Tristan, she didn't need to worry about whether she was pleasing him or whether she was participating enough. As the submissive, she was free to just let go and feel. Her body was his to command. It belonged to him.

She belonged to him.

Sweat dripped down her spine, and damp pieces of hair stuck to her neck. Each thrust pushed her clitoris against the mattress, driving her higher and higher toward another orgasm.

He leaned over and buried his head into the crook of her neck, sinking his teeth into shoulder.

That bite of pain was all it took to push her over the edge. She let out a muffled cry as the tension deep in her pussy unwound like a spool of thread. Hot waves of climax washed over her, and her inner walls clamped down again and again, resulting in eye-rolling pleasure that curled her toes.

"Fuck yeah," he groaned in her ear. "I can feel you coming on my cock." He kept one hand on her hip while the other took hold of her hair and yanked her head back. "Let's see if we can get another one out of you before I blow inside that tight-as-hell pussy of yours."

After two orgasms, she wasn't certain she could climax again.

He quickened his pace, changing his movements from deep to shallow and creating a friction that electrified her from head to toe. His arm banded around her hips, coming between her and the mattress, and his fingers slid down to press on her clitoris.

A pressure inside her lower belly mounted, spiraling tighter and tighter.

He pinched her nub.

And she exploded.

Starbursts flashed behind her eyelids as she bucked and cried beneath him. He wrung every bit of climax from her body, continuing to rub her clit. Mindless, she reached around, grabbing him by the neck, her fingers clutching the ends of his hair.

"I'm coming, Angel," he growled.

His cock twitched inside her, the force of his ejaculation perceptible even through the condom.

Sweaty and heavy, he collapsed on top of her as both of them caught their breath. And like that, she was cocooned. Safe.

She could stay under him forever.

She inhaled the scent of sweat and come into her lungs, savoring it. With a heavy sigh, he withdrew from her body and stood, then gently turned her onto her back. She shivered, instantly missing his weight and heat as the air cooled her fevered skin.

Tristan removed the panties from her mouth and threw them on the floor. "What color are you at, Angel?"

"Green," she whispered, her voice raspy because of her dry throat.

Looking at her affectionately, he caressed her cheekbone. "I know you were worried that I'd change my mind. That's not going to happen. I'm all in, Angel. I promise you. No regrets."

She smiled. "No regrets."

There were a dozen reasons why they were a bad idea. If she sat down and wrote a pro/con list, she was sure the cons would outnumber the pros. But she didn't care.

He was willing to take the risk.

And that meant more to her than all the cons.

Her phone jingled from inside her purse in the living room, alerting her to a new text. She planted a kiss on his cheek and, in all her naked glory, rolled off the bed to grab it. Hopefully, it was Chloe with the news she'd gotten the lead role. She couldn't imagine anyone more deserving than her roommate.

After snagging her cell from the bottom of her purse, she opened up her text messages and stopped cold.

It was as if the ground tipped beneath her feet, shaking her foundation.

Her knees buckled and she collapsed onto the carpet, the phone still in her hands.

Tristan was suddenly beside her, his voice sounding far away. "Isabella? What is it?"

She couldn't answer. As if she was submerged in icy water, she began to tremble uncontrollably.

He took the phone out of her hands and read the message out loud. "See you soon, Izzy." Putting his hands underneath her butt, he scooped her up and plopped her on his lap. His arms banded around her. "Who is this from?"

"Only *he* calls me Izzy." She rested her head on his chest and closed her eyes, hoping it was all a nightmare. A single text had shattered all the peace she'd found through her submission. "It's from Tony." Her teeth chattered. "He's coming for me."

He squeezed her tight. "I won't let anyone hurt you, Angel."

His heart beat steadily under her ear, soothing her like a lullaby. "You can't be with me all the time. If he wants to get to me, he'll find a way. That's what happened before." She shook her head. "God, look at me. One threat and I fall apart."

He rubbed circles on her back. "Are you sure it's from Tony? Is it possible it's from Chloe or one of your family members?"

Her stomach cramped. "No. My family knows better than to call me Izzy. I suppose it could be from Chloe, but she's never called me Izzy before."

"Call her."

With shaky hands, she dialed her roommate. At the sound of her voice, she said, "Hey, Chloe. Sorry to bother you—"

"I was just about to call you! I'm in! I didn't get Maria, but I got Rosalia, which is still a huge role."

She tried to keep the panic from her voice. "You did? I'm so happy for you!"

"I'll probably be out all night, so if I don't make it home, don't worry about me. The cast is going to hang out and get to know each other tonight. But tomorrow, don't make any plans, because I want to take you to dinner to celebrate."

"That sounds great." She grabbed Tristan's hand for support. "Um, did you text me earlier, by any chance?"

"No. Why?"

"No reason."

There was a long pause. "Listen, why don't I meet you back at the dorm?" Chloe's voice was laced with sympathy. "I felt terrible leaving you after you got that phone call from Erin."

"Don't be silly. I'm fine. Just go have fun."

"Isabella—"

"I've got to go. See you tomorrow," she said quickly, ending the call before Chloe could interrogate her. She dropped the phone on the carpet and sighed. "It wasn't from Chloe."

Tristan tucked a piece of hair behind her ear. "Do you trust me, Angel?" he said softly.

When it came to Tristan, she had no doubts. "Yes. I trust you."

His lips brushed her forehead. "Then trust me when I tell you that I'm going to keep you safe. I promise you, Angel. No one is ever going to harm you again."

SIXTEEN

For the second time since his divorce, Tristan slept with a woman in his bed. And not just any woman.

His Angel.

Exhausted by both the sex and the emotional breakdown over receiving that text, she'd fallen asleep in his arms not long after they'd called the police. He held her close, soothed by the feel of her breasts against his side and the sound of her deep breaths. Although she appeared to be sleeping peacefully, her hand was curled into a tight ball on his chest, and every few minutes, she'd whimper as if she was having a nightmare. He wished he could get inside her mind, be her white knight, and vanquish the metaphorical dragons for her. If anyone deserved a good night's sleep, it was Isabella.

Because Tony was still in the hospital, the police didn't see the text as an immediate threat, and without any real evidence connecting the message to him, they alleged their hands were tied. The most she could do was come down to the police station and file a report in the morning. She also left a message for Erin. But likely nothing would happen until Monday, and even then, he had a feeling the text wouldn't be enough to keep Tony in the hospital.

The law had already failed him once. Not directly, but Morgan had known when she'd taken the photos of them that courts rarely accepted consent as a legal argument. If she'd gone to the police with those pictures, it was probable that he would've served prison time for abuse. It was a stigma that would've followed him for the rest of his life. Forget starting Novateur, he would've been lucky to find a job that paid anything more than minimum wage. He would've been ruined.

So he'd given in to Morgan's blackmail.

He'd be damned if he let the law fail him again.

He would do anything to protect this woman.

Especially since no one else would.

No, he wouldn't rely on the cops or the courts to keep Isabella safe.

That was now *his* job.

She'd been right. He couldn't be with her all the time. Not even if he wanted to. But he had the responsibility to teach her how to protect herself. Both emotionally and physically.

Starting tomorrow.

Eventually, lulled by her steady breathing and the warmth of her body snuggled into his, he must have fallen asleep. The sun was low in the sky when the sound of Isabella crying tore him from his dreams.

Her body jerked against him, each limb twitching.

Registering the dampness on his chest, he found her cheek wet with her tears. Her eyes were closed tight, lines of tension pinching the edges. He didn't know whether to wake her, but he couldn't bear to see her cry.

He hushed in her ear and rocked her, smoothing his hand down the length of her hair over and over again as his mother had done to him when he was a child.

After a minute, her lashes fluttered, and her beautiful green eyes stared up at him. "You're here," she said, blinking as if she was imagining him.

"Technically, you're *here*. We're at my place." He sat up, reclining against the headboard, and tugged her along with him so that her head was on his chest, supported by his elbow. "You were having a bad dream, I think. Was it about Tony?"

Her lips pressed together in a line. "I'm not . . . it started out the way it always does. I'm lying in a bed, drugged, unable to move, and he's got a bloody knife in his hand. I watch the sunset knowing it will be my last one." She narrowed her eyes. "But this time, the nightmare changed. He disappeared, leaving me alone in the cabin. My phone was ringing, so I got up from the bed and found it in my purse. When I answered it, all I heard was laughter coming from the receiver. And then it grew louder until it filled the room, and I realized the person who was laughing was inside the cabin with me. I ran to the door, pulled on the knob, but it wouldn't open, so I ran to the window." Her voice cracked. "You were right there on the other side, calling my name. Just as you shattered the window, someone attacked me from inside. This time the knife..." She swallowed and took a deep breath. "...it went straight through my heart."

His stomach soured, acid eating at his esophagus, and his chest constricted as if there were a boulder sitting on it. He ached for her. No one should have to live with the constant threat of violence hovering over her head. She'd left an abusive relationship and had spent over a year healing from it. What kind of legal system allowed for an innocent woman to fear for her life while the man who tried to kill her went free?

No wonder she was worried.

It didn't take a genius to interpret her nightmare.

She didn't have faith in his promise to protect her.

The system had failed her.

He wouldn't.

And he would prove it to her. Starting right now.

"Get up. We're going for a ride," he said, kissing her gently on the lips. He immediately rolled out of bed to keep himself from fucking her until she screamed his name and begged him to stop. There would be time for that later. Right then, she needed something different than his cock.

She raised an eyebrow and followed him out of bed, bending over to pick up her pants and giving him a nice view of the bruise on her right ass cheek. The sadist in him roared in triumph at seeing his mark on her body. Sure, no one else would see it, but he'd know. It said she fucking belonged to him.

She was *his*.

His to cherish.

His to punish.

His to defend.

If she didn't already get that, she would by the end of the day. By the time he brought her back to his bed that night, she'd know exactly what it meant to be his submissive.

Once they were dressed and ready, he grabbed an extra sweatshirt for her, his bag filled with perverted goodies, and a blanket. She still hadn't asked where they were going, and that fact pleased him. It meant a part of her trusted him. Too bad he wouldn't settle for just a part. But as her Dominant, he'd first have to earn it.

She zipped up her coat and allowed the hood to cover the top part of her face. Most people in his building would be sleeping this early on a Saturday, but he was glad she wasn't taking any chances of someone seeing her face.

From there, he drove her straight to the police station, where she spent twenty minutes explaining her past history with Tony to an Officer Hanson, providing a copy of the restraining order via e-mail, and showing the text message. Unfortunately, the officer hadn't been any more concerned about it than the one on the phone the previous evening. But Isabella had taken it in stride, remaining pleasant even when he could tell from the pinch of her lips and the redness in her eyes that she was suffering on the inside.

After picking up two donuts, a black coffee for him, and a mocha latte for her, he headed north on the highway, taking them out of town where no one would recognize them. He cranked up the heat in the car and flipped on the radio, hoping to create a comfortable environment for Isabella to relax.

As they left the town of Edison in the rearview mirror, Isabella angled her body toward him and tucked her hair behind her ear. "Are you going to tell me where we're going?"

He chuckled. "Does it really matter?"

He'd wondered how long it would take her to ask. Control freaks always had a difficult time sitting in the passenger seat. When his mother had been alive, she would stomp her foot on the car floor as if she were stepping on the brake pedal. Of course, back then, she had a reason to... he'd been a terrible driver.

"No, I guess not," Isabella said with a shrug. "But I'm not big on surprises."

"I bet you were one of those kids who couldn't wait until Christmas morning to shake her gifts and try to figure out what was inside the wrapped boxes."

He could just imagine her as a child, her red hair in pigtails, wearing snowman pajamas, underneath the Christmas tree weighing the presents in her hands and holding them up to her ear.

Her lips parted as if she was about to argue, but all at once, they turned up into a smile. "Guilty. I hate surprises for myself, but I love to surprise other people. In fact, one year, I threw Tony..." Her smile melted off her face like candle wax.

"It's hard not being in control, isn't it?" he asked, trying to redirect their conversation from her ex. Thankfully, he'd learned she was easily distracted by confrontation.

She folded her arms across her chest. "Not liking surprises has nothing to do with control."

He chuffed out a laugh. "Doesn't it? Who's behind the wheel of the car? Who knows where we're going? Me. I have the control." He glanced at her, not surprised to see the stubbornness in her posture. "How does that make you feel?"

"You sound like my therapist." She turned her head to look out the passenger side window and grew quiet. "It makes me nervous. Not knowing what to expect. Relying on you."

There it was—the truth.

"And yet you seem to have no problem with my taking control over sex," he pointed out.

"Well...yeah. That's different."

"Why?"

"Why?" Annoyance laced her tone. "I don't know."

Deep down, she did know.

It wasn't *him* she couldn't trust.

It was herself.

He reached over the center console and took her hand. "The first night we met, you trusted me with a flogger. You trusted me to honor your limits. You trusted me inside your body. Why can't you trust me now?"

"I do trust you," she said, a notch forming between her brows.

"Not entirely. Do you trust me not to drive us off the road? Definitely. But why can't you let yourself relax and just enjoy the moment? Why do you need to know where we're going?"

"Because..." She swallowed and ran her hands down her thighs. "Because...the unknown scares me. I can't plan or prepare for it. I've always been that way. But after Tony, it got worse."

Of course. Because Tony had reinforced all her self-doubts.

"Being in control is exhausting, isn't it?" he said quietly.

"Yes."

"When I dominate you, how do you feel?"

"Free."

"It's the only time you cede control," he explained. "That's why the submissive role is so alluring to people with demanding careers. Giving control to someone else doesn't make you weak. I'm sure you know that." He tapped the side of her head. "Up here. Now, we need to make you believe that in here." He placed his fist over her heart.

"And if I do? How will giving up control help me?"

"It's only when you give up control that you'll find your strength and start to believe in yourself again. You want to know where we're going? I'm taking you to one of my favorite spots. I found it when I wasn't much older than you. It will give us the privacy we need for what I'm going to teach you."

The car grew silent, but he could practically hear the wheels of her brain cranking. She was overthinking things. Tense. And that simply wouldn't do. "Unzip those pants of yours and tug them down to your knees. Then spread those gorgeous legs and finger yourself. But do not come, Angel," he warned.

Only a second of indecision flashed in her eyes before her lids grew hooded and she puffed out one of her little gasps. His cock jumped against the zipper of his jeans as if trying to punch its way out. Keeping her gaze on his face, she lifted her butt off the seat and pulled down her pants. She slowly parted her legs, teasing him.

With one hand, she pulled her panties to the side, exposing the pink lips of her pussy, while her other hand delved between them. Her moan filled the car.

He didn't want to take his eyes off the sight, but unfortunately, he didn't want to drive them off the road...especially since she trusted him not to.

The car's engine couldn't mask the sound of Isabella's fingers plunging in and out of her wetness. He marveled at the beauty of her submission. She was completely aroused. Her eyes were glazed and wild. Her skin flushed.

"Don't come," he reminded her, sensing she was close to climax.

Her fingers slowed and she blew out a breath.

He smiled. "Good girl." Keeping her on the edge for the next hour would be torment for them both. "You're dripping for me, aren't you, Angel? Show me those fingers." When she held them up for his perusal, he grasped her wrist and brought her fingers up to his nose. Inhaling deeply, he smelled her arousal as strongly as if his nose were buried in her pussy. "Taste yourself for me."

She bit her lip. "I..."

"You've never tasted yourself, have you?" He wasn't surprised when she shook her head. "Then I'm ordering you to do it."

This time she didn't pause. As she stuck her fingers in her mouth, her lips closing around them on a hum, he imagined it was his cock in her wet mouth she was enjoying.

His head fell back against the seat with a *thunk*.

It was going to be a long fucking drive.

SEVENTEEN

After he'd finally allowed her to climax, she hadn't once asked where they were going. Instead, she'd rested her head against the window and sang along to the radio, her mood both carefree and tranquil. The stress lines marring her face had disappeared, and her eyes were clear. She would likely attribute the change to her orgasm, but he knew the truth.

It was because she'd given up control.

For her, sex worked like a switch in her brain that instantly flipped her from control freak to submissive.

If he had his way, he'd soon replace that switch with his voice, and eventually, she'd submit to him without any provocation at all. Her submission would become as natural to her as breathing.

As they neared their destination, a large sign on the side of the road greeted them, announcing their location.

"Welcome to Paradise," Isabella read out loud. She sat up and cocked her head. "We're in Paradise?"

"The night we met, I promised you paradise, and I always keep my word."

She let out a laugh, her whole body quaking with it. "We drove three hours for that?"

"No, I drove three hours to show you that." He jutted his chin toward the massive tree-capped hills stretched out in front of them. While Edison's trees had also turned from green to the traditional autumn colors, the woods here seemed somehow brighter and more vibrant, as if each leaf had been individually painted on the branches. "We're going to Tahquamenon Falls State Park. Fifty-two thousand acres of mostly undeveloped wilderness and home to one of the largest waterfalls east of the Mississippi."

No longer laughing, her expression turned soft as she looked out the window. "It's beautiful." She curled her hand around his upper arm. "You said you used to come here?"

"Here, I'm reminded that I don't have control over everything. I'm just a man. I might find strength in domination, not submission, but every now and then, I'm humbled by the reminder that there's a greater power than me in this world. It gives me strength when I falter."

"Thank you for sharing this with me."

It was the least he could do for her. He couldn't be the type of guy she probably deserved—someone her own age without baggage or complications. But he could be the man she needed.

He followed the loop through Paradise and turned into the lot where they'd park to see the more populated touristy area of the state park. When they got out of the car, he took her hand, showing her they were free to display their affection for one another here. "It's only a quarter-mile hike to the falls."

Their fingers intertwined, they strolled along the paved path that took them down to the overlook. There were people all around. Couples. Families. The occasional single individual. And not one of them gave him and Isabella a second glance.

Through the heavy scents of leaves, grass, and dirt, he could smell Isabella, a mix of vanilla and sex. She was drenched in it. In him. In the saliva he'd left on her body from his exploration of kisses and licks. And in the perspiration he'd dripped onto her as he'd pounded her pussy to his own explosive climax. In their rush to leave this morning, they hadn't showered.

He brought their linked hands up to his nose and inhaled her pussy's scent from their fingers. Her eyes popped wide, and a blush stained her cheeks as she realized what he was doing.

At the front of the platform that overlooked the Upper Falls, he slipped his arm around her waist and tugged her to his side. "What do you think?"

Fifty feet high and two hundred feet across, the waterfall roared as fifty thousand gallons of water fell per second. The sun's rays bounced off the water, making it look as if the falls were sparkling with hundreds of diamonds. Two squirrels scurried up the nearby tree, and birds swooped in the air, searching for their breakfast. An owl hooted and the trees swayed in the wind.

Being here, with Isabella, was his idea of heaven.

She sighed, resting her head against his shoulder. "Amazing. It's so big."

"Size impresses you?" He nodded once. "Good to know."

Laughing, she elbowed him in his side. "That's not what I meant, and you know it."

He loved hearing her laugh. Cupping her cheek, he turned her to face him. "I'm glad you're here with me." At the sparkle in her eyes, he claimed her lips, stealing her surprised gasp.

She tensed for a moment before sinking into him and ceding control. He angled her head and deepened the kiss, the taste of mocha and his Angel exploding on his tongue.

A gust of wind swirled around them, lightly spraying them with water from the falls. She shivered and moved closer. Wrapping his arms around her, he lifted his lips and just held her, their bodies connected in a way that told everyone around them that they were lovers. His gaze connected with a guy who was holding hands with a toddler, a girl with red curly hair and freckles across the bridge of her nose. Tristan's heart squeezed.

If Isabella had a daughter, was that what she would look like?

The man smiled at him. "Would you like me to take your picture?" he asked, gesturing to Tristan and Isabella.

Isabella tilted up her chin. The indecision that warred in Isabella eyes matched his own internal struggle. Fuck yeah, he wanted a photo of him with his girl. But a picture was worth a thousand words, and if anyone ever saw it, they'd instantly recognize the illicit nature of their relationship.

He shook his head. "Nah, we're good. But thanks for the offer."

Reality shattered the moment, bringing along with it the reminder that the memories they made together could never be recorded or preserved.

When Isabella came to her senses and dropped him for someone who she could bring home for Christmas dinner, she'd leave him with nothing but the memories of her in his mind.

They didn't discuss it. But it hung over them as they left the overlook and ate lunch at a restaurant, her nibbling on a cheeseburger and him drinking a locally brewed beer. They talked about current events and their favorite movies, but stayed far away from anything to do with their relationship.

That would come later. It was an inevitable and necessary conversation to have before they returned to Edison. But for the next couple of hours, he wanted to maintain the illusion that they had nothing to hide.

After returning to their car, he drove them to the far side of the state park, where a much less traveled trail would take them to an unmarked path. He hadn't been there in years, but his memories were as vibrant as if it were yesterday. He nabbed his bag from the trunk and took her hand again. "Come on. You okay hiking a couple of miles?"

"As long as you're with me." She blushed as they ducked under the trees to start on the path. Brown leaves crunched underneath their feet. "I don't have the best sense of direction. When I was ten, I went on a nature walk with Dreama and we had to call the park ranger to come get us when we couldn't find our way back in the dark."

Because they weren't on an official trail, the path was much narrower, and their bodies brushed against each other with each step. "You must have been scared."

She pushed a branch out of her face. "You'd think so, wouldn't you? But Dreama has a way of making everything fun. Instead of freaking out, she kept me occupied by telling stories and cracking jokes. When the ranger did show about a half hour later, I didn't even want to leave."

He was glad that she had her cousin. If he ever got the chance, he'd thank Dreama. She not only saved his Angel's life, but she had brought her to Ryder's. If not for Dreama, he would never have met Isabella. He owed her, and someday, he hoped to repay that favor. "Have you told her that I'm your professor?"

She looked down at her feet and nibbled on her lip. "I was going to. But I got her voice mail and then the thing with Tony happened, and somehow, I just never got around to it."

Hmm. Interesting. He'd gotten the impression she shared everything with Dreama. "Are you worried she'd tell you to stay away from me?"

She stumbled over a rock, but immediately righted herself. "No. She's not like that." She paused. "I guess...I wanted to keep it to myself."

Or was it because he hadn't given her permission to tell her cousin about him?

From the moment he dominated her at Ryder's house,

Isabella started seeing him as her Dom. It didn't always happen that way, but Isabella was new to the scene. Impressionable. She probably didn't even realize it. But subconsciously, she'd keep everything about him a secret until he gave her permission. For now, it was better that they keep their connection under wraps.

For the next twenty minutes, they hiked through the forest and, just as he'd expected, there was no sign of anyone else.

At the sound of a branch snapping off to their right, they stopped. There, only ten feet away, was a deer, its frightened black eyes fixed on them. The magnificent animal stood still, taking stock of them, deciding if they were predators. Its nostrils flared and the deer, having made its decision, galloped away. Only then did he notice the three fawns doing their best to keep up with their mama.

This wasn't his first sighting of deer in these woods, but when he witnessed the wonder on Isabella's face, it definitely became the most special. Her smile lit up the forest.

He probably shouldn't mention the black bears that lived around there.

A few minutes later, the path widened into a small clearing shaped like a circle, with a massive oak tree in the center. It wasn't much, but to Tristan, it was like coming home. How many hours had he spent sitting with his back up against the tree just thinking? Or reading a book that inspired him to become a better man? He'd napped underneath the branches, and once or twice, had masturbated against that tree.

His groin tightened at the vision before him.

Like a forest nymph, Isabella glided around the wide circumference of the tree trunk, her fingers caressing the bark and her long hair blowing behind her. "How did you find this spot?"

"I'd like to say it was divine intervention or because I'd sought solace in nature," he said, joining her at the tree, "but truth be told, I came with a girl and needed a place to smoke a bowl and have sex where we wouldn't get caught."

Her jaw dropped as she leaned against the tree. "It's hard for me to picture you doing drugs."

She couldn't picture it? Marijuana was nothing compared to the hallucinogens, cocaine, and speed he'd done. His days and nights had merged into one continuous blur during that time.

"Why is that?" he asked.

"Drugs tend to make people lose control."

He smiled at her astuteness. "I agree. But I wasn't born a Dominant. In fact . . . ," he said, pausing for effect. "I subbed for a woman before I realized I preferred to be on the other side of a whip."

She put her hand on her hip. "You? A sub?"

"It was after my mother died during my freshman year at Edison. You were right when you said that drugs make people lose control, but they weren't the *problem*. They were a *symptom*." He was walking on a tightrope. While it was necessary to divulge bits of his past, she didn't need to know about all the mistakes he'd made. Besides, today was about her. "And through BDSM and submission, I found discipline. Patience. Control. But it wasn't until I started dominating that I found peace."

Isabella grew pensive. "Will I find it?"

"Yes," he promised. "Some people can submit in the bedroom and that's enough for them." He pulled her against him and gripped her shoulders. "But I don't think you're one of them. I think you'll only find peace when you submit in all aspects of your life."

He'd never had a twenty-four seven Dom/sub relationship before. Never wanted one. Never even considered it. But Isabella needed that from him, and for the first time in his life, he was willing. That kind of relationship would require much more effort and energy on both their parts.

Confusion swirled in her green eyes, and her nose scrunched. "I don't understand. All aspects? Like having someone tell me what to eat and what to wear?"

Hell no. He didn't want a sub who couldn't make a single decision.

He traced his fingers over the frown lines on her forehead. "Some people find success in having a Dom who provides structure and guidance. Almost like a life coach. Together, we can create a schedule and expectations for you to follow. From the moment you woke in the morning until the minute your head hit the pillow at night, everything you did would be under my direction."

The frown lines jumped to the sides of her mouth. "And you think I need that?"

He caressed her cheek with his fingertips. "I do."

"Yes." She covered his hand with her own. "If it helps me live without the constant fear that Tony's going to kill me, I'm game."

"As I told you in the car, strength comes from here," he said, touching her forehead. "And here." He placed his hand over her heart. "But it also comes from knowing you can take care of yourself, and that's what I'm going to teach you right now...self-defense."

Her eyes popped wide. "I don't—"

"There will be times when you're alone." He hated the thought. Wished this wasn't necessary. But she couldn't remain helpless. Hopefully, with a little self-defense, she'd grow confident in her ability to escape if Tony ever did come for her. "I wish I could be with you, protecting you, all the time, but it's just not possible. Having the knowledge to protect yourself is essential."

She nodded once. "What do I need to know?"

He took a step back to give them both some room. "First things first, if you can run away, do it. Even if they have a weapon, most of the time, they won't use it for anything more than intimidation."

"Unless...," she said meekly.

"Noise is your friend," he said quickly, moving on. "Yelling 'fire' will draw more attention than screaming 'help.' That's because people worry more about their own safety than the safety of others."

"Well, that's depressing."

He continued. "Don't move any closer to your attacker than necessary."

For the next hour, he taught her some basic defensive moves that she would hopefully never have to use.

It couldn't have been more than sixty degrees, but sweat rolled down both their faces as they role-played various situations. She began hesitant and fearful, doubtful of her ability to ward off an attacker of Tristan's size. But over time, her movements became surer, more confident. She growled each time he bested her, but it pushed her to work harder.

"Remember, always aim for the part of the body where you can do the most damage," he reminded her. "Eyes, nose, ears, neck, groin, knee, and legs. Let's see what you've learned so far. Pretend you're walking to class." Rather than telling her what moves to use, he wanted to see if she could figure it out on her own. He wasn't stupid enough to think a single lesson in self-defense was adequate, but it was a damned good start.

She wiped her brow and got into character, walking away from the tree toward the path. Staying aware of her surroundings, she kept her head up and her ears open. He didn't give her time to react, running toward her and knocking her to the ground. They hadn't practiced this scenario yet, but with everything he'd taught her so far, she should have enough moves to at least buy her time for help to arrive.

He wrapped his hands around her windpipe as if he was going to strangle her. She didn't show a moment of weakness. She hooked a hand around his wrist, and her other hand came to his opposite elbow while her leg trapped his foot. In two seconds, her head lifted and she'd rolled him over onto his back. Then the heel of her hand met his nose.

"I did it!" she shouted, pure joy evident in her eyes.

He was so proud of her, but even better, she was proud of herself. He grinned and reached up to skim his thumb over the apple of her cheek. "Yeah, baby. You did good." His cock swelled, the weight of her on top of him and the adrenaline rushing through him a heady aphrodisiac. "Now for your next lesson."

Unaware that this past hour had been the easy part of the day, she looked down at him eagerly.

She wasn't the only eager one.

His inner sadist couldn't wait another minute. "Get naked, Angel." He lowered his tone to let her know he meant business. "I want you to take off all your clothes."

EIGHTEEN

Naked?

If it weren't for that wicked sparkle in Tristan's eyes and that deliciously decadent voice that he used, Isabella would have thought he was kidding.

The Dom was back and ready for her submission.

Her heart fluttered and her clit twinged. The arousal at the idea of getting naked in public took her by surprise. Did it make her an exhibitionist if no one but Tristan would see her?

A different thought occurred to her. "Here? What if someone catches us?"

A muscle in his jaw twitched. "Trust me."

"I do trust you," she snapped. Getting off him, she rolled her eyes, not caring that he'd probably punish her for it. She stood up and dusted the dirt off her backside, although why she bothered she wasn't sure, since she was about to be naked.

Although his expression was teasing, his tone was anything but. He didn't like her hesitation. She'd noticed whenever she did, that same muscle twitched. It was kind of funny. One day, she'd have to rile him up to see how far she could push him before his jaw went into spasms.

How many times had he repeated for her to trust him in the last twenty-four hours? Too many to count, that was for sure. Had she done one thing to make him think she didn't?

When she'd gotten in the car with him that morning, not knowing where they were going, she'd trusted him.

When he'd taught her self-defense, she'd trusted him.

When he'd told her she needed to submit from morning until night in order to find peace, she'd trusted him.

Was it so wrong to ask him a question now and then?

Apparently, in Tristan's opinion, it was.

Total submission would take some time to adjust to, but the idea of Tristan having a part in every minute of her day excited her in a way that shocked even her. Her first inclination had been to refuse. She was an adult and on her own for the first time. She didn't need a keeper. But it all came back to trust. If Tristan believed she needed full-time submission, then she'd give it a shot. Her body certainly didn't mind. On the contrary, at the thought of it, her pulse kicked up a notch and her pussy swelled. Or maybe it was because she was about to undress in the middle of a state park where anyone could stumble upon them.

Holding his gaze, she slowly drew her shirt up her abdomen. His pupils expanded, eating up the blue irises of his eyes. He gulped, his Adam's apple working hard to swallow. He might be in control, but he wasn't unaffected.

She ripped off her shirt and shook her head, fanning out

her hair as the shirt fluttered to the ground. The autumn air whirled around her torso like a lover's touch, soft and caressing. There was something sensual in the act of undressing for Tristan as he watched. Power surged through her.

He stood only feet away, his body rigid, stretched tight like a rubber band about to snap. His hands were clenched, making the veins of his biceps bulge, and his nostrils flared, causing his lips to curl into something resembling a snarl. If the deer saw Tristan now, there'd be no mistaking him for anything but a dangerous predator.

"Angel," he growled, warning her.

After removing her shoes and socks, her fingers went to work on the zipper of her pants, down, down, down, as slow as molasses. Tristan's eyes tracked every millimeter of its descent, his arousal almost tangible. He might punish her for her tease, but no matter what he admitted, he loved it.

She hooked her thumbs around the waistband and, with a shimmy of her hips, bent forward, giving Tristan a clear view of her cleavage as she tugged her pants down her thighs. Now clad only in her sheer bra and panties, she straightened her spine and threw back her shoulders, exulting in her feminine power.

Her hard nipples poked through the fabric of her bra. Her breasts felt heavy and swollen. Sensitive. Reaching behind her, she unclasped her bra and allowed the lace to slide down her torso.

A quiet moan passed her lips at the blatant heat banked in Tristan's eyes. Hunger. Possession. Desire. It was all there for her to see.

Her clit sizzled. Her hair stroked the tops of her breasts and the wind tickled her nipples. Starting at her belly button, she skimmed her fingertips up the length of her abdomen, that simple touch lighting a fire along its path. Goose bumps popped up on her skin. As if offering her breasts to her lover, she cupped them in her hands, shivering at the sensation of her cool skin on her warm, sensitive flesh.

Tristan growled, the noise emanating from deep in his chest. Like a lion about to pounce, he stalked toward her, his gaze on her tightly pebbled nipples. "Cold?"

She shook her head. "The opposite." He followed the movement as she skated her hands down her rib cage to the top of her panties. "I'm burning up inside." With his full attention on that shadowy V between her thighs, she dragged the damp lace down her legs and stepped out of them, baring herself completely to him.

"That was quite a show you put on for me."

Some of the confidence she'd felt from her striptease leached out of her. "I hope you enjoyed it."

His lips pressed together. " 'Enjoy' isn't the word I'd use. More like 'torture.' "

She deflated like a week-old balloon. "You didn't like it?"

"Like? He chuckled and shook his head. "I fucking loved it." He took her hand and placed it on the giant bulge behind his pants. "You did this, Angel," he said gruffly. "And now it's time to pay the price for it."

A frisson of excitement shot through her veins, not knowing what to expect or what price she'd have to pay.

She'd known before she started her striptease that she was playing with fire. But hearing that he'd loved it, feeling the evidence of his lust for her under her palm...that made it all worth it.

He picked a piece of errant hair off her cheek and rubbed it between his fingers. "I want to try something with you, but I understand if you're not ready." His lips whispered against hers. "I want to tie you up," he said softly.

She inhaled sharply. Just over a month ago, it had been a hard limit for her. She still remembered the panic of waking up in the cabin unable to move. The excruciating pain of Tony's knife slicing into her skin. The agony of waiting to die as the blood drained from her wrists onto the white sheets.

"It scares me," she admitted.

His large hands cradled her face, and compassion flared in his gaze. "I know it does. But that's what we're doing here today. Eliminating your fears, so that no matter what happens at Tony's hearing next week, you'll know that you're strong enough to handle it."

Was it that simple?

When she thought about Tony, it was her loss of power that she feared the most. Submission gave her the ultimate control because she always had the capability to stop the scene with the utterance of her safe word. She had other hard limits that would always remain that way, but those had nothing to do with fear. Before the incident, thoughts about bondage turned her on. She wasn't ashamed to admit there were nights she masturbated to fantasies of a man tying her spread eagle to a four-post bed and having his wicked way with her. But in every variation of that fantasy, there was always underlying consent to it.

Since the cabin, she'd banished any idea of bondage from her imagination, not because it didn't arouse her, but because she was afraid. And she was so, so tired of Tony's hold on her.

"Okay," she said, determination like a fire in her belly. "I'll try."

Oh my. Tristan's gaze turned molten as his eyes raked over her, from her eyes to her feet and back up again. "What's your safe word, Angel?"

She cleared the thickness in her throat. "Red."

"If you need it, use it," he said firmly.

"Yes, Tristan."

Leaving her a naked, aroused, and trembling mess, he strode to his bag underneath the tree. The material of his jeans stretched as he bent over and rifled through the duffel, showcasing his rounded ass and his powerful thighs. His shirt rode up, giving her a glimpse of the golden skin of his back. Aching need bloomed in her pussy.

He beckoned her over with a curve of his finger.

Her mouth dried and her clitoris throbbed as she heeded his call.

Coiled white rope hung from his hand. He turned sideways and gestured for her to move beside him. "Stand here and lift your arms up over your head."

She took a deep breath and planted her feet, raising her

arms straight above her. He looped the rope over a thick tree branch and, within minutes, had both her hands restrained and completely immobile. She'd expected the rope to be scratchy and uncomfortable, but it was surprisingly silky. Caressing.

There was no mistaking that she was scared. Her heart thumped wildly in her chest, and her entire body shook. But mixed in there was fervent desire. In this moment, she would do absolutely anything to feel his hands on her, even if that meant allowing him to bind her. Because the rope itself became an extension of him.

As he crouched to secure her feet with rope and metal stakes that were usually intended for tents, she couldn't stop herself from looking over her shoulder and scanning the woods around them for any sign of approaching people.

He never stopped to look up, but somehow he saw her anyway. "Whose job is it to make sure we're not discovered?" he asked, his voice stern and admonishing.

Shame punched her chest. Her action had negated her promise to trust him. "Yours, Tristan."

"That's right," he said, tying the rope so it brought her to her tiptoes. His warm breath drifted over her backside. He kissed her tenderly on her right butt cheek before sinking his teeth into it.

She whimpered, the pain a delicious aphrodisiac that only served to arouse her further. He rubbed his day-old stubble all over her behind, lighting up the nerves until her head rolled back from pleasure.

"Let go," he crooned. "You only need to do what I tell you." He stood straight, his covered groin pressing against her spine. "I'm going to make it easier on you."

She groaned as he moved away from her. He pulled a piece of dark fabric from his bag.

"A blindfold." She swallowed. "That makes it easier?"

He rubbed the satiny material on her chin. "Your only job is to take what I give you."

Not asking for permission, he covered her eyes, plunging her into darkness, and tied the blindfold behind her head. Opaque, the fabric completely blocked out everything.

Without her sight, her other senses blossomed. She heard the leaves rustling in the breeze and birds chirping. The sun's rays shone down on her, heating her right shoulder, while dirt cooled the bottoms of her feet. Tristan's shoes crunched over the leaves, telling her he'd walked away from her to go to his bag again.

She sensed Tristan's eyes on her, as if he was greedily drinking in the image of her bound to a tree, exposed and vulnerable. The sound of his footsteps announced his return.

He lifted her hair off her shoulder and pressed his lips there. He cupped a breast in his hand and rolled her nipple between his fingers. She sighed, relieved to finally have his hands on her skin.

A sharp, piercing pain in that nipple stole her breath. "What did you do?"

It felt as if he'd bitten down on her flesh with sharpened teeth.

"Nipple clamps," he said with a touch of sadistic glee. "How do they feel?"

She was almost about to complain, when she realized the pain had disappeared, leaving a tension on the center of her nipple "When you put it on, it hurt, but now..." The tension morphed into a pleasurable throbbing that radiated outward. "Oh God, it feels so good."

He played with her other nipple, getting it good and erect before attaching a clamp. This time, she didn't care about the pain, knowing that in seconds, she'd be rewarded with overwhelming pleasure. He tugged on them, eliciting a spark that shot straight to her pussy. Arching her back, she fruitlessly struggled against the rope. The need to rub her clit consumed her.

"Wait until they come off." He chuckled darkly, as if he couldn't wait for it.

How did she not know he was a sadist? Sure, he'd enjoyed spanking and flogging her, but this...this was...*amazing*.

Crack!

Her head snapped up in alertness. That noise sounded familiar. Did he have a whip? "Is that a—"

"Shh. I'm warming up."

It was one thing to wear nipple clamps, but whipping was a different story. Her BDSM trainer had explained the amount of pain depended on the kind of whip used and, without her sight, she had no idea what instrument Tristan wielded. "Warming up? I don't—"

Crack!

"Oh!" The searing bite of the whip sank its teeth into the

back of her right thigh, making her instinctively hop up on her toes. Blistering heat wrapped around her leg and arrowed up straight to her pussy.

"Don't worry about what I'm doing...," he demanded as he struck her again, this time on her left thigh.

Crack!

"...or what I'm doing it with. Just feel it." His voice was hypnotic, leading her away from the forest and the whip to the sea, where she floated weightless on the tall waves.

Crack!

The pain was there just under her right butt cheek, but just as it had with the clamps, it changed. Now she welcomed it. Craved it. Because the brief sting was worth the tremendous pleasure that followed. Her whole body pulsed in time with her heart.

She felt alive.

Intoxicated.

Free.

"Accept it and make me proud," he said, striking her thigh again.

She could do that. She wanted to do that. For him. And more importantly, for herself.

Again and again, the whip left its brutal kiss on her skin. Her body jerking, she vibrated with an overload of sensations and groaned from the inability to squeeze her thighs together. She didn't need her sight to know that her labia and inner thighs were slick with her arousal. She could smell it. Feel it cool on her skin as the breeze swept over her. Her heart hammered in time with the pulsation deep inside her pussy. She was one giant exposed nerve, every cell awake and wired directly to Tristan.

Panting, she hung her head, sweat dripping down her cheeks. "Help me, Tristan," she begged. "Please."

As the whipping ceased, she wasn't sure whether she was relieved or disappointed. There was a long silence before she heard his heavy breathing right behind her.

His hands gripped her shoulders. "What do you need, Angel? I'll give you anything." He nipped her earlobe, and as sensitive as she was, she felt it all the way to her clit. "Everything."

"I need you. Just you."

She nearly wept at the rustle of clothes being removed. Liquid need pooled in her belly. He ran his hands down her neck, her breasts, her stomach, her hips. His hands rotated until he was in front of her. Hot breath fanned her pussy. She could see him in her mind's eye, on his knees, staring at her puffy labia.

Without warning, his mouth was on her. Until now, she'd never understood the expression "eating out." But that's exactly what he was doing. His chin was *inside of her*, his stubble rubbing against the wet flesh as his tongue, teeth, and lips feasted on her clitoris. Rough and urgent fingers dug into her sore butt cheeks, pressing her against his hungry mouth.

Feet spread, she was swinging in the breeze, her arms overhead and straining against the ropes, the sun hitting her face with the man she desired on his knees in worship of her pussy.

She didn't have a second to process it all before the tension in her core unwound like the world's largest spool of thread. Her channel convulsed around his chin, but he didn't pause, continuing to lash at her with his tongue. When the contractions stopped, he dipped his fingers in her pussy and wet them before dragging them between the cheeks of her butt. She stilled, alert and just a little bit scared.

He pressed a finger against her rosette and slowly pushed it inside of her. "Relax."

Relax? Easy for him to say.

It fucking burns.

But it also feels fucking fantastic.

He swiped his tongue along her slit, ending at the bundle of nerves at the top. His lips covered it, sucking her clitoris into his mouth as he inserted his thick fingers inside her pussy and curved them. And then he rubbed and tapped a spot that electrified her. On a moan, she jerked her body, not quite sure whether she was trying to move closer to Tristan or move away.

He bit down on her clit. "You will take it, Angel."

As if she had a choice.

She was so open. Exposed. Vulnerable.

At his mercy.

With the skill of a master, he gently moved the finger in her ass, manipulated her G-spot, and sucked on her clit all at once, depriving her of the capability of thought. Of breath. Of everything.

He owned her body, playing it as if he'd done it for years.

She was a lit firecracker, sizzling and burning. Her limbs

shook. She exploded into millions of shards of light, heat bursting out from her pussy to every part of her. Over and over, again and again, pleasurable contractions wracked her. Never ending. One climax spilling into another.

If she could sag, she would have. She was exhausted, overloaded by the myriad of sensations hitting her body all at once. Sweat trickled down her spine, and the blindfold was soaked. But they weren't done. She knew that as easily as she knew her own name. When he withdrew his fingers and removed his face from her pussy, she held her breath, waiting for it. Waiting for him.

He didn't make her wait long.

Her pussy stretched around the thicker intrusion, making room for his cock. From this angle, he felt huge.

One hand curled around her throat, collaring her as the other banded around her middle.

He slid his cock almost all the way out before slamming back inside of her, forcing her to take him. Take all of him. He held her prisoner in his arms, but there was no place she'd rather be. Furiously, he pistoned his cock, his balls slapping against her ass, and his pubic hairs tickling her skin. She was incredibly full.

Full of cock.

Full of Tristan.

Full of peace.

He fucked her relentlessly, using her pussy with a single intent—to get himself off.

The fact that she loved it was just an afterthought.

He swept one hand down her belly to her nub and pressed

on it, the edge of his fingernail scraping her sensitive skin. His other hand left her throat, trailing a path down between her aching breasts. Without warning, he quickly removed both clamps, one after the other.

Pain stole her breath and, at the same time, pushed her into the strongest orgasm of her life. She screamed as she splintered into a thousand jagged pieces, stars exploding in her eyes.

Tristan cried out on his own completion, fucking her with shallow strokes as she actually felt the hot streams of come bursting from his cock into the condom.

From self-defense to overcoming her fear of bondage, she'd learned a lot about herself today.

But by far, the most significant thing she'd learned was that she was unequivocally, undeniably, in love with Tristan Kelley.

NINETEEN

She wasn't sure how she'd gotten there, but the next thing she knew, she was in the car, and felt as though she'd just woken up from a long nap. There was a bottled water in her hands and a half-eaten chocolate bar on her lap.

Had she gone into subspace or passed out from exhaustion?

Her skin was sore, especially on her butt. Like a mild sunburn. She couldn't wait to look in the mirror and see if he'd left any bruises.

Did it make her a freak if she was aroused by that thought?

The idea that she'd be sitting in his class this week, wearing his mark like a badge on her skin, with everyone around her unaware of it, made her pussy throb. It would be their dirty little secret.

When he called on her, would he be thinking of how she tasted? Would he get aroused at the sight of her pencil in her mouth, imagining her lips around his cock?

Breathing heavily at the idea, she squeezed her thighs together to quell the ache.

Maybe she should be worried about Tony's hearing, but at that moment, she was only concerned with how and when she'd see Tristan outside of school again. "What happens when we get back to Edison?" she asked, taking a bite of the candy.

Reaching over the center console, he took her hand. "This afternoon was a beginning, not an ending. I want more, Angel. More of you. More of us. I want to make love to you over and over, until I know your body better than my own. I want to fall asleep with you in my arms and wake up to your beautiful face. I want it all."

She smiled. "I want all that too."

"I'm sure this goes without saying, but we have to keep our relationship a secret. If anyone finds out about us—"

"I won't tell anyone," she said quickly.

"That includes your roommate, Chloe. You might have to lie to her."

Other than Dreama, Chloe was her closest friend. She didn't want to lie to her, but she knew that in order to have a relationship with Tristan, she'd be forced to hide a huge part of her life from those she cared about, Chloe included. She also knew it would be worth it. "I know, and while I prefer not to lie, I understand what's at stake."

"Do you? There are real repercussions if we get caught. I'll not only lose my job, but any chance of getting the business loan—"

"I get it." She shrugged, playing it casual even though she felt anything but. "If it's not worth it to you, I'll under—"

"It is worth it." He pulled off to the side of the road and put the car in park. He turned to face her, his eyes blazing. "*You're* worth it. But if our relationship is discovered, you not only risk your chance of getting into the business administration program, but you could get thrown out of Edison University. People could find out about your participation in the BDSM lifestyle. Are you sure you're willing to take that risk?"

It wasn't as if she hadn't considered that, but hearing him say it made it that more real. Admittance into the prestigious program at Edison was her dream. Her stomach clenched. What would happen if she lost it?

She shook her head. That wasn't going to happen. No one would find out about them. They'd be careful. Take precautions.

Even if Chloe did somehow find out, she would never tell the university administration about it. But it was the second part of his question she preferred to answer.

"There's no shame in participating in BDSM. What happens between two consenting adults is no one else's business. Would I be embarrassed if my parents found out I take the submissive role during sex?" She shuddered. "Yeah, they shouldn't know anything about my sex life just like I pretend I was the product of an immaculate conception."

He shook his head and rubbed the ends of her hair between his fingers. "You're so young."

"What's that supposed to mean?"

"It doesn't work like that in the real world," he said.

"People hear you like to tie women up and paddle their asses until they bruise, you're thrown in prison for abuse."

"I'm not naive. I realize that society has misconceptions about the lifestyle."

"You of all people should know that the legal system doesn't always work the way it should. The guilty go free and the innocent serve twenty to life."

She paused at the bitterness in his tone. "You sound as if you have personal experience with this."

He turned away and put the car into drive, returning to the road. "We're getting off topic. This is about you. What happens if we're caught and you get expelled from Edison? Are you willing to risk your dreams for sex?"

She folded her arms across her chest. "Why are you trying to demean what's going on between us? Did I misinterpret it? Am I nothing more than a convenient piece of submissive ass to you?"

His eyes narrowed. "Fuck no. I haven't had a committed relationship with a woman since—in a long time. I didn't want one. No-strings sex with a trained submissive. That's all I needed. All I wanted." He lowered his voice. "Until you walked through Ryder's door. One look. That's all it took for me to change my mind."

His words seemed to contradict each other. On one hand, he was almost pushing her to break up with him, and on the other, he said things that made her pulse race and her head swoon. There was something she was missing. Something he was keeping from her. She felt it down to her very soul. But she'd leave it alone...

For now.

"And is that what we are?" she asked. "Committed, I mean?"

He placed a hand on her thigh. "I told you before, I'm all in. I can't make any promises or predictions about the future. You've got four years of college and a lifetime of opportunities in front of you. My path is already set. One year in Edison and back to the city and Novateur."

And what happened then? Would he still want her when she lived twelve hours away? Her heart pinched in pain. Why couldn't she help feeling their time together had an expiration date? "I won't risk my education for sex. But I will risk it for you."

* * *

Later that day, she lay on her bed and stared up at the ceiling as darkness fell. On the ride home, Tristan had created a studying schedule for her and had prohibited her from masturbating unless he ordered her to. Beginning next week, her weekends belonged to him, and she'd stay at his apartment from Friday night through Sunday night.

"Hey, are you okay?" Chloe asked, standing at the entrance to her room.

She hadn't even heard her come home.

"Yeah, just tired," she said.

Chloe started to leave. "I'll let you sleep."

"No, that's okay," Isabella said, sitting up. "I don't have the energy for dinner tonight, but I want to hear about your audition."

Chloe bounded into the room and plopped herself down next to Isabella. "I couldn't believe it. There were amazingly talented people auditioning for the show. I thought there was no way I'd even get in, much less a lead. I'm the only freshman who got a speaking role."

Her roommate's excitement bordered on mania. She barely took a breath between sentences.

"The girl playing Maria is a senior and she told me that she's never heard of a freshman getting a lead role. Everyone is so nice. We just hung out at her apartment last night and today, reading the scenes and learning the music." She grinned, looking sheepish. "And there may have been a little bit of drinking too. I should be hungover and exhausted, but I'm just too happy."

She threw an arm behind Chloe's shoulders. "I'm so happy for you, and I'm not surprised at all that you got a lead. Forget what your music teacher and your mom said. You have a gift. You deserve the lead."

"Thank you." Chloe's smile fell. "Oh, Isabella, I'm so sorry. I don't want you to think I forgot about your phone call from the prosecutor. How are you holding up?"

If it hadn't been for Tristan, she'd be freaking out, but she couldn't share that with Chloe. Even though she was bursting at the seams to tell her.

"Surprisingly...okay," she answered honestly. "I hope he doesn't get out, but if he does, I'm not going to cower in fear."

Chloe jerked back a little, her brows crinkled. "Oh, well, wow. I'm impressed with how calm you are about it." She patted her thigh and stared at her mouth. "But if you ever need to talk about it, you know I'm here for you, right? No matter how busy I might get with the show, you can always count on me."

She gave her friend a smile. "I know."

Chloe stood from the bed and walked toward the exit before turning around. "Hey, why did you ask if I texted you Friday night?"

She tried not to make a big deal out of it. "I got a weird text from an unknown number."

Chloe giggled. "And you automatically thought of me?"

"I was just checking."

"What did it say?" Chloe asked, now serious.

Instead of telling her, Isabella handed her the cell phone and let her read it. Chloe's eyes popped wide. "You don't think it's from Tony, do you?"

She shrugged. "He's the only one who calls me Izzy. Yeah, I think it's from him."

"Then why aren't you freaking out? You need to make sure his psychiatrist knows about this so he doesn't get released."

"I already filed a police report and left a message for Erin. That's all I can do right now. Otherwise, I'll obsess over it."

Hands on her hips, Chloe seemed outraged on her behalf. "They won't let him out. Not after he sent you the letter and the text."

"I can't prove the text was from him. It's from an unknown number and there's nothing incriminating in the message."

"You said it yourself. He's the only one who calls you Izzy."

She understood Chloe's confusion over the apathy of the legal system. After all, hadn't she felt the same?

"It's my word against his. He's in the hospital being supervised by medical personnel. Mailing that letter was one thing, but even I don't understand how he'd have access to a cell phone."

"So you're not going to fight his release?" Chloe asked, clearly surprised.

"I'm going to provide the information I have and see if Erin can get him charged for violating the restraining order. That's all I can do. It's out of my hands."

Chloe stood slack jawed in the middle of the room. "Where did all your strength come from?"

She couldn't help the smile. "I took a walk in the woods."

TWENTY

No one on campus had blinked when the first snowflake fell.

If it were the city, the local news would hail it as the next 'snowmageddon,' the prediction of six inches bringing everything to a halt.

But there in the Upper Peninsula, it was just another six inches. Students threw on their winter boots and trekked their way across campus to get to class on time. Professors cleaned the snow off their windshields and fought for closer parking spaces to their buildings.

Until today, Tristan had forgotten that winter lasted an extra three months in Edison. Back in the city, it was completely dry. They probably wouldn't see snow for another couple of months. Just in time for a white Christmas. The Edison campus would have at least two feet of snow on the ground by then.

Thank goodness it was Friday. When the clock struck five, he and Isabella would leave the office—separately—and meet up a couple of blocks away, where he'd pick her up in his car and take them both to his apartment for the weekend.

After glancing at the clock, Tristan snatched his prized baseball off his desk and tossed it in the air.

Where the hell is she?

Isabella was an hour late for her work-study. He'd already tried calling her but it had gone straight to voice mail. They were supposed to be together when she called Erin to find out what had happened at Tony's hearing.

His gut burned with apprehension. What if she'd gotten the call earlier and had fallen apart? His fingers clenched around his baseball as he dismissed that idea. All week she'd been calm and prepared for any outcome, but even if she did break down, she would've reached out to him.

Maybe the weather had delayed her.

That had to be the reason. And he'd tell himself that until he believed it.

He threw his baseball into the air again, when a knock fell upon his door. It wasn't Isabella. She wouldn't knock. He swore under his breath. He was in no mood to listen to one of his students whine about their grade today.

"Enter," he growled. He missed the ball, and it smashed down onto his desk and bounced off the wall beside him before zinging toward the door.

"Who pissed in your Wheaties?" Ryder said, strolling through the entrance and catching the ball with ease as if he'd been expecting it. Just like old times, he tossed the ball back to Tristan. "Or did you already hear the bad news?"

He frowned as he caught it this time. That was the last person he'd expected. "Ryder. I didn't know you were coming."

His friend lumbered toward him waving a thick docu-

ment in his hand. "I didn't either. But since I have that conference on Mackinac Island this weekend and some things
shouldn't be discussed over the phone, I figured, what the
hell, I'll just drive a few extra hours and check out my
partner's new office." He surveyed the office, nodding in approval as he approached. "Nice decor, by the way. I really
like what you've done with the place."

It had to be really bad to have Ryder drive an extra five
hours out of his way in the snow. The Michigan Innovators
Convention was one of the largest trade shows of its kind in
the state, and Ryder had been making plans to unveil their
designs for Novateur there for weeks. "What bad news? Did
you hear back from the bank?"

"No." He slapped a document onto his desk. "We got
served."

"Served. You mean, we're being sued?" He snatched up
the stack of paper. "By whom?"

"Lucifer," Ryder deadpanned, dropping into the chair in
front of Tristan's desk and slouching, his legs spread wide.
"Excuse me. I mean, Morgan."

He should've known she had something up her sleeve
when she'd come up there the first week of school. "She's suing us? You and me?"

"You, me, and Novateur," Ryder clarified.

"For what?" he asked incredulously.

"Fraud. She's alleging that not only did she come up with
the idea behind Novateur, she's claiming she has an interest
in all of our business assets, including both company shares
and the patents."

Damn it. Between Tony's hearing, Isabella missing, and this, could the day get any worse?

He could wring Morgan's damned neck.

Why wouldn't she just leave him the hell alone?

She'd already taken everything he owned, and now that he'd finally begun climbing out of the trenches, she wanted more?

Did one of them have to die before it ended?

Frowning, he quickly flipped through the causes of actions laid out in the complaint. "She was long gone before you and I gave up our consulting business and turned our attention to kitchen automation."

"You don't have to convince me, remember? I was there."

As Tristan read over the stated facts of the case, his chest tightened as if a ton of bricks had fallen on it. He shook his head and pushed the document away from him.

The woman may be the devil incarnate, but she had the memory of a steel trap. "Over dinner one night at our favorite bistro, we had a conversation about automation replacing chefs. She suggested the food would taste better without human intervention tweaking with the recipe." He snorted in derision. "Then again, she also expressed the need to replace the waitstaff with robots. But that was it. Certainly nothing about designing and implementing small kitchen automation systems was discussed."

"Keep reading," Ryder said, almost sounding amused. "You haven't gotten to the part where she claims you fraudulently induced her into signing away all rights to any of your future earnings."

"*She's* claiming fraud? After she fucking blackmailed me into giving her all the money my mother left me? She fucking took everything, from the house to the damned outdoor grill. And she doesn't even barbecue."

"She must have found out that we'd applied for a loan to expand our business. Now that it's on its way to becoming profitable, she realizes she divorced you too soon."

As much as it pained him, he punched her number into his cell. It didn't even ring once before she answered.

"Tristan," she crooned. "What a surprise."

"Cut the bullshit, Morgan. You knew I'd call the minute you had Ryder served."

"Oh, you mean the lawsuit?"

He gnashed his teeth and growled a warning at her. "Drop it, Morgan. I'm warning you. You have no rights to Novateur."

"My attorneys say otherwise."

"Novateur isn't worth a fraction of what it's going to cost you in attorneys' fees," he pointed out, attempting to reason with the unreasonable. Even if she won the lawsuit, he and Ryder would stop working on behalf of the company, and its shares would be worthless. Sure, if she sold the patents, she could make a third, but the attorneys' fees would easily eat the earnings up. So what was her angle?

"Good thing I'm not the one paying them then," she said cryptically. "Oh shoot, someone is at my door. But I'm sure I'll be seeing you soon."

She hung up before he could ask her who the hell was paying for her lawyers. He checked who she was using and was shocked to see two of the best litigators in metro Detroit, each from a different law firm. Was her position so strong that they'd agreed to be paid on contingency?

He quickly dismissed that possibility. These lawyers would at least demand a hefty retainer to get started. Morgan had already blown through the money she'd won off him. Which meant someone had to be bankrolling her.

And if she'd found someone with their own money, why in the hell did she need to go after Novateur, especially when the business wasn't worth anything yet?

Who in the hell had she hooked up with?

Tristan ran his hand down his face. "We don't have the money to defend this lawsuit, do we?" he asked Ryder.

His friend twirled a pen in his hand. "I've got enough to hire an attorney to at least answer the complaint and try to get it dismissed, but after that, I'm tapped out."

"Doesn't matter. She knows this will never be fought in court." The woman was pure evil. "She must have been feeling things out when she came here last month," he said, more to himself than Ryder.

Ryder's brows shot up. "Morgan came all the way up here? What did she want?"

"To remind me she still has the photos." He shook his head and sat back in his chair. "She's blackmailing me again."

"Actually, she's blackmailing both of us," Ryder pointed out. At Tristan's glare, he put up his hands in surrender. "Sorry, but did you ever think you may be better off just letting her release the pictures?"

Was Ryder crazy?

"Why the hell would I do that?" he snapped.

"As long as she can use them against you, you'll never get rid of her. I checked the laws in our state, and chances are, the statute of limitations for criminal charges have run out even if the district attorney wanted to charge you with something like battery. Same for the civil statute for battery, which is probably why she chose to allege fraud. There's a six-year statute of limitations on that. Let her claim you physically abused her during your marriage. What's the worst that can happen?"

Jesus, Ryder had done his homework. But what did it matter when Morgan had Tristan by the balls? Not only would she do everything in her power to destroy him, she was going to make sure she took his best friend down with him. And it was all Tristan's fault.

That was the problem with giving in to blackmail.

It never ended.

"Assuming I don't go to jail?" Filled with nervous energy, Tristan drummed his fingers on his desk. "How about the loss of my reputation? My job here? Our business? Do you think Isaac could keep me on as an adjunct professor if word got out that I used to beat up my wife? And let's face it, the defense that she consented to it would not fly with the students' parents or the school's benefactors. The stigma would follow me around for the rest of my life. I can't allow her to get away with it. I won't be blackmailed. Not again. Morgan is a dead woman walking, because the next time I see her, I'm going to kill her."

"You're being blackmailed?" Isabella asked from the doorway.

Tristan spun toward her. "Isabella."

"I'm sorry." She stared at him with what looked like disappointment in her eyes.

Exactly why he'd kept his past from her in the first place. Who trusted a Dom with the kind of baggage he came with?

He wanted to find out why she was late and if she'd heard from Erin, but that wasn't a conversation for Ryder's ears. When her eyes fell on Ryder, he reluctantly waved her forward to introduce them. "Isabella Lawson. This is Ryder McKay. Ryder, Isabella."

Ryder stood up as if he was a gentleman. Which he wasn't. "Ah, the infamous Isabella. How's our favorite professor treating you?"

Tristan sighed. "You don't need to answer him. He's just fucking with you."

"No, but I'd like to," Ryder said on a wink.

"Behave yourself," he warned his friend. "This isn't one of your parties."

Ryder gave him a little smirk.

"Who's Morgan?" Isabella asked, setting her backpack on top of her desk.

The silence screamed as he thought of a way to get out of telling her.

He blew out a breath. "My ex-wife."

Her eyes widened. "You were married?"

"Unfortunately," he muttered.

She moved to stand beside him, her hand reaching out as

if to comfort him before she yanked it back to hang at her side. "And she's blackmailing you?"

"She wasn't just my wife. She was also my submissive for more than two years. At least she played the part of one. Turns out it was all an act so that she could use it against me in our divorce. She hid a camera behind a pillow and took shots of our sessions, making sure they showed her bruises and welts. And now that Novateur is taking off, she's using the photos again. She's suing me for fraud."

Isabella folded her arms across her chest. "What. A. Bitch."

Ryder pointed his thumb at her. "What she said." He laughed. "I like her."

Yeah, Tristan bet he did. Isabella was just his type. *New.*

Tristan shot his friend a warning to back off. He wouldn't share. She was his. "Isabella's working on creating a plan for us to expand automation into the bakery business."

"I'm impressed. You should come down to our warehouse and see how it works." Standing, Ryder slid a glance at Tristan, his lips twitching with humor, before returning his full attention to Isabella. "I'd be happy to give you a tour. Maybe take you to dinner and pick your brain about designing an automated kitchen for a small bakery."

Before he could blink, Tristan was on his feet, his hands clenched into fists at his sides. Friend or not, Ryder had better keep his hands off Isabella.

"Maybe I should give you some privacy." Isabella's gaze ping-ponged between the two men. "I'll give you a few minutes while I run over to the student union for some coffee."

As soon as they were alone, Ryder grinned. "Beautiful and smart. She's the complete package."

"Back off. She's just my student," he warned through gritted teeth. "Dinner and a tour of Novateur? Don't think I didn't catch how you were looking at her."

Ryder faced him head-on. "How was I looking at her?"

"Like you were picturing her in your bed."

Ryder shrugged. "If you want to get technical, she was bent over your desk."

Tristan's fist went flying and with a satisfying crack, caught Ryder right below his left cheekbone.

Asshole. He shook out his hand. That had probably hurt him as much as it had hurt Ryder.

Rubbing the spot where Tristan had popped him one, his best friend only smirked. "Nice shot. Just your student. Would you punch me over any of your other students?"

Understanding dawned. "Fuck. You did that intentionally."

Ryder shook his finger at him. "Doesn't do you any good to lie to yourself or to me. I've known you for a decade. It's obvious to me that you're fucking her. Besides, if she was just your student, I doubt you'd tell her about Morgan." His friend placed a hand on his shoulder. "Look, man. I'm not judging you. But no matter how special she might be, it's not worth it. We're this close to achieving our dream. Don't blow it on a girl who's not even old enough to drink the champagne when we celebrate our success. We've got enough to worry about right now with your ex coming after us."

Morgan would mow down anyone in her path to destroy Tristan. If she found out about Isabella, she'd drag the girl into the bowels of hell with the rest of the people he cared about.

Ryder grew serious. "Maybe you should—"

"Don't say it." Tristan wouldn't break things off with Isabella. "I'm not going to let Morgan's threats dictate how I live my life. I've got it all under control."

Ryder's lips parted as if he was about to argue but instead, he gave Tristan a nod of understanding.

If Isabella had met Tristan a few years ago, he'd had it all. A promising future and a life free of complications. But now, what did he have to offer her other than stolen moments?

Tristan returned to his chair and threw his prized baseball to his best friend. "What do you do when you find the right girl at the wrong time?"

Even while keeping his eyes fixed on Tristan's, Ryder caught the ball. "Hold on until it's the right time."

* * *

Walking back to the business school, Isabella sipped her coffee, holding a tray with two others in her free hand, in case Ryder was still in Tristan's office. The snow was bad enough, but as the day progressed, the temperature had plunged twenty degrees.

Despite the coffee, she couldn't stop her teeth from chattering. Her head pounded after everything that had happened today. First, she was pretty sure she bombed her exam. Okay, maybe not bombed, but she couldn't have done better than a C. No matter how hard she'd tried to concentrate during it, she couldn't stop herself from wondering what would happen at Tony's hearing. After that class, she'd gotten the bad, but not surprising, news from Erin. And then, she'd overheard Tristan and Ryder's conversation.

Tristan had been married?

To say Isabella had been shocked to learn that was an understatement. When she'd met him, he came off as a player and made it clear that he only did one-night stands.

Was Morgan the reason?

In her BDSM class, the leader had counseled them all to carry a wallet-sized card that defined the differences between BDSM and abuse in case they were ever in the position of having to explain themselves to an officer of the law. But honestly, she hadn't thought much about it. After all, whatever happened between consenting adults was nobody else's business. She'd never considered the ramifications or how it could affect her life if someone exposed her participation in the lifestyle.

To think that Tristan could go to prison over it made her throat constrict.

What kind of person would blackmail their spouse?

She and Tristan may be almost a decade apart in age and at different points in their lives, but they weren't so different.

They'd both been burned by people they trusted.

And it just made her fall for him a little more.

Her heart pinched. She'd told him everything about Tony. So why did he keep her in the dark about his ex?

An hour after Tristan had introduced her to Ryder, she returned to the office, hoping she'd given them enough time to finish whatever conversation she had interrupted. She'd sensed a tension between the two men and couldn't help thinking it was about her. Ryder seemed to have a perpetual smirk on his face the entire time she was in the office, as if he'd known something was going on between them. Had Tristan told Ryder about their relationship?

And did it matter to her if he did?

In front of the business school, she threw her empty coffee cup in the trash and headed inside.

All week, she'd been floating on a cloud of happiness, barely spending more than a minute here and there worrying about Tony. When she wasn't in class or studying, she was thinking about Tristan. Even in class her thoughts tended to stray to him, especially in his. She'd nibble on the end of her pen and stare at his mouth, recalling how he'd used it to bring her to climax over and over. She tried to separate the passionate man she privately knew him to be from the professor he portrayed to everyone else, but it was more difficult than she'd anticipated.

Now she wondered if she wasn't exaggerating their relationship in her head.

He had no problems sharing himself sexually and physically with her. But emotionally? Before today, she'd had a gut feeling he was holding back with her, but finding out about Morgan had been confirmation of it. How could he not have told her?

She had to admit, finding out about it that way had hurt her. It was something he should have willingly chosen to share with her rather than her overhearing it by chance. If she hadn't walked in when she had, would he ever have told her?

Shaking the snowflakes from her hair, she turned the doorknob of Tristan's office and let herself inside. Deep in thought, he was sitting in his chair with his back to the door and staring out the window at the falling snow. He was so beautiful, sometimes it hurt her to look at him.

She set the coffees down on his desk and took off her gloves. "Do you trust me?" she asked, her teeth still chattering from the cold.

Tristan's head snapped up as if shocked to see her there. "Isabella." Standing, he frowned as he removed her snowy coat. "Why are you asking me that? You know I trust you."

His current actions spoke volumes. As her Dom, he saw her as his responsibility, but not as an equal. "No, you tell me that you do. You've gone on and on about how important trust is on both sides of a Dom/sub relationship. So why then have you never mentioned you were married?"

That damned muscle in his jaw ticked. "It's not relevant."

"Really? Is the fact you're being sued also not relevant? Were you going to keep that from me as well?"

He tossed her coat on the desk and brushed his hands up and down her arms, warming her.

It was sweet.

Caring.

And it was pissing her off.

"If you want to know the truth...," Tristan began hesitantly. "Yes. It has nothing to do with you."

At least she'd expected him to apologize for it and promise not to do it again. Not to so nonchalantly brush it aside like she was snow on a coat.

She stilled his warm hands and took them in her cold ones. "What happened to your fight is my fight? Doesn't that work both ways?"

He looked down at their joined hands, his brows lowered in a severe slash. "You don't need to take on my baggage. You have enough of your own shit to deal with."

The words were like a punch to the gut. She tore her hands away and took a step back from him.

He hooked his arm around her waist and tugged her to him, enveloping her in a hug and holding her tightly as if he feared she'd run if he didn't. "I'm sorry. I just meant I didn't want to bother you with stuff that didn't matter. Morgan is a parasite who will suck the life of everyone she comes across. I wanted to keep you out of it."

At his chest, she clutched his shirt in her hands and burrowed into his warmth. He was her safe place. She couldn't bear to lose him. "You're like a puzzle that I'll never complete because you're intentionally keeping pieces from me. If we're going to really do this, you have to let me in."

"I don't know that I can," he said quietly.

Now that he'd spoken the truth, she almost wished for the lie.

"Wait," he said, pushing her back a few inches and looking down at her. "Why were you late earlier? Did you hear from Erin?"

She nodded, still holding on to him as if he was her lifeline. "I didn't think I'd hear from her so quickly. He was out as of one thirty today. The judge reminded him the restraining order still applied. He's got two hours of outpatient therapy five days a week and has agreed to continue taking his medication. That's it."

"How are you doing?" He tipped up her chin. "I was concerned when you didn't answer your phone."

She winced, knowing she'd messed up. "Sorry. I didn't mean to worry you. I went for a walk to clear my mind, but I'm actually doing okay with it." She gave him a little smile. "No fear."

"I'm glad. But you're still going to be punished for not calling me."

She winked at him. "I wouldn't have it any other way."

He'd effectively changed the subject for now, but she wouldn't give up on him. Someday, he'd have to start opening up to her.

Because she wouldn't settle for anything less.

TWENTY-ONE

On Saturday afternoon, Isabella set the last batch of mini pecan pies on the cooling rack. Word of her baking skills had spread throughout Edison, and thanks to having access to Tristan's kitchen, she'd be able to earn money on the weekends baking pastries for professors and others in the community. Soon she'd have enough padding in her bank account that she would no longer have to worry about money.

Thank goodness for the schedule Tristan had helped her create, or she'd never buckle down to get her work done. Of course, he wasn't going to be pleased when she told him about messing up on yesterday's exam. Hopefully, she could keep it from him for a little longer.

Tristan came into the galley kitchen and moved behind her, banding his arms around her middle. He lifted her hair off her shoulder and pressed soft kisses against her neck. Shivering, she tilted her head back to give him better access, resting against the hard planes of his chest. Instantly, she grew damp, her body preparing itself for his magnificent cock.

Back at the beginning of high school, she and her friends would Google photos of naked men and giggle over the strange-looking penises. Short and long, straight and curved, cut and uncut, thick and thin. The girls couldn't understand what was so great about them.

Thanks to Tristan, she got it now.

She was grateful that not only was he long and thick, but he knew how to use it.

His hands dipped lower and her inner muscles clenched in celebration. Just a little further and he'd find out how wet she was for him.

It was ridiculous. They'd made love well into the early morning hours in bed and had fucked in the shower that morning. She should be sated. Instead, her pussy was already throbbing and dying to be filled.

Too bad it was going to have to wait.

"*Ugh,*" she groaned, turning around and pushing him away with her hands to his chest. *God, his chest.* Maybe one day, he'd let her explore him. She couldn't stop thinking about what he'd do if she bit down on his—no. She had to be strong. She'd made a promise to both of them that she wouldn't allow anything to interfere with her schoolwork.

Her poor, sex-addicted vagina would just have to wait until tonight to get its fill. At least she knew it would be worth it.

"I've got two hundred pages of *Madame Bovary* to read if I don't want to fall behind in lit class. I'm just going to park myself at a coffee shop for the day. You don't mind, do you?" She slid to the side, trying to escape before she jumped him. "I know you've got plenty of tests to grade, so I'm—"

"Lose your clothes and get on the dining room table."

His low, commanding voice sent tingles through her breasts. That voice. She swore sometimes she could come from his voice alone. He didn't use that tone often in class, but when he did, her nipples perked up as if they were ready to play. It was a voice that demanded respect and one that her body simply couldn't resist.

But her will was stronger than her body.

She took a couple more steps away from him. "Tristan, I have to study."

He caught her, reaching out and hooking his arm around her waist, then tugging her toward him. She should've known he would. His hard cock ground into her belly. "Oh, you're going to. Trust me. I'll make sure of it. There's no reason for you to leave."

"If I stay, especially naked, I doubt we'll get any work done."

He clucked his tongue. "How little you trust your Dom. I always have your best interests at heart."

"Oh yeah? How about last night when you left me waiting naked by the door, on my knees for an hour while you took your sweet time getting home from campus? How was that in my best interest?"

"Patience. Discipline. Two qualities that will not only aid you as my lover but in business as well. What did you feel as you knelt waiting for me?"

She thought back. "At first, I was excited, thinking of what you had planned for me. Then as I imagined different scenarios, I got...horny. I wanted to touch myself, but I didn't."

"Why not?"

Why indeed? What was it about Tristan that made her want to please him? Yes, she was a submissive and he was a Dominant, but that alone wasn't enough to compel her to submit. "Because you told me not to and I didn't want to disappoint you. But as the minutes passed and you didn't arrive, I got pissed. I mean, you told me when you dropped me off that you'd only be a few minutes at the store. I thought about getting out of position and stretching or giving up and taking a shower."

"But you didn't, did you? You waited the entire hour for me."

"Yes."

"And what did you get in return?"

He'd casually walked through the door, as if he hadn't known to expect her on her knees, but the moment his eyes fell on her, she saw the hunger in them. There had been nothing casual about the way his body grew rigid and his cock bulged against his pants. He'd unzipped himself and wrapped her hair around his hand as he brought her mouth to him. She'd opened willingly, sighing in contentment as she took the head of him inside, the last hour completely forgotten. All she'd wanted in that moment was to please him. To watch him lose control until his essence slid down her throat. But rather than finishing, he'd pulled her off him and scooped her up, then carried her to his bed, where he'd eaten her out thoroughly and eagerly, not stopping until the sheets were drenched with her wetness. The next hours were a blur of desperate fucking, their need for each other insatiable. By the time he'd changed the sheets and cleaned them both off, she'd fallen asleep, sore and content, tucked into Tristan's chest, where she listened to his strong heartbeat.

When he'd arrived home and found her as he'd demanded, he was proud of her. And that in turn made her feel proud of herself. It gave her the confidence that had been missing from her life for years. What had she gotten in return for her submission?

More than he'd ever know.

She smiled and threw her arms around his neck. "I got rewarded. With you."

"Your patience and discipline paid off, didn't it? So why would you doubt me now? You can safe word if you really want to go to the overpriced coffee shop where you'll blow ten dollars on mediocre cappuccinos and probably get nothing done because your mind will keep wandering as you try to figure out what I'd planned for you this afternoon. But like I said, feel free to safe—"

"No. You're right." But no matter what he believed, there was no way she'd be able to concentrate on her reading. Oh well. She'd just have to stay up late Sunday night. "I won't get any work done now that you've planted that little seed in my brain. You're very wicked, you know that?"

She wasn't sure what to make of the gleam in his eyes. It

promised mischief and so much more if only she listened. Safe wording didn't even cross her mind when he got into this kind of mood. Experience had taught her in the weeks they'd been together that there was always a method to his madness. But studying naked on a table? That surpassed even her wildest imagination.

Since they'd been lazing around his apartment all morning, she hadn't bothered changing out of her pajamas. "I don't know how comfortable it's going to be lying on a table to read."

"You always read lying down."

"In bed or on the couch. My head is elevated."

"Good point. I'll be right back. When I return, I expect you to be naked."

She grabbed the bottom hem of her tank top and pulled it over her head, her already erect nipples hardening into tighter buds. Her panties soon followed, soaked and useless.

She didn't know why she bothered wearing them when she was here since they did nothing to prevent her arousal from coating her inner thighs. She was a constant horny mess around Tristan.

Maybe it should embarrass her but it didn't. Instead she reveled in the claim of her sexuality. A year ago, she could barely touch herself, the idea of sexual pleasure frightening. Tristan had done so much for her in the short time they'd been together. There was no way she could ever repay him.

But she'd spend every precious moment they had together trying.

Carrying a pillow and his comforter, Tristan strolled back

into the room. He folded the blanket in two and laid it out on the middle of the kitchen table. After placing the pillow at the top of the "bed," he slapped the table a couple of times. "Grab your book and hop on up."

She scurried to her backpack and retrieved the book, then climbed on top of the table, her heart pounding in anticipation. Lying back, she realized it wasn't as uncomfortable as she'd expected. Flat on her back with her legs straight ahead, she cracked open her book and began to read. Tristan placed the unmarked tests on the table beside her, then left the room again. What was he up to? She read the same paragraph over three times, none of it sinking in, her thoughts constantly straying to Tristan. She didn't want to doubt him, but all signs pointed to this being a great big fail. She'd play around for an hour, but then she really did need to go out to get her reading done.

When Tristan returned, her eyes flew to a strange metal bar in his hands. And that wasn't the only thing he brought with him. Hung over his shoulder was that black duffel bag, what she'd come to know as his Dom bag, implements of pain and pleasure hidden inside. She had a Pavlovian response to it, instantly becoming aroused.

"What's that bar? Planning on swinging me from a trapeze?"

"Not today, but I'll keep that in mind. This is a spreader bar for your legs."

He dropped the bag onto his chair, then turned to her. "Knees apart. Feet flat on the table."

He couldn't be serious, right?

Rather than question him, she did as he asked, wholly throwing herself into the scene with the trust required of her. She put the book on her chest, inhaling deeply in surrender.

His cool hands settled on the inside of her thighs and pressed. "Wider."

After she'd complied, he affixed the cuffs hanging off the bar onto her thighs. She waited for the panic to hit, but instead, all she felt was a hunger for more.

"What color are you at, Angel?"

"Green. I'm good."

"Yes, you are. Today we're going to work on your ability to concentrate. I'm going to teach you how to concentrate on your task in any situation. You may have to make a deal at a baseball stadium or read over contracts while you're at a rock concert. Business doesn't wait for convenience."

Her body flushed hot as she watched him pull a U-shaped vibrator from his bag.

His smile turned pure Machiavellian. Hell, she could practically see him twisting his pencil-thin mustache as he tied her to the railroad tracks. He was a sadist. What else could he be when he expected her to concentrate on reading her book as she lay out for him like a feast, a spreader between her legs and a vibrator inside of her. Maybe he wouldn't turn it on. He couldn't be that evil. He was overestimating her ability to concentrate. But she'd hate to fail him.

He didn't give her any explanation before inserting one end of the vibrator inside her slick channel and setting the other end over her clitoris. Then he took a step backward and stared down at her as if she was a piece of artwork he was admiring.

"You'll have to let me know what you think of the vibrator. The lady at the store said it won all sorts of awards."

"What kind of awards do they give for vibrators?"

"The kind that stimulate both the G-spot and clitoris simultaneously?"

Her mouth fell open. "Seriously? You think I'm going to get any reading done while that thing is buzzing inside of me?"

"Hmm. I'm not sure. But it will be fun to find out, don't you think?"

"Tristan—"

"Professor. Call me professor for this scene, Ms. Lawson. And I do believe you'll get your reading done."

Professor. She pulled in a ragged breath. "How can you be so certain...Professor?"

The side of his lips twitched as if he was suppressing a smile. "Because I demand it of you, and you don't want to disappoint me. More important, you don't want to disappoint yourself. College can only teach you so much. These lessons will prepare you for the real world. If you can complete your task with, as you said, a vibrator buzzing inside of you, you'll realize there's nothing you can't accomplish."

"You want me to read while I'm coming?"

"Oh no. I'm not that cruel."

"Thank God.

"You're not allowed to come."

"But...but...," she sputtered.

He palmed the small remote with way too much glee for her comfort. "Don't worry. We'll start it on low, Ms. Lawson."

TWENTY-TWO

Isabella exhaled, relieved. Tristan had set the sex toy on low to a tolerable hum. It wasn't much stronger than her cell phone when it vibrated with an incoming call. She could handle it. "Thank you, Professor." She lifted her book. "I won't disappoint you. Two hundred pages of *Madame Bovary*, here we come."

"Nice choice of words, Ms. Lawson."

She just gave him a little smile letting him know two could play at this game. She couldn't imagine he'd get much done with her lying here, her pussy open and wet in front of him. He sat in the chair and pulled out his red pen, beginning to grade.

Ignoring her.

Was it possible he'd learned the lesson he was trying to teach to her? Could he actually concentrate in any situation?

She bit her lip as she read the first page of her book, ignoring the subtle buzzing on her clit. She'd show him she could concentrate every bit as much as he could.

For the next several minutes, she sank into her task, find-ing the book both compelling and heartbreaking. Other than her Intro to Business class, English Literature was her favorite, the professor a proponent for women's rights around the country and especially on campus. While it wasn't technically a women's studies class, her teacher had chosen all female-focused books and spent a considerable amount of time drawing comparisons between historical and current times. At first, the guys in her class had groaned about what they deemed a female conspiracy to reduce men's rights in order to become the dominant gender, but it hadn't taken them long to appreciate the hypocrisy in so-ciety.

Before *Madame Bovary*, they'd read *The Scarlet Letter*, a book she'd read in tenth-grade English class. Her professor had compared Hester Prynne to Monica Lewinsky, the young intern who had had an affair with President Clinton. In both cases, the women had been blamed for their sexual-ity while society ignored that the men had been in positions of power, being that of priest and president of the United States. Surprisingly, it was the guys in the class who ex-pressed that Hester and Monica had gotten a "raw deal," and that the men should have taken the bulk of the respon-sibility for the affairs, having been the ones to break their vows. The women in the class, however, felt that to negate the women's responsibilities for their actions was sexist.

Isabella couldn't help but draw comparisons to herself in that discussion. If word about her affair with Tristan got out, would she become the Hester Prynne of the campus, or would she be banished from the school? Her thoughts drifted and she found herself staring at Tristan. Lines marred his forehead, and he shook his head as he marked the paper with red. She hoped that wasn't her test. Good thing they were only identified with their twelve-digit student numbers and not their names.

As if he sensed her gaze on him, he lifted his head from the paper. Frowning even deeper than he had while grading the paper, he lifted something off his lap and raised it in the air.

Whack!

A fiery pain erupted on her outer thigh. "Oh!"

"Read, Ms. Lawson, or the next time I'll hit you with this ruler somewhere much more painful."

He'd hit her with a ruler?

Suddenly, the professor-and-student scene took on a whole new meaning.

She didn't know whether she wanted to bite him or kiss him.

Maybe both?

"Yes, Professor," she muttered as she returned her eyes to the page of her book.

For the next hour or so, she read in silence, the only sound the scraping of Tristan's pen on paper and his occasional grunt of disgust. She wasn't the fastest reader, but she'd made a decent dent into her two-hundred-page assignment. At that rate, she'd be done by dinnertime. She smiled to herself. Perhaps she could concentrate in any situation.

It couldn't have been more than five minutes later that

Tristan set his hand on her navel. He didn't move it, but it was like a lead weight just the same. A little lower and he'd touch her pussy. Was it time for a sex break?

Unconsciously, her hips lifted a bit off the table. He chuckled and pushed her back down.

Damn him.

His hand drifted upward, tickling her ribs and brushing over her breasts, but bypassing her nipples. He was playing a game, and she feared it was one she'd lose. Her eyes drifted closed, waves of heated pleasure washing through her. His finger caressed her nipple, and a loud moan fell from her lips.

Game over.

He'd proved that when it came to concentration, she had none, at least if his hands were on her skin.

He tsked, removing his hand from her body, and whacked her stomach will the ruler. "Concentrate, Ms. Lawson."

She hissed at the sting and took a breath. "How am I supposed to concentrate with you touching my nipple? Could anyone?"

"Maybe you need a better incentive than merely pleasing me." He stood from his chair and paced, rubbing his chin as if deep in contemplation. He didn't fool her for a second. The sadist knew exactly what he was about to do to her. In fact, she'd bet anything that he'd had this "lesson" planned for a while, and that any added incentive he gave her would come at a steep price. "Since positive reinforcement hasn't helped, I'll have to do the opposite, I'm afraid," he said in an obviously mocking tone. "Orgasm denial it is."

"For how long?"

"As long as it takes," he said, cranking up the motor of the vibrator.

"I don't see how this will help me learn how to concentrate. So far all it's done is prove that I can't."

He tilted his head, as if truly considering her words, and retook his seat at the table. "We have all day for you to learn. Until you do, you will not have an orgasm. If you do, you'll be punished. Thoroughly. And Ms. Lawson..."

Her eyes practically rolled back in her head as tension wound deep in her belly, one tip of the vibrator rubbing against her G-spot and the other massaging her clit. She clenched her teeth, adjusting to the pleasure. "Yes, Professor?" she ground out.

"We won't stop until you learn your lesson, so I suggest you learn it quickly." He shifted in his seat, demonstrating he wasn't as immune to the scene as he'd appeared. "For the both of us."

She breathed in through her nose and out through her mouth, working through the pleasure just like she worked through the pain when she exercised. If side cramps and shin splints didn't keep her from running a 10K, then why should the threat of an orgasm keep her from reading?

Over the next couple of hours, Tristan didn't play fair, bringing her to the brink of orgasm time and time again. It hadn't been easy to concentrate, proof of that in the dozen or so whacks of the ruler on her skin. But her desire to succeed, as well as her overwhelming need to come, kept her from giving up on Tristan's lesson.

Between the perspiration coating her skin and the arousal spilling between her legs, she'd soaked the blanket beneath her. Considerate of her comfort, Tristan had raised the heat in the apartment, warding off a chill.

By late afternoon, she'd won the war over her body and found the power inside of herself to remain completely focused on her book, lost in the world of the adulterous Madame Bovary and her oblivious husband. Tristan and the toy inside her body did their best to distract her, but in the end, she finished her two hundred pages of reading and laid the book beside her on the table.

Reclined in his chair with his legs spread, Tristan lazily stroked his exposed cock as he stared at her. He gripped himself hard, pulling and twisting the reddened skin taut over his considerable length, pearly beads of pre-come aiding his ministrations. Her heart picked up speed, the book forgotten.

He was so beautiful it hurt, and at times like these, watching him exult in his blatant sexuality, she didn't understand what he saw in her. She didn't miss the way other professors would flirt with him at the dean's monthly gatherings, or the way her peers would stare in admiration at him as he walked across campus. It killed her not to have the ability to kiss him or touch him in public. The need to stake ownership in him and show those women he wasn't available grew stronger and stronger with each passing day.

"Don't I get a reward for finishing my homework, Professor?" she asked. If he came at his own hand in front of her, she'd cry. She needed him with a desperation that bordered on insanity.

He didn't stop, but rather moved his hand faster. *Damn him.* He was going to deprive her after she'd worked so hard. "You do, Ms. Lawson. Have a little something in mind?"

"No. Something big. Your cock in my mouth would be a good start."

A look of lust passed over his face as he tugged hard on his balls. "I do love that dirty mouth of yours. It would be a shame to waste it."

He stood and walked around the table, stopping on her left side and offering his cock to her like a treat. She knew better than to reach for him. Holding his gaze, she opened her mouth and waited.

She didn't have to wait for long. He rolled her to her side, then rocked up on his toes and fed her his cock, sliding it along her tongue until he bumped the back of her throat and she gagged. He pulled back a couple of inches, making her as comfortable as she could get while lying on her side on a hard table and being face-fucked by a cock that was so thick it just barely fit in her mouth.

Her lips stretched over him and she relaxed her jaw, allowing him to use her mouth as the vessel to get himself off.

There was something so sexy about Tristan taking his own pleasure from her body. She didn't have to worry about pleasing him or whether she was doing it right.

He set the pace. He determined the rhythm. All she had to do was submit.

Tristan tasted like sex and candy, both sweet and spicy. *Addictive.* God, she was addicted to him and that cock of his. She'd never get enough.

He moved powerfully in her mouth, plunging and retreating with even strokes, completely controlled. She didn't want that. She wanted him out of his mind and lost to his desire to come. She wanted him to break apart and shatter. To spill his seed down her throat.

When the vein on the underside of his cock pulsed against her tongue, she prepared herself for his essence to fill her mouth. But he deprived her, withdrawing his cock and slapping her on the thigh.

"Lie on your back," he demanded.

She wasn't about to argue. If he didn't want to climax yet, who was she to argue, especially after he'd kept *her* on edge all day?

He shifted to the front of the table and grabbed her by the ankles. He pulled her until her butt was almost off the table, and then he lifted her bottom half into the air, hooking her bound ankles over his shoulders. She groaned as he removed the vibrator still lodged inside her.

Beyond sensitive after a day of foreplay, her clitoris fluttered as if the vibrator were still working. Arousal covered her mound and inner thighs. She was so wet, she should be embarrassed.

But she wasn't.

Tristan lowered his head. "Feel free to come as many times as you want."

The moment the tip of his tongue hit her sensitive bundle of nerves, she went off like a lit firecracker on the Fourth of July, her inner muscles clenching and releasing with so much force, she swore she saw stars. But Tristan didn't stop. If anything, he took her climax as a signal to ramp up his ministrations. He shoved two fingers inside her still-spasming channel and worked them in and out of her, fast and hard, keeping her orgasm going. She cried out, the sensation almost bordering on pain, and tried to get away from his mouth. But his hands clamped down on her thighs, keeping her locked in place and at his mercy.

A second orgasm hit her before the first one had ebbed, sharp and powerful. Tears rolled down her cheeks, but she wasn't sure if it was the result of pleasure or pain. At this point, was there a difference?

Before she thought she'd lose her mind for good, he dragged his mouth away from her pussy to stand between her legs. He bent over her, and his tongue, slick with her essence, made love to her mouth, taking her in a way that left her unable to think. Only sensation remained.

The softness of his lips.

The tang of her arousal on his mouth.

The rough hairs tickling her legs.

Her heart soared at the possession in his kiss.

As soon as he removed the spreader bar, she wrapped her legs around his waist, planting her heels at the base and his spine. He shoved his hands under her butt, lifting off the table and carrying her to their bed.

Their bed.

When had she begun to think of it belonging to them both?

Maybe it was because she spent every waking moment with him here on the weekends, the two of them shuttered up behind closed doors with the world outside almost forgotten.

She had to admit, the risk of getting caught added to some of the excitement, but at the same time, it was like a noose around her neck, threating to tighten at any moment.

Chloe was proof of that. When she'd interrupted them in the office, Isabella thought Chloe had figured it out. And as the weekends progressed and Isabella spent more and more time away, Chloe would demand to know where Isabella was sleeping.

It was only a matter of time before she put it all together.

One slipup and someone could find out about them. How long would their luck hold out?

Tristan dropped her onto the mattress and took a step back, a pensive look on his face. He strode to his closet and returned holding two of his ties.

He didn't say a word, but he didn't have to.

She knew what he was asking.

Her pulse kicked up a notch and a tremble broke out all over her body, but it wasn't from fear.

It was from excitement.

Desire.

Arousal.

"Green," she said, giving her consent.

Tristan's pupils dilated, swallowing his blue irises. "Get on your knees and hold on to the top of the headboard."

She flipped over and crawled up the bed until she reached the pillows. Once she got into position, she peered over her shoulder at Tristan and smiled seductively.

He pulled his shirt over his head in one swift motion, then dropped his pants to the floor. As always, the sight of his naked body took her breath away. His impressive erection stood out from his nest of trimmed hair, aimed straight for her like an arrow. And while she loved that part of him—really, really loved that part of him—it was the sight of his arms that did it for her. They weren't overly muscled like a gym rat's, but they were firm and they were strong, and when they were wrapped around her body, she felt as if nothing could ever go wrong.

"You're so fucking beautiful." He rounded the bed to stand by her side. "And so fucking *mine*."

He wound the soft silk around her wrists, binding her to the slats of their bed. Every part of her pounded and pulsed, the eroticism of the moment sending her soaring to the edge of climax.

She was at his mercy.

And she wouldn't have it any other way.

The bed dipped as Tristan got on it and moved behind her, the heat of him radiating onto the skin of her back. His cock bumped up against her behind as he reached around her to cup her breasts in his hands. He teasingly ran his fingers back and forth over her nipples, making them tighten before he plucked and twisted and pulled and pinched. She gasped and moaned, growing restless as her pussy clenched hard. When his hands left her body, she whimpered in desperation.

"You need something Angel?" he whispered in her ear. "Let me hear you beg for it."

She bit her lip and threw her head back. "Please, Tristan. I need you inside of me."

"Not good enough, Angel. What in particular do you want inside of you?"

"Your cock, damn it."

"Where?" He teased the crack of her butt with the tip of his cock. "Here?"

Without meaning to, she pushed back against it. "Um..."

"You like that idea, huh? Not tonight, but soon I'm going to take you there. But right now, where do you want it, Angel? Tell me. Beg for it."

"Please, please, please, I need your cock in my pussy, Tristan. Make the ache go away. You're the only one who can."

"You're right. I am." He grabbed her thighs, pushing them open a little wider, then tilted her body and, in one brutal thrust, buried himself inside her channel. "Because you belong to me." He withdrew almost all the way out, dragging his cock along all the nerve endings inside of her, before slamming back in. "And I belong to you."

With a relentless pace, he drove himself in and out of her body.

Possessing her.

Owning her.

Branding her as his.

His sweat-slicked chest covered her back as his hand curled around and pressed her clitoris. It was just what she needed to push her over the edge, and she exploded, flashes of color bursting in front of her eyes and her body shuddering. He screamed her name as he found his own climax. Holding her chin, he turned her face toward him and kissed her, at first tentatively, but then passionately.

He undid the knots of the ties and dragged her down to lie in his arms, resting her head on his chest. His heart pounded furiously underneath her as he caught his breath. Gazing into her eyes, he cupped her cheek. "I'm falling into you, Angel."

"I'm falling into you too," she said, not ready to tell him what she'd recognized last weekend. That she'd already fallen and was in love with him. She covered his hand with hers. She hadn't known it possible to feel such overwhelming happiness.

How could she have fallen so hard, so fast?

She'd been with Tony for four years and never felt one iota of what she felt for Tristan. This man had penetrated her deepest defenses and had embedded himself inside her heart. She hadn't bargained for this when she'd made her decision to spend the night with Tristan at Ryder's party. College was supposed to have been filled with days of studying and working, not falling in love. And here it was, not a year into her education at Edison, and she'd fallen so hard, she wasn't sure she'd ever recover from it.

But she wouldn't give up a moment of this time with him, regardless of the outcome.

His phone rang, breaking the peacefulness of the moment. He rolled over and checked it, swearing as he read the display.

"It's Morgan."

TWENTY-THREE

Less than thirty minutes after admitting to Isabella that he was falling in love with her, Tristan had been forced to leave her naked in his bed while he met with Morgan.

The snow from yesterday had already mostly melted, but it wouldn't be long before the campus was plunged in a winter wonderland. Right now, it was a balmy ten degrees Fahrenheit, beyond cold to most people, but when you lived in the Upper Peninsula of Michigan, it was a way of life. Locals laughed at the droves of students and staff who moved up here and froze their asses off because they weren't prepared.

It was odd that he'd moved back to the city years ago, but a couple of months living here again, he felt like he'd never left. When he inhaled, it was as if he could breathe easily for the first time in years. Some of it could be attributable to Isabella. Hell, he could admit, most of it was attributable to her. He couldn't remember a time when he'd smiled so much. But it was also the town and its people, the environment of academia. Sharing ideas and debating policies, the students at Edison University were optimistic about their future. Their excitement was infectious and Tristan loved being a part of it. For the first time that he could remember, he felt as if he was a part of something bigger than himself.

He felt humbled.

Did he still want to make Novateur a success? *Abso-fucking-lutely.*

Not just to prove that he wasn't a failure, but for his best friend.

Ryder had stuck by his side since their freshman year of college. Hell, he'd been his best man at his wedding to Morgan and a couple years later had taken him to get plastered when she served him the divorce papers. Ryder was the brother he'd never had, and aside from each other, neither one of them had any other family they could rely on. Tristan because he had none that he spoke to and Ryder because he couldn't escape them. Didn't mean he didn't constantly try, and Novateur was a big component of that. At any time, Ryder could have used his family's money to fund Novateur or at least use it to attain a loan, but he refused to use his family connections on his loan application.

Tristan wouldn't disappoint him.

He approached the bridge, seeing that Morgan had already arrived. Dressed in a black full-length fur coat and fur boots up to her thighs, her makeup and hair perfect as if she was preparing for a night on the town rather than standing on a bridge in the middle of a college campus, Morgan managed to look even colder than the autumn night air felt. How had he ever found her beautiful?

She turned his way as he stepped onto the bridge.

"I thought I'd made it clear I didn't want to see you again," he said, doing away with pretenses. After all, she'd pulled him away from his night with Isabella and he was eager to get back to her.

"Oh, you did. You made it perfectly clear," she said with so much glee it immediately set him on edge. "That's why I hired someone else to follow you." She waved her finger at him. "You've been a very, very bad boy, Tristan. Fucking a student. Whatever will your friend Isaac say when I tell him how you seduced a child and introduced her to your depravity?"

His chest tightened, and a surge of adrenaline coursed through his veins. She'd hired a private detective. Fuck, he should've known she'd do something like that. "I don't know—"

"Isabella Lawson. God, I knew you were sick, but preying on an innocent freshman and introducing her to your abusive sex games is beyond demented."

Time and time again, he'd foolishly underestimated the lengths this vindictive woman would go to. A hundred different emotions hit him all at once, but he focused on his anger. Like any predator, if she smelled his fear—fear for Isabella and all she stood to lose because of him—she'd go in for the kill. "Despite what you accused of me in our divorce, you know I don't abuse women."

"It doesn't matter. It's all about public perception." She

patted her large Louis Vuitton purse. "I have pictures of you and your precious Isabella that would make a porn star blush."

That wasn't possible. She had to be bluffing. "I don't believe you."

She shook her head as if she pitied him. "You should have a talk with your leasing manager. It didn't take more than a hundred bucks to get him to unlock the door and let me inside your apartment."

Tristan pictured the potbellied, cigarette-smoke-scented man and knew immediately she wasn't lying. He thought back to his lease agreement. If his memory was right, management had the right to enter his apartment only in certain circumstances. Allowing a stranger inside his apartment to set up a camera had to be against the law. "You took the photos illegally."

Apparently, Morgan had been prepared for that accusation. She shrugged and checked out her nails. "So? You think your friend the dean or the rest of the university staff will care how the photos were taken? No, they'll be too busy figuring out how to cover their own asses so that they don't get sued by the Lawsons."

He jolted, stunned by the lengths to which Morgan would go to get what she wanted.

White-hot rage shot through his veins as he curled his hands into tight fists. Anger consumed him, anger directed not only at Morgan, but himself.

He'd fucked up.

He'd promised Isabella he'd keep her safe.

And he'd failed.

Morgan pursed her lips and shook her head. "And after everything that poor girl went through with her boyfriend, to have it happen again," she said, her voice laced with mock sympathy. "Her parents will be devastated. At least this time, they'll have someone to sue. Settling with the university should set them up quite nicely. But they're not the only ones who will need money."

His tightly reined control was slipping with every word Morgan uttered. Red clouded his vision, and the urge to squeeze the life out of her overwhelmed him.

"Once word gets out that she slept with her professor," Morgan continued, "she'll never find a decent job after graduation. *Poof!* All her dreams gone over a man who would've grown bored with her before the end of the year and moved onto his next victim." Venom dripped from her voice. "I should know."

He hadn't thought he could hate the woman any more than he already did, but he was wrong. How could she threaten to ruin an innocent girl she didn't even know? He pointed a finger at her. "Don't play the victim card. You were the one who cheated. Not me."

She lifted a shoulder, completely blasé. "So you say. But a wife knows when her husband no longer desires her. I couldn't give you what you needed. How long before you went out and found a woman who would?"

He'd never cheated on a woman in his life. Even after he'd grown disenchanted with Morgan, he'd remained faithful, hopeful they could make their marriage work. "Hell, Morgan, when I married you, I loved you. I'd planned to spend the rest of my life by your side. My desire for you only disappeared when I discovered I had married a woman who didn't exist. But *you* knew exactly who you were marrying before we even met, didn't you?"

She had the audacity to bristle, looking over his shoulder to avoid his gaze. "I don't know what you're referring to."

"My reputation for kink wasn't a secret. Nor was the fact that I'd inherited all my parents' money. You targeted me right from the start." The guilt in her eyes was all the proof he needed to confirm his suspicions were true. "Were you ever faithful to me?"

She slowly slid her gaze to his. "For a few months when we first married, I thought I might love you. I'd even considered staying in our marriage. But once you began talking about investing everything we had into a new business venture, despite my vocalized concerns, I knew it was time to get out before you lost all of the money."

He took a deep breath through his nose to restrain himself from wringing her neck. In losing control, he was giving her what she wanted and playing into her hands. It was time to wage an offensive and remind her who really held the power.

Folding his arms over his chest, he smiled. "And yet here you are, blackmailing me for a piece of Novateur. Guess you underestimated me."

Probably thrown by the change in his demeanor, she bit down on her lip, silent. A notch appeared between her brows, and her gaze darted left and right.

"I made a mistake walking out on our marriage." She

moved closer and softened her voice. "It was real. At least for a little while. We could have it again, you know. The marriage. The house in the suburbs. The babies. Everything you wanted. You'll never get those things with Isabella. She's a child. You need a woman." She laid her hand on his chest and looked up at him. "You need me."

She was right.

He did need a woman.

Covering her hand with his, he lowered his head, bringing his mouth within inches of hers. With a victorious grin, she tilted her head to the side and curled her hand around his neck in preparation for his kiss.

And that woman was Isabella.

He made sure to enunciate so she didn't misunderstand him. "You're really delusional, you know that?" Gripping her wrist tightly, he ripped her hand off his body and lifted her arm in the air. "You divorcing me was the best thing that ever happened to me."

She sneered and broke his hold on her, clawing her sharp fingernails into his cheek. "Because of your precious little Isabella."

He felt the telltale warmth of blood dripping down his face. "I'm warning you," he growled. "Stay away from her."

"You honestly think you're in love with her," she said incredulously.

"What I am is none of your business."

"You're going to ruin that girl, Tristan. We both know it. If you really love her, take my deal. Give me half of your Novateur shares."

Fury burned in his gut. "Over my dead body. Better yet, *over yours*."

"Then I guess you don't really love her, because I will expose your affair."

"If you do, I'll lose the funding for Novateur. You'll get nothing," he spit out.

"I'll get the satisfaction of destroying you and saving that poor child from a lifetime of abuse at your hands. Someday she'll thank me. I'll give you twenty-four hours to make the right decision and sign the paperwork."

"You're heartless."

"Better heartless than poor." She stood on her tiptoes and kissed him gently on his bloody cheek. "See you soon, partner."

She turned to go, but he grabbed her by the arm and spun her around.

Her pupils dilated in fear.

Good. She should be scared.

Did she really think he'd allow her to do this to him? To Ryder? To Isabella?

If so, she had another think coming.

TWENTY-FOUR

Isabella was worried. And when she was worried, she baked. The minute Tristan had walked out the door to meet his ex-wife, Isabella had raided the pantry for her choice of drug.

Sugar.

An hour later, she'd baked two dozen double-fudge-mocha brownies and one Kahlúa cheesecake.

But he still hadn't come home.

So now, at nearly midnight, she was onto her next creation—a pecan-walnut pie with a brownie crust. Needing to chop the nuts to the right size, she grabbed a cutting board from under the sink and a sharp knife from the block Tristan kept on the counter. After sprinkling the variety of nuts on the board, she began chopping them, thrilled to have an outlet right now for her aggression. Quickly and efficiently, she moved from one end of the board to the other, pretending each of them represented Tristan's ex-wife. How long would Tristan allow that witch to play her little games? It scared her that one of these days, the woman would push him too far. What if he did something he later regretted?

She shook her head. No, he was too controlled to do something stupid. Between Ryder and Tristan, they'd find a way to stop Morgan once and for all.

The sound of the front door slamming startled her. Her knife slipped, slicing into the fleshy pads of her pointer and middle fingers. She felt the sting of it only seconds before the blood streamed down her fingers and onto the nuts. She dropped the knife on the floor and went to pick it up, knocking the cutting board into her. Nuts went tumbling down her shirt, spattering blood on it.

When she looked up, Tristan stood in front of her, his face white as a ghost except for the red scratches on his cheek.

"What happened to your face?" she asked.

He blinked at her as if she was crazy. "What the hell happened in *here?*"

Thank goodness he was home. She grabbed some paper towel and a spray bottle of cleaning fluid. "Don't worry, I'll clean up the mess. What happened with Morgan?"

He stayed her with a hand to her bicep. "Jesus, Isabella. I don't give a shit about the kitchen. You're hurt."

"It's just a couple of little cuts. Tell me what happened with Morgan."

"Maybe your version of little is skewed because you're bleeding all over the damned place. Let's get it under water," he said, steering her to the faucet.

"It's fine. I just need to keep pressure on it to stem the

blood flow." She wrapped the paper towel around her fingers and held it tight. "Cutting yourself is a hazard of being a chef or a baker."

He stared at her—no, through her—with haunted eyes.

Whatever had happened with Morgan, it wasn't good.

She laid a palm on his cheek. "Talk to me."

He clenched his hands. "I don't want to talk."

"Then what do you want?"

"I want to lose myself in you," he said hoarsely. "I need you."

"You have me. Always. Whatever you need, it's yours. I'm yours."

"Dangerous words to say to a Dominant."

"I mean it. I trust you."

He sank his fingers into her hair, tugging her head back while he suckled on that sensitive spot between her neck and shoulder. With a growl, he lifted her onto the counter. Forehead to forehead and breathing heavily, they looked into each other's eyes.

Her heart ached as if Tristan held it in his hands and was softly squeezing it. She wanted him more than she wanted her next breath. But it hurt so damned much. Why would something so beautiful, so wonderful, make her feel this way? It was almost as if she was grieving, the tugging sensation in her chest similar to the days following her dear grandma's death. And yet at the same time, she couldn't remember ever being this happy. It didn't make sense.

Her stomach twisted into knots, a foreboding she couldn't ignore settling into her bones. Even with everything that they risked, she wouldn't give up a single minute of their time together. Despite it being against the rules, what they shared was rare and precious.

And at any moment, he could be ripped away from her.

He pulled back, despair on his face. "Morgan—"

Before he could say anything more, there was a knocking on the door.

Tristan put his hands on her waist and set her on her feet. He put a finger over his lips in the universal signal to stay quiet. "Go hide in the bathroom."

"Why? What's going on? You're scaring me," she whispered.

"Just do it. Don't question me," he said, somehow able to use his *don't mess with me* Dom voice while whispering.

Heart racing, she darted into the bathroom and shut herself in. She heard the sound of Tristan opening the door to his apartment.

"Tristan Kelley?"

"Yes, Officer, what can I do for you?"

Officer? As in the police?

What were they doing here?

"At approximately eleven fifty-five tonight, a body was discovered in the parking lot near the campus bridge. The driver's licensed identified her as Morgan Kelley . . . your ex-wife."

* * *

Isabella sat on the edge of the bathtub and put her head between her legs to avoid a full-blown panic attack.

What the hell just happened? Had the police really taken Tristan to the station for questioning?

Morgan had been murdered.

There was no way the man she knew could intentionally kill someone, especially a woman he'd once loved. But what if he had done it accidentally? He'd acted so strangely when he came home after seeing her.

Why hadn't she pressed him to tell her what had happened tonight?

What was he hiding?

A ribbon of icy fear tightened around her chest, making it hard to breathe.

There was no time to fall apart. Tristan needed her.

But what should she do?

Regulating her breathing and counting back from one hundred, she forced herself to calm down so she could make a plan. When she felt her heart return to its near normal rhythm, she got up from the tub and went to the sink, where she splashed some cold water on her face.

As much as she wanted to, she couldn't go to the police station. Her arrival would raise too many questions she wasn't prepared to answer.

But what if the police arrested Tristan?

Depending on when Morgan was murdered, Isabella might be his alibi.

She'd have no choice but to tell the police she was with him in his apartment tonight. Everyone would find out about her relationship with Tristan. They'd both be ruined. Even if she were allowed to stay at Edison, she'd never get into the Lancaster Business School. Her dreams would go up in smoke. Sure, she could transfer to a different school and hope they'd ignore her indiscretion and admit her into their second-rate business school, but it wouldn't be the same.

Still, she wasn't selfish enough to stay silent when Tristan needed her the most. Not when his freedom could be at risk.

She strode into the bedroom and snatched her cell phone. Whom should she call?

There was only one person she could trust.

Thank goodness Tristan had given her his phone number so that she could call if she had any questions about Novateur.

Her fingers shook as she dialed and waited for him to answer.

"Ryder McKay."

She opened her mouth and nothing came out but a rush of air. She swallowed, lubricating her dry throat, and tried again. "Ryder? It's Isabella. Tristan needs you. I think he was just arrested."

"Arrested? Tristan? What the hell for?"

She heard the shock in his voice and she could completely relate, because she couldn't believe the words she was about to utter. "Murdering Morgan."

There was a heavy silence that went on for far too long.

"Ryder, are you still there?" she prodded.

"I'm only a few hours away. Don't do anything stupid like go to the police station on his behalf. The last thing he needs is to explain why his student is there."

Guess that confirmed he knew she was more than Tristan's student. "I won't." She closed her eyes and exhaled.

"Thanks for calling me, Isabella. I'll be in touch as soon as I know something." He disconnected without saying good-bye, but considering the circumstances, she'd forgive him for his rudeness.

She looked around the apartment. She couldn't stay here. If the police came back to search for evidence, she didn't want them to find her here. Finding it soothing, she cleaned up the kitchen, scrubbing the bloodstains with bleach, and tossed away the desserts she'd baked. Then she shoved everything she could find of hers in her bag, wiping any evidence of her existence in his apartment. She didn't want to walk in the dark of night, especially knowing that a woman had been murdered, but what choice did she have?

By the time she got back to her dorm room, her entire body was covered in sweat despite the cold temperature outside.

She let herself in the room, careful not to make any noise. Chances were Chloe wasn't even there—she'd had plans with the other cast members from *West Side Story*—but in case Isabella was wrong, she didn't want to wake her.

After changing her clothes, she got under the covers of her twin bed, leaving her cell phone on her chest. Heart thumping and her hands shaking, she knew there was no way she'd ever sleep.

She couldn't help thinking about the way Tristan had looked when he'd gotten back from seeing Morgan tonight.

Those scratches on his face.

Had *she* done that to him?

Were those...defensive wounds?

Her lungs seized with terror.

What if Tristan really had killed Morgan?

TWENTY-FIVE

Two hours of questioning and Tristan thought his head was going to explode. Still in the interrogation room, waiting for the detective to return, he hung his head in his hands and rubbed his temples.

Morgan was dead.

Murdered.

And he was the police's prime suspect.

Especially since he had those cuts on his cheek.

When they'd asked him about it, he'd told them the truth and had allowed them to swab the scrapings as evidence.

After, it had occurred to him he shouldn't have given them permission without a warrant, but at the time, he was still in shock.

Besides, he was innocent.

That had to count for something, right?

They hadn't arrested him. No, they'd made it clear he could leave at any time. But they'd also made it clear leaving would only make him look guilty, throwing out that as Morgan's ex-husband, he should want to find the real killer.

And he did. It was terrible, but a small part of him wanted to thank the son of a bitch for it.

He'd thought about doing it himself a thousand times.

He'd even thought about it tonight when he'd knocked her to the ground and retrieved the photos from her purse. He'd never felt such uncontrollable rage as when he saw the photos of his private moments with a naked Isabella. Morgan had turned something beautiful and special into something sordid and deviant.

He wanted her to pay. To suffer. To fucking disappear.

He'd wanted her dead.

But he wasn't a killer.

In the end, he'd turned and left her crumpled on the wet ground.

There was no doubt in his mind that Morgan had pissed off more than just him. The fact was, anyone who truly knew the woman would probably want to kill her.

But to do it in Edison?

The cop who'd questioned him had said there hadn't been a murder in the town since 1942.

Tristan had played their conversation on the bridge over and over in his head. Had he missed a clue, something that might lead them to the real killer?

A poor student had found Morgan's body by her car. There was no sign that Morgan had brought anyone with her on the twelve-hour drive, but there must have been another person. It didn't make any sense that someone would have followed her all the way up here to kill her.

When the shock had worn off sometime during his police

interview, he'd clammed up, refusing to say anything other than that he'd met with her on the bridge and that when he'd left, she was alive. He knew it made him look guilty. But the cops didn't have anything other than a witness who had seen him arguing with Morgan on the bridge around eleven that night and his DNA under her fingernails. That wasn't enough to prosecute him, was it?

Just like they did on those television procedurals he enjoyed, they played their mind games in an attempt to break him down, offering different scenarios, hoping he'd let something slip.

They obviously assumed he'd done it. It would make their job a hell of a lot easier if he had. He just hoped they didn't allow their assumptions to keep them from doing their job and investigating the facts.

They'd only brought him in as a witness. At this point, he wasn't in police custody and therefore wasn't entitled to an attorney. Not that he'd hire one. No, his only option was to keep his mouth shut.

They'd find the real killer.

He had to believe that.

When the door to the room opened, Tristan lifted his head, expecting the detective, but reared back to see Ryder sauntering in with bloodshot eyes. Tristan ran his hand down his face and stood, wondering if he looked as tired as his friend. "Ryder. How the hell did you know I was here?"

"Isabella called and told me."

Isabella.

It had pained him to leave her hiding in the bathroom

when he went with the police, but he knew if they had started questioning him there in his apartment, she would've made her presence known in order to protect him. And he just couldn't allow that to happen. Not when the consequences of her exposing their affair would end in her expulsion from school. "Sorry to pull you away from the conference."

"Are you fucking kidding me?" Ryder asked, his eyes flashing with rage. "You should've called me yourself. When the hell are you going to get over that goddamned inferiority complex of yours and start asking for help?"

He didn't have an inferiority complex, and he certainly didn't need anyone else's help. There may have been a time when he was weak and needed both Isaac and Ryder to pull him back from the brink, but those days were long over. He'd spent the last ten years proving that he could take care of himself.

The detective in charge of the investigation returned, a cup of what Tristan assumed by the scent was coffee in his hand. "Mr. Kelley, you're free to go. I'm sure we'll be speaking soon, so be sure to stay in town for the time being."

The cop didn't have to tell him twice.

Tristan put on his coat. "Of course, Detective."

Five minutes later, he was sitting silently in the passenger seat of Ryder's car, on his way back to his apartment.

He should call Isabella. She had to be worried.

She should be.

Not for him, but for herself.

"Now that we're alone, tell me what happened to Morgan," Ryder said, his voice raspy with exhaustion.

Tristan relayed the information the police had communicated to him. "She was stabbed to death getting into her car. The police haven't received the official report from the medical examiner yet, but based on the amount of blood around her body, the police say she most likely bled out."

Ryder grimaced and shuddered. "I can't say I didn't wish her dead a thousand times, but that's a harsh way to go. What do the cops think? Mugging gone bad?"

If only it were so simple. Tristan shook his head. "Credit cards and over five hundred dollars were still in her wallet."

"Maybe they panicked and ran off without it?" Ryder suggested.

"The cops don't think so." In fact, they seemed to have already decided on a scenario. "They're going on a crime-of-passion angle. Judging by the amount of stab wounds, the killer was likely angry at Morgan."

Ryder snorted. "Well, hell. Morgan could make the pope angry enough to kill her." He paused. "What was she doing up here, Tris?"

Tristan filled him in on what had happened on the bridge, then revealed the final nail in his coffin. "The usual. Blackmailing me. She has...had...photos of a naked Isabella and me in my apartment. I tossed them in the garbage right after I met with her. Guess I don't have to worry about any copies now that she's dead." He touched his cheek. "These scratches. They're from her. I couldn't lie to the police. They have my DNA, and it's going to match the skin under her fingernails. Not to mention, I was also covered in blood. They got a samples of that too."

"Maybe you shouldn't be telling me all this," Ryder said.

"Jesus, I didn't do it," he shouted. "The blood was Isabella's. Came home from dealing with Morgan and found her bleeding all over my kitchen from a cut on her hand. But I couldn't tell the police whose blood it was. I refuse to bring Isabella into this mess."

Ryder blew out a breath, his gaze meeting Tristan's. They both knew what Tristan had to do. "It won't match then. Yeah, you had an argument with her and she scratched you, but other than that, they've got nothing."

Tristan pinched the bridge of his nose as the dark, cold reality began to set in. "I hated her and I was the last person to see her alive."

Ryder parked the car in front of Tristan's apartment building and shut off the engine. "That's not true." He turned to Tristan. "That privilege goes to the person who killed her."

* * *

Isabella groaned, turning over in her bed to escape the loud noise.

A familiar chiming threatened to split her head wide apart, and it took her a moment to realize the noise was coming from underneath her pillow.

She bolted awake, wincing at the sharp pain in her temples. She'd been up all night waiting for Tristan or Ryder to call her, but she must have fallen asleep sometime after daybreak.

What time was it?

A quick glance at her alarm clock said it was eleven a.m. She'd slept four hours.

She snagged her phone without looking at it, expecting to hear Tristan or Ryder's voice. "Hello?"

"Isabella? It's Erin. I don't want to alarm you, but Tony's missing."

She sat up, her pulse skyrocketing. "Missing?"

"He hasn't been seen since he left his parents' house yesterday morning, and he isn't answering his phone."

She closed her eyes and took a deep breath. Really, she wasn't surprised. Hadn't she known this would happen? Prepared for it?

Erin continued. "Now, there's no reason to panic."

She laughed. The only reason she wasn't breaking down was because of Tristan. Just knowing she had his support was enough to get her through this. But that didn't mean she wasn't worried. "No reason? Are you kidding me? Put yourself in my shoes and tell me if you wouldn't panic," she said, proud of herself for keeping her voice calm. "Has anyone called the police?"

"No. The only reason I found out was that his parents gave me a courtesy call. They don't believe their son is dangerous, but just in case, they thought you should know."

She used to consider Tony's parents as part of her family. But after the incident, they'd been forced to choose a side, and of course, they'd chosen their son's. She never blamed them for it, but it had hurt just the same. At least they'd had the decency to warn her.

"The police can't do anything, because he hasn't broken any law," Erin needlessly reminded her. "Unless he violates the restraining order, there's nothing I can do at this time."

After ending the call, she hung her feet over the side of the bed and put her head in her hands. She had to stay strong. She'd made a promise to herself and to Tristan that she wouldn't allow Tony power over her anymore.

Still in her hand, the phone rang again.

Tristan.

"Are you okay?" she asked immediately.

He hesitated. "I'm fine."

She exhaled. "I was so worried. Where are you?"

"I'm home," he said. "I need to see you." His monotone voice gave nothing away. Maybe someone was with him and he couldn't speak freely.

That had to be it.

She wouldn't entertain any other option.

"I'll come over right now," she said, rolling out of bed. She had to tell him about Tony. "Listen, I need to—"

"No, don't come here. Meet me at the bridge by your dorm in ten minutes."

The next thing she heard was a click.

He'd hung up without saying good-bye.

Her stomach churned with nervousness. Not only because she didn't want to walk by herself with Tony on the loose, but because of the way Tristan had spoken to her on the phone.

If he *had* killed Morgan? Could she stay with a man who'd stabbed his ex-wife?

She loved him. There was no question of that. But having been a victim herself, she couldn't imagine a circumstance other than an accident where she'd be able to forgive him for killing Morgan.

She immediately dismissed that idea.

She knew in her heart he never could have done something so awful.

After throwing on some sweats and her winter gear, she headed out toward the tower. As a result of not enough sleep, her body ached, and her eyes felt as if they had sandpaper in them. She stepped outside and immediately started shivering. It was so cold, her breath was visible in the air. At least it helped wake her up.

Without a home football game, Sundays were quiet on campus. There was hardly anyone around as she hurried to the bridge, but her neck prickled with awareness. She shivered again, but this time, it was from the sense of being *watched*.

Tristan was leaning with his back against the wall of the bridge, his eyes closed, and his hands in his pockets. He looked so fragile and vulnerable like that. She just wanted to wrap her arms around him and assure him that everything would be okay.

It would be. It had to be.

She couldn't lose him.

Not now. Not ever.

"Hey," she called out as she approached him.

His eyes popped opened and he pushed off the wall, meeting her halfway.

Disregarding the possibility of being seen, she did what she wanted and threw her arms around his middle, resting her head on his chest. "I was so worried." He didn't return her embrace, but instead stood frozen, his limbs like ice. She took a step back and peered up at him, noting immediately that he wouldn't look at her. In fact, he was looking at everything but her. "What's wrong?"

He clenched his jaw, the muscles around his mouth twitching from the tension. "I came to tell you I can't see you anymore."

The bottom fell out below her feet and the earth spun around her. She couldn't have heard him right. "You mean just for a little while. Just until the police find the real killer."

His gaze slowly made its way to hers. "No."

She took a deep breath to steady herself. He didn't want this. No, he was playing the martyr. "You're doing this to protect me," she said confidently. "Well, I refuse to let you. I don't care if everyone finds out about us. I'm going to tell the police the truth."

"And what truth is that?" he asked, his expression hard as granite.

She stumbled back, the rage radiating off him almost palpable. "That I was with you when Morgan was murdered. That the blood on your clothes was mine."

He grabbed her by the arm and pushed her up against the wall. Whether it was to give her support so that she didn't fall or because of his anger, she didn't know. And that scared her. He was scaring her. "No. You're not saying anything to the police. It's not your fight. Stay out of it."

"What do you mean it's not my fight?" She laid her palms on his cheeks. "Your fight is my fight."

He shook his head and removed her hands, rejecting her comfort. *Rejecting her.* "Not this time. My fight is my fight and mine alone."

She felt as if she were grappling with the rocks on the edge of a cliff, unable to gain purchase. "I told you, I know what you're doing. You think you're protecting me, but I don't need it."

"Protecting you? How am I protecting you?" he spit out with clear contempt. "Because I don't want you to ruin my life by telling the police I was with my fucking my student when my ex-wife was murdered? I'll lose my job and lose any chance to expand Novateur. That's why I'm here at Edison. It's the only thing that's important."

Every word he uttered was like a physical blow to her heart. How could he minimize what they'd shared together? He made their relationship sound so sordid. This wasn't the Tristan she loved. The man she'd come to know would never say these things to her. "Well, if you go to prison for murder, you're not getting the loan either."

He folded his arms across his chest. "They'll figure out the blood on my clothes isn't a match for Morgan and start looking in another direction."

"And you call me naive? You had the motive and opportunity to kill her," she pointed out, careful to keep her voice down even though she wanted to rail at him at the top of her lungs and beg him to see reason. "They're not going to look at anyone but you."

"You think if you tell the police you were with me around the time of Morgan's murder it's going to clear me? If anything, it will only give them another motive." His eyes darkened as he fixed his gaze on her. "She was fucking blackmailing me over you."

The resentment in his voice nearly bowled her over. "What?"

"She had photos of us together. Naked photos," he clarified. "Thank fuck she didn't have them on her when she was murdered."

Nausea gripped her. "How do you know she wasn't lying?"

"Because I took the set she had on her and destroyed them," he said coldly. "Actually, 'took' is too nice of a word." He looked her in the eyes. "I wrestled her to the ground and ripped her purse away from her. Still think I'm a nice guy?"

Is that what this was about? Guilt over the fact he'd manhandled Morgan? "I think you did what you needed to do, and lots of people would have done a lot worse. Case in point. She's dead."

"If you and I hadn't been so weak, this never would've happened. She might still be alive."

She flinched at the accusation. He blamed *her* for Morgan's death. All the air in her lungs disappeared and her eyes stung with fresh tears. "What happened to no regrets?" she whispered.

"It was stupid to think we could make this work."

"Why are you doing this?" She had to make him see that

he was wrong about them. That they were better together than they'd ever be apart. "All I have to do is go to the police—"

"Providing me an alibi isn't going to help," he repeated. "What it will guarantee is me losing my job and you getting kicked out of school. Is that what you want?"

She couldn't hold back the tears, allowing them to spill over onto her cheeks and leave an icy path. "No. It's not what I want. But I can't sit back and allow you to be charged with a crime you didn't commit."

He ground his teeth. "How do you know I didn't do it?"

"Because I know you," she said softly, taking his hand in hers. "You're not capable of killing anyone."

He looked down at their joined hands. "You're wrong. I'm not only capable, but I wanted her dead. You heard me threaten her."

"You didn't mean it. You were angry."

"You're so naive, Angel." Giving her hope, he tucked her hair behind her hair like he had so many times before. "You see the best in everyone even when all the signs are right in front of you."

"That's not true. Maybe it was at one time, but—"

"I could have done anything I wanted the night we met. You didn't know me and yet you trusted me enough to have sex."

Anger sliced through her. "Don't throw that back in my face. Maybe it was naive, but I'd never regret my decision. It was our beginning. We wouldn't be where we are now."

"Where do you think we are? You're a freshman. How long did you think we were going to last? I'm only here for another few months and then I'm going back to the city. Permanently."

There had been a few times over the last couple of months that she'd allowed herself to think about that, but she'd chosen to remain optimistic. "So? Plenty of people have long-distance relationships. We can make it work."

He let go of her hand and took a giant step back, creating a chasm between them that she feared could never be crossed. "No. I don't want to make it work. Our affair always had an expiration date, Isabella. It's time you accepted that."

"I don't accept that. You said you were falling into me. Well, I've already fallen," she admitted. "And I think you have too."

For a second, she thought she'd gotten through to him. His expression softened and she saw it there. Love. But then, like a mirage, it was suddenly gone. "Another time, another place...you and me, we might have had a chance. But we were doomed from the start. I'll always care about you, Isabella." He swallowed. "But I can't do this anymore."

"This?"

"Us." He raked a hand through his messy hair and blew out a breath. "I haven't been fair to you. I made you believe you meant more to me than you do."

An ache settled into her bones as a long shadow fell on them. She searched the space behind Tristan, but was unable to find the source. "I don't believe you," she said even as she was plagued with doubt. He'd never actually said that he loved her. Had she been so eager for someone to take care of her that she'd read something into their relationship that wasn't there?

"Why? Because you don't want to believe someone you care about could hurt you? Didn't you learn your lesson with Tony?"

She winced. "How could you say that? You're nothing like Tony."

He nodded. "You're right." Cold steel glinted into his eyes. "He loved you."

She swore she heard the sound of her heart shattering into a million pieces and covered her ears to make it stop. "Stop. Just stop. I know what you're doing. You're trying to push me away because it's your misguided way of protecting me. But I won't let you do it."

In two strides, he was right in front of her, ripping her hands away from her ears and holding them tightly. "You need to hear this. You're wrong about me. You've put me on this pedestal and I don't belong there. You had some romanticized notion about me and for a while, I thought maybe...maybe I could actually be that man, but it was all a lie. Do you know why I found you so attractive that night at Ryder's?"

She shook her head, but he ignored her.

"I'd fucked almost every other female sub there already and you were new," he said darkly. "You were like a fucking lamb stumbling inside a hungry lion's den. I wanted your innocence and I took it. That's it. There was nothing magical about that night or what's happened between us since then. It's just sex. Great sex, but sex just the same. It's not enough for me. It's not what I want. Before I met you, I had plans. Big plans. And for a while, I got distracted, but Morgan's murder reminded me what matters most. That's Novateur. So you see, this has nothing to do with protecting you. This is all about me finally doing what's best for me." He dropped her hands. "It's over."

As she slid down the wall to her knees, no longer feeling the cold, no longer feeling anything but emptiness, the man she loved turned from her and walked away, taking all the pieces of her shattered heart with him.

TWENTY-SIX

When her phone rang, Isabella wasn't sure how long she'd been on her knees. She looked around, confused. Everything was dark and gray. It was snowing. The sun must have disappeared behind a wall of clouds, because it couldn't be any later than noon. She was submerged in darkness, the shadows having disappeared along with Tristan. It was as if he'd stolen all the light from her world when he'd left. How could she have been so wrong about him? The pain of Tony's knife had nothing on the pain of Tristan telling her that he didn't love her.

She'd been so certain she'd found her soul mate, the man who helped her be the best version of herself. But she had just been a temporary distraction for him, someone to keep his bed warm until he finished his exile in Edison and returned to his real life. She would've been better off if she'd never met him. At least that way, she wouldn't have known how much it hurt to love someone who didn't love her back. There was a huge, gaping hole where her heart used to be.

How could she have been so blind?

The worst part was she couldn't avoid him.

He was still her professor for a few more weeks.

And if she wanted to stay in school, she'd have to continue as his assistant next semester.

It was going to be agony.

She told herself everything she was supposed to: She was a survivor. The pain would lessen over time. Her heart would heal. She'd fall in love again someday.

Blah, blah, blah.

Her phone rang again. She frowned as she answered. "Hey, Chloe. This isn't a good time."

"Isabella?" Her roommate's voice sounded funny. Far away and shaky as if she'd been crying. "I need you."

Isabella jumped to her feet. "What's wrong?"

"Everything," Chloe said hoarsely. "I've lost everything."

She turned in the direction of the dorm. "Are you in the room?"

"No. I'm on top of the bell tower." Chloe sobbed. "Isabella? Why does it always have to hurt so much?"

What was she talking about?

Tristan must have left a piece of her heart behind because it had started to beat faster. Something in Chloe's tone frightened her. "What do you mean? What hurts?"

"No matter how hard I try, I lose everything. I'm tired of losing."

Isabella's scars tingled. She recalled her conversation when Chloe had confided she'd once tried to kill herself.

She wouldn't.

Ice slithered down her spine. "Oh, hon. I'm on my way. Promise me you won't do anything stupid."

There was a long pause.

"It's too late."

Chloe hung up.

What did she mean it was too late?

Looking at her cell phone with the intention of calling 911, she took a couple of steps toward the tower and smacked straight into a wall. She put her hands on the wall to steady herself, realizing at once it wasn't a wall but a person. Her head snapped up and she reared back at the blue eyes that met hers.

She took a step backward, her heart skipping a beat in fear. Her throat frozen in terror, his name came out no louder than a whisper. "Tony."

Noise is your friend.

She hadn't seen a soul on campus. Would anyone hear her scream out here?

"Hey, Izzy." He moved toward her with his arms out as if he was about to give her a hug.

Don't move any closer to your attacker than necessary.

She held up her hands, and her eyes darted for an escape route. "Stay away."

He nodded, his own hands up in surrender. "I will. I promise. Just don't run away."

If you can run away, do it.

She should run. Run fast. Run and scream.

Would he chase her?

Knock her to the ground and beat her?

Take out a knife and slice and stab and cut?

Why wouldn't her fucking legs move?

Even without him giving her drugs, she was immobile.

Eyes, nose, ears, neck, groin, knees, and legs.

She wouldn't let him hurt her again.

She wasn't going down without a fight.

"Give me one good reason why I shouldn't run," she ordered, buying some time to get herself together.

"Because I'm not here to hurt you. I'm here because I'm worried."

He looked older than the last time she'd seen him. The hair she used to run her fingers through was gone, replaced by a military-style buzz cut. Even though he'd avoided it during his teenage years, he had acne on his slightly swollen face. He was still handsome, just...different. She wondered if his meds had caused some of the changes in his appearance.

"What a coincidence. I'm worried too. You're not supposed to be here," she reminded him. "How did you find me? Did you follow me?"

He tilted his head to the side as if weighing how best to answer her. "Most freshmen live in your dorm. I just figured I'd start there and ask around if anyone knew you. Then I saw you run out of there like your feet were on fire, so yeah, I followed you."

She frowned, something about his explanation sparking a hazy recollection of a similar discussion, but she couldn't grasp it, the memory just out of reach.

Tony brushed his hand down his face. "Look, I know I'm

not supposed to contact you, but I had to come. I didn't send you a letter."

"Tony, I recognized your handwriting."

"I'm not denying that I wrote it. I just never sent it to you." He linked his fingers together and put his hands behind his neck. "And I never sent you a text. I didn't even have access to a cell phone in there."

Her blood went cold.

He had to be lying.

There was no other explanation.

And yet as she really took him in, she saw a glimpse of the Tony of her childhood in his relaxed posture and clear eyes.

Her best friend.

"The first few months I was in the hospital were difficult to say the least," he said, his voice calm and without the mania she'd become accustomed to hearing in it. "My doctors wouldn't medicate me until they had a firm diagnosis, and then after, it took several tries before they found the right cocktail that took away my delusions but didn't make me a walking zombie. The only thing that helped me get through those days were the letters I wrote you." His arms fell to his sides and his shoulders slumped.

It was clear to see *he* believed he hadn't sent the letter.

But she wasn't as easily convinced. "You're claiming someone else sent me the letter? Why? What possible reason would someone have?"

He threw his hands up in the air. "I don't know, all right? I realize it doesn't make any sense, but I'm not lying to you. The last thing I ever wanted to do was hurt you."

She lifted up her wrists and slid down the sleeves of her coat, baring the scars to Tony's gaze. "But you did."

Tony's teary eyes shone. "I'm sorry. I'm so fucking sorry," he said, his voice breaking. "I know words will never be enough and I don't expect forgiveness, but I thought you should know. I'll always love you, Izzy." Looking away, he brushed away a tear that had escaped. "I saw you with that guy on the bridge. Are you in love with him?"

She curled into herself and put her hand over her heart, almost feeling it shatter all over again.

Sometimes words cut deeper than any knife.

But she couldn't bring herself to deny it. Even if Tristan no longer wanted her, her heart belonged to him. "Yes," she answered.

Tony's mouth pursed as if he'd eaten a lemon. "I know I have no right to judge the guy, but I'm worried that he's fine with you running around campus with your crazy ex-boyfriend on the loose. I mean, look how easy it was for me to find you."

Again, something about how Tony had found her unnerved her. Chloe had told her—

"Chloe!"

She had to get to her. Only a couple of minutes had passed, but what if she was already too late?

Tony frowned. "Who's Chloe?"

"My roommate. She's in trouble. I need to go."

The tower was behind Tony. She'd have to pass him in order to get to Chloe.

Don't move any closer to your attacker than necessary.

His posture grew rigid. "Wait, your roommate's name is Chloe?"

Confusion over his reaction caused her to pause. Hadn't he already known her roommate's name? Despite his earlier assertion, that had to be how he'd learned her address. Otherwise...he couldn't have sent the letter to her at the dorm. "Yes. Why?"

"What's her last name?" he asked urgently.

"Donahue. Why does that matter?"

He exhaled loudly, his shoulders dropping in relief. "There was a Chloe at the mental hospital. Different last name, though. She and I were...friends for a while," he said sheepishly.

By his tone, she got the impression that they were more than friends. "What happened?"

"The more I improved, the more I realized she never would." Blushing, he shuffled back and forth on the balls of his feet. "It was when I was at my sickest. When I got better, I realized she was obsessed."

"Obsessed with *you?*" she asked, unease spreading through her.

"No." He looked down at a patch of snow in front of him before lifting his head. "She was obsessed with *you*, Izzy. I shared stories about you in group. I guess that piqued her interest because she was always bringing you up. Asking me what you looked like. Your hobbies. Your favorite things. There was nothing she didn't want to know. It was almost..." He shook his head and laughed. "I don't know...it was like she was in love with you."

He took a step toward her. "Izzy, she knew about the letters."

She inched backward, keeping a good-sized distance between them.

Eyes, nose, ears, neck, groin, knees, and legs.

The ground beneath her feet tilted, and the bridge swayed as if there'd been an earthquake. She grabbed the railing for support.

It was all too much.

Morgan.

Tristan.

Tony.

Chloe...

She was stuck in a nightmare she couldn't awaken from.

It couldn't be true.

And yet...

"I have to go," she said, taking the risk and running past him toward the bell tower.

"Izzy..."

When he started after her, she flipped around and shot him a look that stopped him in his tracks. "Don't follow me or I'll call the police. I'm glad you're doing better, Tony, but please, don't contact me again."

Racing down the path, she called 911 to report a possible suicide at the bell tower, hoping, praying, that Chloe was safe and Tony had been lying.

But she couldn't shake the feeling that everything she thought she knew was wrong.

Up was down.

Left was right.

Front was back.

Nothing made any sense.

Her nightmare had returned—only he'd come to *warn* her. And the man she'd believed would keep her safe?

Gone.

How could she have been so wrong about Tristan?

I wish I could be with you, protecting you, all the time, but it's just not possible.

As the bell tower came into view, clarity hit her like a thunderbolt from the sky.

She *had* been wrong about Tristan. Wrong to believe that what he'd said to her on the bridge was the truth.

What they'd shared in the forest...when he'd made her confront her fears and had helped her find her strength...that had been the truth.

He loved her.

And that scared the hell out of him.

She wouldn't allow him to use Morgan's murder as an excuse to avoid facing his own fears.

Disappointment slammed into her when she got his voice mail. "'Trust me.' That's what you said. Now I'm telling you to do the same. Trust me, Tristan. You can pretend what we feel for each other will pass, but I'm not willing to lie to myself or to you." At the foot of the tower, she swung open the door and headed into the darkness. "I just saw Tony. He told me that..." She took a ragged breath. What would she find when she got to the top? "Please. Meet me at the bell tower. I need you."

TWENTY-SEVEN

Tristan stood under the cold, punishing spray of the shower, his head hanging down to his chest. He was numb and it had nothing to do with temperature of the water.

And everything to do with Isabella.

He couldn't get the image of her at the bridge out of his mind.

Her tears would haunt him until his dying day.

She'd haunt him.

My Angel.

Walking away from her had been the worst moment of his life. Every word he'd spoken was a lie to keep her safe. It had been selfish of him to think he could have it all.

No one got it all. Especially not him.

But Isabella...she deserved the chance.

Which was why he had broken up with her.

It was crazy of him to think for a moment that they could have lasted. Not when the deck was stacked against him. Every time he thought he'd finally gotten his head above water, life put its big ugly hands on his shoulders and pushed him back under.

In the end, Morgan had gotten the last laugh. Even dead, she'd taken the person who mattered to him most.

Novateur. His job. Money. Without Isabella, it was all worthless.

His suffering meant nothing. But he would march into the deepest fiery pit of hell to save Isabella.

He turned off the water, and getting out of the shower, he wrapped a towel around his waist. After changing into his work clothes, he went to the kitchen to grab a coffee, shocked when he saw his friend Ryder sitting on the couch with two steaming mugs in front of him.

He'd thought he'd left.

"We need to talk," Ryder said firmly, passing off one of the coffees to Tristan. "Sit."

"What's up?" Tristan asked before taking a sip from the mug.

Ryder casually crossed his legs, but the tension radiating off him was palpable. "You broke things off with Isabella, didn't you?"

Tristan scratched his cheek. After Ryder had warned him away from Isabella, why did the asshole even care? This had nothing to do with him. "I don't see why that's any of your business."

His friend scowled, his eyelids narrowed into slits. "Fuck you," he spit out.

Tristan reared back, almost spilling his coffee. "Excuse me?"

"You heard me the first time." A red-faced Ryder jumped

up from the couch. "Fuck you," he said, this time enunciating each word. "Fuck you and your need to punish yourself for something that was never your fucking fault in the first fucking place."

What the hell had gotten into him? He wasn't the one under suspicion for murder.

Tristan set his coffee onto the table and stood, folding his arms in front of him. "That's a lot of fucks, even for you. Why don't you stop the fucking swearing and get to the fucking point?" Then leave him the fuck alone the way he fucking deserved.

"Your mother," Ryder said, lowering his voice. "You couldn't have prevented it. Nothing you did led to your mother's death."

What did Ryder know about it? Ryder's mom might have died when he was a baby, but he'd always had his father and plenty of other family. It was his choice to cut them out of his life.

He didn't know what it was like for Tristan and his mother. His entire life, they'd only had each other.

Tristan shook his head as if the action could erase his memory of her ashen, emaciated shell of a body lying in her coffin. "I know that. I also know my mother has nothing to do with my breaking things off with Isabella."

Their only commonality was his reluctance to discuss either of them with Ryder.

Disappointment banked in his friend's eyes. "Doesn't it?" He paused and tilted his head. "What do you get from being a Dom?"

Tristan chuffed out something resembling a laugh. He should have known his friend would eventually bring the subject back to sex. "I'm not having that conversation with you."

Ryder being Ryder refused to drop it. "Know what I think? You use it to keep women at arm's length."

He let out a snort. "That's ridiculous." Like Ryder was one to talk. Tristan wasn't the one who refused to have sex with the same woman twice.

Wringing his hands, Ryder strode toward the door, then turned back to Tristan. "You're like that one family member who always takes the photos at the holidays. You might be there, but you refuse to be a part of it. Being a Dom means you make the rules. You demand the honesty. You become the protector."

And what was wrong with wanting control? Having rules meant each party had clear expectations. Honesty led to open communication and trust. And as for him being the protector? It was his role to ensure the safety of his sub.

"Morgan preyed on that," Ryder said with disgust. "She didn't demand anything from you other than your money." He smirked. "But Isabella? She's won't let you get away with that, will she? Ten minutes of being in the same space with you two and I saw it. She's not one of those subs who obediently complies without asking questions. She won't let you stay behind the camera, and that scares the shit out of you."

Ryder didn't know what the hell he was talking about. Nothing about Isabella scared him except for the fact he didn't want to drag her underwater with him. "I'm still not understanding what any of this has to do with my mother."

His friend slowly walked across the room until he stood right in front of him. "Even if you had been there, she still would've gotten cancer. She still would've died," he said softly. "You didn't do anything wrong by going to college and having your own life. You couldn't have saved her. And it's not your job to save Isabella now. You owe her the truth, man." He clutched Tristan's shoulders. "Let her in. Let her help you."

He didn't need anyone's help. He'd made his bed and now he would have to lie in it. No matter what Ryder believed, he had done the right thing by breaking it off with Isabella. She never would have done it herself. No, she would've sacrificed her dreams for him. She wouldn't see it now, but someday, she'd appreciate that he'd made the decision for her.

Tristan's gaze fell onto his phone sitting by his coffee cup, and noted the message emblem was lit. "Did my phone ring?"

"Oh yeah." Ryder squinted, thinking about it. "'Bout five minutes ago. While you were in the shower."

Tristan didn't bother checking to see who had called before listening to the message. His heart galloped upon hearing Isabella's sweet voice. He closed his eyes, expecting her recriminations and tears. There here was none of that. Only strength...and love.

But it was her next words that made his blood run cold.

Tony.

His eyes met Ryder's. "It's Isabella. She's in trouble."

TWENTY-EIGHT

Isabella was out of breath and a hot sweaty mess by the time she reached the top of the bell tower. She listened for the sound of sirens, but it was eerily silent on campus. What if they hadn't believed her? What if Tristan didn't get her message or, worse, ignored her plea?

Her chest constricted, not from the exertion of the climb but from trepidation.

She had to know.

And only Chloe could provide the answers.

This time, she couldn't run away. She couldn't keep her distance.

Not until she confirmed that Chloe was safe...

And that Tony had lied.

The light breeze cooled her sweat as she walked around the tower counterclockwise in search of her friend.

She found Chloe sitting on the ground, staring at the wall in front of her. In her hand was a large kitchen knife, its blade sliding back and forth across her wrist.

Hot adrenaline coursed through Isabella as she remembered the pain of when Tony had cut her. She couldn't get enough air into her lungs. Dark spots floated in front of her eyes. She couldn't lose it now. Not when her friend obviously needed her help. "Chloe, honey?"

Chloe looked up at her with red, swollen eyes. "You came. I knew you would. Best friends always take care of each other."

"They do," she agreed, searching Chloe for evidence of blood, but not finding any. "Why don't you put the knife down and tell me what happened." Not wanting to spook her friend, she fought her instinct to go to her and instead stayed a few feet away.

Chloe exhaled, but continued moving the knife, almost as if she wasn't aware she was doing it. "I didn't get into *West Side Story*."

She was confused. "That's not true. You told me you got Rosalia. You hung out with the other cast members last week."

"I lied," Chloe mumbled, dropping her gaze. "I never even auditioned."

Why would she lie about that? "But you left me up here to go to it. When I called you that night about the text..."

Chloe had offered to come home, but Isabella hadn't wanted to go back to the dorm room or to Chloe.

She'd only wanted Tristan.

Just like she wanted him now.

Had he gotten her message?

"When I got to the auditions," Chloe continued, "I heard

them sing, and I just couldn't do it." Tears trickled down her cheeks. "They were so much better than me. The director called my name and I panicked. I ran out of there..." She gazed up at Isabella. "...and went back to the tower."

Chloe dragged her knife across her skin once more, this time pressing hard enough that dots of blood welled on her skin. "I saw you there with Professor Kelley," she snarled. Her pupils shrunk to pinpoints as her voice rose to an accusatory pitch. "I followed you to his apartment. How could you do that me?"

Isabella opened her mouth to speak, but nothing came out but air. She didn't understand why Chloe was so upset.

Her stomach rolled, nausea choking her.

Unless Tony had been telling the truth.

She tempered her words, wary of offending her friend. "I'm sorry, but what happened between Tristan and me had nothing to do with you."

Chloe jumped to her feet and waved the knife in the air. "How can you say that? I love you, Isabella. I love you and I know you love me too."

She took a giant step backward, her fear that Chloe would harm herself changing to the fear that Chloe would use that knife on her. Where the hell were the cops? "I do love you, Chloe. As a friend."

Chloe tore at her hair, pulling on it harshly with one hand while the one holding the knife dangled at her side. "No, no, no. That's just what *she* said. After everything we'd shared, she just denied it. She told the school board that nothing had happened between us and that I was a sick girl with an unhealthy fixation on her. No one believed me. She lied to keep herself from a prison sentence and threw me under the bus." She bit her lip hard enough that blood trickled down her chin. "Tell me you believe me."

"I believe you," Isabella said immediately.

Chloe smiled, a dreamy look entering her eyes. "I knew you would."

Sirens rang out in the distance. *Thank God.* She just needed to keep Chloe talking until they got there. She didn't think Chloe would hurt her—after all, she thought she was in love with her—but then again, Tony had loved her too.

"I know you'd never do anything to hurt me, so I'm confused as to why you sent me Tony's letter," she said gently.

Chloe's eyes darted from side to side. Bits of blood and hair were stuck to her palm, but she didn't seem to notice as she gripped the hilt of the knife between both hands and raised the blade to chest level with the tip pointing to the sky. "Would you ever have told me about him if I hadn't sent it? It brought us closer together. We bonded over our tragedies. Tony talked about you. How beautiful, sweet, and loyal you were. And when he said you were going to attend Edison, I realized it was destiny. So when I got out of the hospital, I gave destiny a little push and contacted you about rooming together."

"And the text? That was from you, wasn't it?"

Rocking back and forth on her heels, she smiled, blood staining her teeth. "That was to help you. I thought if you brought that to the police, they'd keep Tony in the hospital." Her face crumpled. "You were supposed to cry on my shoulder. Not Professor Kelley's. Everything I've done was to protect you! You have no idea how far I would go for you. How far I have gone!"

Isabella's heart stopped. Chills racked her body as if she were submerged in ice.

The siren sounded close by, but the cops would have to park a couple of blocks over and walk the rest of the way. She was no longer worried about Chloe. Now her only concern was whether she would make it off this tower alive. Her pulse hammered in her neck as she prayed the police would get there in time.

She slowly inched her way toward the stairs, careful not to make any sudden moves. She didn't think Chloe would take it well. "What else did you do to protect me, Chloe?"

Her eyes narrowed. "She had naked photos of you, did you know that? She would've told Dean Lancaster about your affair with Tristan, and they would have thrown you out of school. I couldn't let them do that. I couldn't let them tear us apart."

Bile rose in her throat. *Oh God.* "Morgan," she said on a whisper. "You killed Morgan."

Chloe nodded. "After Tristan left, I followed her to her car. I had this knife in my backpack."

"Why..." She sucked in a breath. "Why did you have a knife?"

"I waited all night for you to leave his apartment," Chloe said, tears again rolling down her face. "In the morning, after you left, I had to know. I thought...maybe there was another explanation why you spent the night there. I still had that wire on me, and since it had opened the tower door, I tried it on Professor Kelley's. When I saw the tangled sheets, smelled the sex in the air, I . . . I just wanted the pain to stop, and I thought I could end it." She slashed at her wrist. Once. Twice. Fresh red blood spilled down her arm. "I took a knife from his kitchen, but I couldn't do it. I couldn't leave you. So, I slipped the knife into my bag and left."

With every word Chloe spoke, Isabella took a step backward, widening the distance between them as she waited for her chance to run.

Chloe got a faraway look in her eyes. "Killing her was so easy. Her back was turned and she was fumbling through her purse for her keys. I came up behind her and plunged the knife into her." She raised the knife above her head and repeatedly jabbed the air. "Over and over and over."

Lost in the memory, Chloe took her attention off of Isabella.

Now was her chance.

She turned and bolted for the stairs.

"No!" Chloe screamed, her voice echoing all around Isabella. "Don't leave me!"

Only a foot from the door, Chloe tackled Isabella to the ground. Stars danced in front of her eyes as the world began to darken around the edges.

Crying, Chloe rolled her onto her back. "I'm so sorry. I didn't mean it."

Through the haze, Isabella saw Chloe hovering above her.

What happened?

Throbbing pain like she'd never experienced exploded

into her right side, just above her hip. She touched the spot and brought her hand to her face, shocked to see her palm covered in bright red blood. "You stabbed me."

"You made me do it." She lifted her knife into the air, blood dripping from the blade. "I'm ready for my happy ever after now. Are you?"

* * *

Tristan raced up the steps of the bell tower, his heart pounding in his ears. Hopefully, those sirens in the distance were in response to Ryder's phone call to the police.

Tony was *here.*

So why the hell was Isabella on top of the tower and not with the police? Did Tony have her? Had he chased her up here?

Since getting her message, Tristan had called her again and again, but each time, it went immediately to voice mail. He shivered, struck by the feeling that Isabella was in danger at that very moment. He pumped his legs harder, using every bit of strength to get to her as fast as possible.

He had to get to her in time.

He wouldn't let her be another one of his failures.

At the sound of a female scream, he flew past the carillon and outside. "Isabella!"

Icy tentacles squeezed his chest at the sight of Chloe standing over Isabella with a bloody knife in her hand, raised and poised to strike.

He didn't take time to assess.

Without a warning, he tackled Chloe, knocking her backward.

The knife clattered to the ground and skittered away as her head hit the wall with an awful *thunk*. Chloe's eyes rolled back and she went limp.

He ran back to Isabella and dropped to his knees. Blood poured out of a wound in her side.

"Isabella? Angel?" He put two fingers at her neck to check for a pulse, and almost cried in relief when he felt it. It was weak, but it was there.

From the corner of his eye, he saw a movement. On a battle cry, a blood-drenched Chloe charged him, her gleaming knife overhead. He surged to his feet as the knife arched through the air, nicking his cheek. He launched himself at her, grappling for possession of the knife, as she screamed in a voice that barely sounded human. With a tight grip on her damaged wrist, he dug his fingers into her wound. She howled in pain and loosened her hold on the knife just enough for him to seize it from her grasp.

Shouts came from the foot of the tower, announcing the police's arrival.

Chest heaving, Chloe stared at him with intense vitriol before glancing longingly at Isabella. She turned toward the wall and, before he could figure out what she was doing, hopped up on the ledge and swung her legs over the railing.

What the fuck?

He dropped the knife and lunged for her just as she hoisted herself off the edge. He snatched her left wrist with both hands. "Hold on, Chloe. I won't let you fall."

"It's your fault Isabella's dead! I can't let you get away with it!" Dangling from one hundred feet in the air, she looked down at the ground. "No, don't kill me, Professor Kelley!"

She twisted in his grip and then she was gone, leaving his hands empty and bloody.

She screamed all the way down. A scream that seemed to go on forever before a sound too terrible to process reverberated in his ears as she hit the ground.

Chloe was wrong.

Isabella wasn't dead.

She couldn't be.

He raced back to her, finding her lips blue and her skin so pale, he could see all the veins beneath it. He pressed his hands over her side to stem the bleeding. "Isabella? Angel? Come on. Wake up. Wake up for me, baby."

Her eyes fluttered. "Tristan?"

She spoke so quietly, he'd almost thought he'd imagined it.

"You're safe," he said, his voice breaking. "I've got you now."

"It hurts," she whispered. "It hurts so much."

If he could trade places with her and take her pain, he would. He'd die for her, didn't she understand that? "I know, Angel. Just hold on a little longer and we'll make that pain disappear."

Her eyes opened wide in panic. "Tristan? I can't breathe. I can't..."

He kissed her forehead. Her cheeks. Everywhere he could. "I love you, Angel. I love you so fucking much. Do you hear me?"

Isabella stared at him, eyes unblinking and fixed. Her chest wasn't moving.

"Isabella?" *No. no. no. She's not breathing.* "God no." He started chest compressions. "You are not going to die. I won't let you, do you hear me? I refuse to let you die."

"Step away from the girl."

He barely bothered to glance at the police, not caring that they had their guns pointed at him. Nothing mattered but his Angel. He wouldn't stop administering the chest compressions.

"No. She's not breathing," he shouted, sweat dripping off his brow. Or were those tears? "I can't leave her."

Hands fastened onto his shoulders and yanked him away. "You need to give the EMTs room to do their jobs."

Someone pulled him away from Isabella. He turned and, fists flying, clocked the officer in the nose. Another officer pinned his wrists behind his back as he twisted and swung and fought to return to his Angel's side. "I . . . No. Damn it. Let me go. Isabella. Isabella!"

The EMTs swooped in to take his rightful place.

As the police dragged him away kicking and screaming, he heard the words that shattered his world into a million pieces.

"I can't find a pulse. We're losing her."

TWENTY-NINE

Alone in the interrogation room, a handcuffed Tristan sat at a small table. They'd charged him with assaulting a police officer and obstruction, allowing them to hold him for seventy-two hours while they combed through the evidence and tried to figure out how to pin Morgan and Chloe's murders on him.

It had been hours since he'd been here, and no one would tell him a damned thing about Isabella. They'd entered him into their computer system, treating him like a criminal. Subjecting him to fingerprinting and evidence collection and having his mug shot taken. They'd traded his blood-stained clothes for a gray jumpsuit.

He hadn't even gotten to make a phone call yet.

The police walked leisurely around the station, in no hurry to do anything other than drink coffee and talk about the Detroit Lions game.

Head pounding, throat aching, and eyes burning, Tristan had done nothing but silently pray for Isabella. The image of her lifeless body lying on the cold, hard concrete was burned onto his retinas.

Chloe was right.

It was all his fault.

If he hadn't broken up with Isabella, none of this would've happened. She would've been with him instead of on top of that tower.

Because of him, she could be dead.

There would be no absolution.

He'd never forgive himself.

The door to the room opened, and a portly officer entered.

"I want to know the status of Isabella Lawson." After all his yelling and raging, Tristan's voice came out raspy and hoarse.

The cop plopped down on the chair. "Why, want to make sure she can't finger you?"

Tristan slammed the table with his fists. "Fuck you. I didn't hurt her." Somewhere inside, this guy had to be a shred of humanity. "Please. Tell me she's alive."

The cop paused, scrutinizing him as if he were a bug on the windshield. Then he nodded once and put his hands out in front of him as if attempting to placate Tristan. "She's alive. That's all I know. Maybe if you answer all my questions, we can make a call over to the hospital for an update."

Fuck that. "How 'bout I answer your questions once you tell me how Isabella is?"

"Doesn't work that way," the cop said gruffly. "You have a few choices." One by one, he ticked off a finger. "You can make this complicated and drawn out, refusing to answer our questions, and then you'll never find out what you want to know. You can invoke your right to an attorney and all questioning will stop, once again, delaying information about the girl. Or you tell us everything I want to know, and I'll make that call. The ball is in your court. What's it going to be?"

Goddamn it. For Tristan, there was only one choice. "I'll answer your questions."

"Good. That's good." The cop signaled to someone behind the tinted window. "This interrogation is being videotaped under Michigan law. Mr. Kelley, have the police read you your Miranda rights?"

"Yes." *Twice.*

"And you have waived your right to an attorney at this time?"

"Yes."

"Thank you. Mr. Kelley, can you tell us what happened on the Edison Tower this evening preceding the death of one Chloe Donahue?"

He flinched. Watching that girl plummet one hundred feet to her death would plague him for the rest of his life. "When I arrived, Chloe was standing over Isabella with a knife in her hand, and Isabella had a wound to her abdomen."

The cop frowned. "Let's back up a moment. How did you come to be on that tower?"

"Isabella called me and left a message to meet her there."

"Do you meet all your students on top of the bell tower?" the officer asked, raising an inquisitive brow.

Tristan didn't respond, not willing to state the nature of his relationship with Isabella. It wasn't relevant.

"See, when you don't answer, I'm forced to use my imagination to fill in the blanks." The cop leaned forward in his chair. "Would you like me to tell you what I think, Kelley? I think those girls knew you had killed your wife, so you decided to get rid of them before they had the chance to report it to the authorities."

Tristan growled. "That's not what happened."

"Then tell me what did."

The door opened, and another officer poked his head in. He pointed at Tristan. "His lawyer is here."

Shocking Tristan, Isaac strode into the room. "Questioning is over. My client is invoking his right to remain silent."

Tristan had forgotten that Isaac had gone to law school and passed the Michigan bar back in the day. As far as he knew, his mentor had never practiced. Guess there was always a first time.

A muscle ticked in the cop's jaw, but he didn't argue as he left Isaac and Tristan alone.

"How did you know I was here?" he asked, unable to look his mentor in the eye.

"Ryder called me a few minutes before I received a phone call from the Edison president informing me there had been an incident on top of the bell tower involving one of my professors and one of my students."

His chest tightened. "Isabella? Is she . . ."

"She's alive. Her body went into shock from the blood loss, but the knife didn't hit any major organs. They gave her a transfusion, and the last I heard, she was in serious but stable condition."

Relieved, Tristan blew out a breath and ran his hand down his face. Thank God she'd recover. The world would have been a dark and dismal place with the loss of his Angel.

"Who is she to you, Tristan?" Isaac asked.

Keeping his gaze on his hands, he shook his head. "Believe me, as my boss you don't want to know."

"I'm not here as your boss, damn it," Isaac said firmly. "I'm here as your friend."

Tristan pressed his lips together.

Isaac settled into his chair as if he were at home rather than in a police station. "Let me tell you a story. About five years ago, I had an affair. I'm not proud of it. At the time, Cassandra and I were essentially separated. We shared a home but not a bed. Rarely a meal or even a conversation. We'd become strangers. I tried doing everything I could. I suggested therapy, taking a vacation, having a re-commitment ceremony, but she refused it all. I thought I'd lost her. In a moment of weakness, I slept with a student's mother. Over the next two months, we met several times, but it didn't make anything better. It was just sex, and it turns out, that wasn't enough for me. I needed my wife. When I finally realized that, I ended my affair, and this time, I didn't ask Cassandra to go to therapy. I forced her to go."

Tristan didn't understand what this had to do with him, but he played along. He lifted his gaze from his hands to look at his mentor. "Did you find out what had caused the rift in your marriage?"

"Years ago, when Cassandra and I learned that we couldn't have children, we both agreed that it was okay. That we were enough. And it was, until her friends started becoming grandmothers. Then for the first time, she regretted our decision not to adopt. She felt like a failure as both a woman and my wife." He smiled. "Ridiculous, I know. Except, I get it. I'm the third generation to have a presence on this campus, and the legacy ends with me. I had hoped..."

"What?" Tristan prodded.

"That maybe you'd discover your love for teaching and consider staying on at the school. Maybe even work toward becoming a full professor or go into administration. Carry on my legacy."

Tristan was shocked. It had never occurred to him that Isaac had ulterior motives for offering him the position at Edison.

"Anyway," Isaac continued, "I never did tell Cassandra about my affair. But someone else knew."

Tristan didn't have to ask. The answer was there in Isaac's eyes.

"Morgan."

His friend dipped his chin. "Yes. She had me followed around the time of your divorce. Why, I have no idea. But she's held it over me, asking for a little money here and there, waiting for the time to use it fully to her advantage."

Tristan recalled Morgan's taunts that Isaac wasn't a saint. "That's why you met her for breakfast when she was here. She'd decided it was time to call in her marker. What did she want?"

Isaac's eyes hooded in shame. "Fifty thousand dollars."

So that's how she'd gotten the money to pay for her attorneys. He should've known it was nothing legal.

"I was weak," Isaac continued. "Cassandra and I had finally found our way back to each other. I feared if Morgan told her about my affair..." He shook his head. "Because of that, I gave in to her blackmail."

For a millisecond, Tristan considered the possibility that Isaac had killed Morgan, but the thought died as quickly as it had arrived. "Why are you telling me all this, Isaac?"

A little smile tugged at the corners of his mouth. "Because as smart as you are, there's one lesson you haven't learned." He steepled his hands and leaned forward as if about to divulge the world's greatest secret. "No one is perfect. Not even me. Does knowing my weak moments make you think any less of me?"

"No. Of course not," he bristled.

"Then why do you believe I'd think any less of you? You may not be my son," Isaac said, tearing up, "but I couldn't be any prouder of the man you've become."

Tristan laughed, the act making his throat feel as though he'd swallowed sandpaper. Any other time, he would've happily eaten that line of bullshit. "How can you say you're proud of me? My life is in shambles."

"Once you're cleared—"

"Being arrested is just the rancid icing on the poisoned cake." There was an ocean full of differences between himself and his mentor. "Look at me, Isaac. I've failed at everything."

"You're only twenty-eight years old, Tristan. Did you really believe you wouldn't make a few mistakes along the way to greatness?"

The damage Tristan had caused to everyone who cared about him was more than a few mistakes. Like a black hole, he sucked them into his gravitational pull without the chance of escape. Because of him, Morgan had been given the opportunity to blackmail Isaac. Because of him, Ryder couldn't grow Novateur into the company he deserved. Because of him...

"Isabella is in the hospital because of me." His throat thickened with emotion. "She could die, just like my—"

"Mother," he said softly, reaching out to cover Tristan's handcuffed hands with one of his own. "You didn't put Isabella in the hospital. Chloe did that."

Chloe may have been ultimately responsible, but he'd set the pieces into motion. "If I'd just been stronger, stayed away from her..."

"You're a Dom, not God," Isaac quipped.

He knew?

"Don't look at me like that. I make no judgment when it comes to sex. Or love." His tired eyes softened. "We can't help who we love. You couldn't have prevented yourself from falling in love with Isabella any more than I can keep it from snowing. Some things are out of our control. Including your mother's death."

"Ryder said something similar," he said.

And Tristan disagreed with them both. No, he didn't blame himself for falling in love with Isabella. Anyone who really knew her would have fallen just as easily. But if he'd done something—anything—differently, Isabella wouldn't have been injured. If he'd stayed home instead of going away to college, he would've noticed his mother was sick.

Isaac was wrong.

The commonality between the two women was Tristan's failure to protect them.

"I lost a married friend to pancreatic cancer," Isaac said, patting the top of Tristan's hand sympathetically. "He went as quickly as your mother, even having a wife by his side the entire time. Your being there wouldn't have changed anything."

It would have changed everything. "She wouldn't have died alone!" How could she have kept that from him? While she'd been wasting away, he was having the time of his life. "She should've told me she was dying!"

"I can't pretend to know what was in her mind, but I could guess what was in her heart. You were happy at Edison. She didn't want to take that away from you. If you'd known she was dying, you would've spent every day at her side, watching her grow weaker and weaker, mourning her before she was even gone. She didn't want that for you."

He'd always loved his mother, but after receiving a call from hospice about her passing, he'd hated her as well. "What about what I wanted? She made the decision for me."

She'd stripped him of control and had sent his life into a tailspin that he'd never recovered from.

"Like you did with Isabella?"

Tristan's jaw dropped. How did he know that he'd broken things off with her when he shouldn't have even known they were together in the first place?

Isaac shrugged. "Ryder."

Fucking prick. "He shouldn't have told you."

Isaac nodded. "I agree. *You* should have told me."

If only it were that easy. But just like now, handcuffed and under arrest, he'd had no choice. His hands had been tied. "My relationship with Isabella broke the university's rules. I couldn't tell you."

Something glittered in Isaac's eyes. "You could always tell me. It was *your* decision not to."

"To protect Isabella."

Isaac didn't pull any punches. "And yourself."

"At first." He'd always worried about Isabella's future, but yeah, he'd worried about his own ass too. "I didn't want to risk my job or my chances at qualifying for a business loan."

"And now?"

"Nothing matters but Isabella."

For her happiness, he'd give it all up.

No matter what it cost him.

Isaac leaned back in his chair and exhaled. "It's time you let people in, Tristan. Ryder. Me. Isabella. You might be surprised at what happens."

THIRTY

Time crawled in a jail cell, each minute lasting an hour and each hour lasting a day. It was nothing like it was portrayed on television. He wore gray not orange. Ate meals with plastic sporks. No one threatened him with a shank. And he didn't have a cell mate named Bubba who wanted to make him his teddy bear. No, instead he got Buddy, who smelled as if he'd never taken a shower in his life.

The cell he called his temporary home was smaller than any Edison dorm room and came with two single beds and a toilet. In jail, prisoners were tortured by boredom. Tristan had never read so many magazines in his life. Ones on golf and weight lifting, entertainment, a year-old *Time* and decade-old *National Geographic*. If this was going to be his life, he'd definitely need Ryder to bring him better reading material.

But reading filled only so many hours. The rest of the time, he spent thinking. Thinking so much he'd swear his brain would explode.

It was as if he was playing home movies of his life in his head. All he needed was popcorn, a Coke, and a package of licorice to make it complete. Some memories made him laugh, several memories made him cringe, and a few memories almost brought tears to his eyes. Those were the ones that lingered with him well after lights-out, when he lay on the thin mattress with a scratchy excuse of a blanket over him and tried to sleep.

He wondered about why Isabella had been on that tower and why Chloe had stabbed her.

But mostly, he thought about what Isaac had said to him in the interrogation room.

Was he really not to blame for his mother's death?

When he'd gotten into Edison, his mother had been so proud. After all, his father had also graduated from there, and look at how successful he'd been. Why his mother cared about anything to do with the dishonorable Winston Kelley, he had no idea. If anything, it made a stronger argument to go somewhere else for his education. He could've stayed local and lived at home, or at least have gone to a school closer to home. But the truth was he was eighteen and seduced by the idea of being on his own for the first time in his life.

No one would've ever called him a mama's boy—at least not to his face—but with no other family, he and his mother had always been a team of two. But he was tired of always worrying about her, and he wanted the opportunity to spread his wings.

Four months after he'd started at Edison, he got the

phone call that had changed his life. He'd learned later from her physician that she was diagnosed shortly after he'd left, when she was taken by ambulance to the hospital because of severe back pain.

And she had never uttered a fucking word of it to Tristan. Every phone call had been the same. *I'm fine, everything's fine, tell me about you.*

Already at stage four at the time of her diagnosis, there had been no option of chemo or surgery. Only treatment for the symptoms. Lying in her casket four months after the last time he'd seen her, she must have lost thirty pounds off of her petite frame. No wonder she hadn't wanted him to come home for Thanksgiving. One look and he would've known. He never would have returned to school that semester. And he would have stayed and cared for her until the bitter end.

But she'd taken that right from him.

She'd taken his *control*.

Was that why Ryder had asked about Tristan's reasons for being a Dom? Why Isaac had made a point of telling him he was only a Dom and not God?

Tristan lay back on his cot and put his arms behind his head.

Before now, he'd credited BDSM with helping him quit the drugs and get his life back on track, but he'd never wanted to think about what had made him jump the rails in the first place.

Were they right? Had he actually become a Dom to re-gain the control he'd lost because his mother had kept his illness from him and to do what Ryder had suggested? Keep women at arm's length?

If it wasn't so tragic, he could've laughed. Ten years of beating himself up and it was all because he had mommy issues.

He'd been content to stay with Morgan because he'd never really cared about her in the first place. If he had, he would've seen through her shiny veneer to the cold, calculating bitch underneath. She had given him what he'd needed at the time...

The illusion of control.

But he'd never been happy with her. How could he have let himself be when he didn't feel he deserved it? If anything, Morgan had been his misguided repentance for failing his mother. He'd married her because he knew deep down that he could never love her. And that had kept his heart protected and his conscience clear.

Because if you didn't love someone, they couldn't disappoint you and you couldn't fail them.

A BDSM exchange of power between a Dom and sub required honest and open communication on both sides. Over the years, he'd negotiated dozens of scenes with dozens of subs, but until Isabella, he'd always kept his guard up. Honesty had only gone as far as sexual limits and boundaries. But his first night with Isabella had been different. She'd challenged him. Even with her shyness, she'd demanded as much honesty from him as he demanded of her. And he'd given it, at least as much as he was able.

It had been easy that night because he wasn't supposed

to see her again. But then she'd turned up here in Edison, and honesty became harder to come by. After all, if he let her in as Isaac and Ryder had suggested, she would see him, warts and all. She'd see that he wasn't worth the effort. Even worse...he'd destroy her.

He'd done everything in his power to keep her safe. Taught her self-defense. Shown her to find her strength through submission. Broken up with her. And still, she'd been injured.

It was as if no matter what action he had taken...no matter what he'd decided...even if he and Isabella had never met...Isabella would have still been hurt.

Despite what he'd told himself, there were some things out of his hands. For some unknown reason, Isabella had made the decision to go up to the top of the tower, and Chloe had chosen to commit suicide. His mother had kept him in the dark about her cancer.

People had the right to self-determination.

Ultimately, the only person he could control was himself.

Whether those things were a result of destiny, fate, or a series of random acts, he didn't have the power to stop them. So why then was he holding himself responsible?

The bars of his cell slid open and a cop waved a hand. "Tristan Kelley, please come with me."

Not needing to be asked twice, Tristan rolled out of his cot and followed the cop down the hall. Isaac had promised to visit him today to go over the details of his upcoming arraignment and, more importantly, to bring news about Isabella.

The officer ushered him into a tiny room and then left, closing the steel door behind him. Inside the dim room, there was a single chair bolted to the floor and in front of it, was a window.

And on the other side sat an angel with fiery red hair and a smile that lit up the darkest night.

* * *

"Isabella." Tristan stared at her in shock with bloodshot eyes.

She hated that they were separated by a pane of glass. In an awful pale gray jumpsuit, he looked haggard, as if he hadn't slept in weeks. In the couple of days since she'd seen him, he'd grown a short beard and the beginnings of a mustache. But the facial hair couldn't mask the deep lines etched around his eyes and mouth.

She wanted to wipe away those lines with her fingertips and put the light back into his eyes.

He didn't deserve to be in jail.

But if she got her way, he'd walk out with her today.

"Why aren't you in the hospital?" he asked, his voice carrying through the windowpane. The sound rolled over her like a caress, working better than her prescription medicine at alleviating the pain in her side.

"I just got out." She saw the worry for her in the rigid set of his jaw. "I'm fine. A bit fatigued, a lot sore, but otherwise unharmed." Her doctor had told her that on the tower, she'd gone into shock from the blood loss and had been dead for nearly a minute before the EMTs had revived her. "And I needed to see you. There are some things you should know."

"If this is about us, I've done a lot of thinking in here, and—"

"Chloe killed Morgan," she blurted out before Tristan could say another word. Before he made any decisions, he deserved to know the truth about what had transpired on the tower. For the next ten minutes, he sat quietly, giving away nothing as she filled him in about everything Chloe had admitted to her. When she finished, there was a long silence.

His gaze slid away from her, and he sighed with his whole body.

She waited for him to wrongly take the blame.

For him to thank her for visiting before dismissing her.

For him to lie to her about what he'd told her when he thought she was dying.

But *she* remembered. Those words had been her lifeline as she fought against the darkness of death to get back to him.

He turned his head to look her straight in the eyes, with his nostrils flared and his lips parted. "I love you," he said. "And my life doesn't make sense without you in it. Chloe, Morgan, the university, Novateur, none of it matters anymore. What matters is you and me and where we go from here."

Damn this wall of glass.

Tears slid down her cheeks. "I love you too. Which is why I wanted to talk to you before I give my statement to the police. I can't be with you unless you're willing to give me everything, so I need to know . . . Do you trust me?"

He lit up the dim room with his smile. "Yes. Without a doubt, yes."

"Then you have to let me tell them the whole truth. I won't have you making stupid sacrifices on my behalf anymore. I'll give you my submission, but I can't agree to you making decisions for me that haven't been negotiated. I know your heart was in the right place when you said those awful words to me on the bridge, but from now on, I deserve your honesty." She put both hands against the window. "Because your fight is my fight, Tristan."

Making his pledge, he matched her motion, placing them palm to palm. "From now on, we fight together."

EPILOGUE

Isabella set the cookies on the cooling rack and bumped the oven door closed with her hip. The scent of brown sugar and vanilla made her mouth water, but these weren't for her. After baking for Professor Weaver's party, she'd scheduled enough events to keep her busy for the rest of the school year. These were for the students of Edison Elementary School's Springtime Celebration. She wouldn't make any money on them, but after learning that the school had eliminated parties because it put an undue financial burden on parents to supply treats for the kids, Isabella had volunteered to bake for the event.

A pair of arms wrapped around her waist from behind to grab a cookie. She slapped his hand. "Those are for the kids."

"They won't miss one," Tristan said, nibbling on her neck.

She relaxed against him and closed her eyes, bathing in his heat. "You're insatiable."

"For you." He turned her around and claimed her lips, kissing her passionately before pulling back.

She glanced at the oven clock. They had less than an hour before they'd planned to leave, and she still needed to drop off the cookies before she and Tristan headed down to the city. "Are you packed?"

"Mm," he answered, chewing on his cookie as he leaned against the counter. "Are you sure your parents are okay with my staying at their home for the holiday? I could always sleep at Ryder's."

For the last several months, Isabella had made a concentrated effort to repair her relationship with her family. She called home weekly and text messaged with her mom almost daily. After Isabella had revealed to them everything that had occurred leading up to her stabbing, they'd begged Isabella to return home for college, placing the blame on the university and the man who'd "seduced" their daughter. She'd left the decision to fate. If she were expelled, she would've moved back.

But thanks to some creative maneuvering, Dean Lancaster had been able to negotiate a deal that allowed her to remain a student at the university. She'd had to drop her Intro to Business class, but luckily, she was able to take it at the local community college this semester. As for her work-study, Dean Lancaster had taken it over temporarily until Professor Weaver had gotten an available opening. Unfortunately, she'd probably lost any chance to get into the business administration program.

Her parents hadn't been pleased with her decision to stay

at Edison. To say it was tense during her visit home at Christmas would be an understatement. Her parents had refused to consider even meeting Tristan, much less invite him to Christmas dinner. So, she'd divided her winter holiday between her family and Tristan, spending Christmas in the city and New Year's Eve with Tristan in Edison.

But over time, her parents' anger had ebbed, especially after Dean Lancaster had paid them a visit. She didn't know what he'd said to change their minds, but from that point, they'd been more receptive to the idea of her and Tristan being a permanent couple.

Isabella swiped the tins from the pantry and scooped the cookies into them. "I told you, they want you there. Mom has already cleaned out a room for you." She snorted. *Poor guy.* "Hope you don't mind sleeping on Super Mario bed-sheets."

He ran his fingers through her hair. "I've gotten used to having you sleep next to me. It's going to feel strange sleeping alone."

Only days after leaving the hospital, she'd moved into his apartment. The reminder of Chloe had been too strong in the dorm room, especially with her things there. And once the school's administrators became aware of her relationship with Tristan, there was no reason to sneak around anymore.

She walked her hands up his chest. "I'll just have to sneak into your room after everyone else has gone to sleep."

He frowned. "No. You can't do that. It's disrespectful."

She laughed and inched closer, feeling his erection against her pelvis. "It's par for the course in my house. All my siblings have done it." She wrapped her leg around his thigh and rubbed her pussy against him. "What my parents don't know won't hurt them."

"But it might hurt you." He tilted up her chin and playfully snagged her bottom lip between his teeth, gently biting down before releasing it.

Heat surged through her lower belly. She swiped her tongue along her lower lip, tasting the cinnamon he'd left behind.

"How's the insulation in your house?" he murmured. "If I decide to spank and fuck that delicious ass of yours, is everyone going to be able to hear?"

Her pussy clenched and her clit pulsed. "I seem to remember my panties work wonders as a gag." She dragged her hand down his torso. "So I was thinking...since Ryder and Dreama are both going to be at Easter dinner, maybe I could—"

His head fell back as she cupped his cock through his jeans. "I thought she was in a committed D/s relationship."

She continued to torment him, enjoying their little power play. "That's been over for ages. So what do you think? Should I try to fix up Ryder and Dreama?"

On a moan, he bucked up into her hand. "Ryder's still obsessed with that woman he met on Mackinac Island."

The night of Morgan's murder, Ryder met a woman who pulled a Cinderella and disappeared on him. Naturally, Tristan loved to give Ryder shit about it. Not that he was one to talk. She'd done the same thing to him once upon a time.

"He still doesn't know who she is?"

"Not a clue," he said, reaching behind her to grab a cookie from out of the tin.

What the hell?

She took her hand off his cock. "Stop eating the cookies!"

His eyes heated with lust, and his voice went as thick as honey as he laid the cookie on the counter. "You offering me something sweeter to eat?" His quiet laugh, low and deep, heated her skin. He curled his hand around the back of her neck and tsked. "Talking 'bout our friends when you got my cock in your hand. Had to shut you up somehow." With his free hand, he untied the drawstring of her plaid pajama pants, his fingers brushing the skin of her belly as he did it.

He could have all the cookies he wanted so long as he kept touching her. Teasing him was fun, but submitting to him was much more rewarding.

"Hop up on the counter, Angel," he demanded, tugging her pants off her legs. "I'm hungry for your pussy."

Said pussy was totally down with that idea.

He put his hands on her waist and hoisted her onto the counter. The surface felt cold underneath her fevered skin. As Tristan kneeled, she spread her legs open wide, the flesh between them quivering and wet.

On a loud groan, he yanked her toward him until most of her ass was hanging off the counter and threw her heels over his shoulders. He stared crudely at her pussy. "Nothing better than the taste of your pussy except for the taste of your pussy covered with your come." He looked up at her as he inserted two thick fingers inside her channel and twisted, finding her G-spot with ease. "You gonna give me that?"

His lips covered her clit and his tongue snaked across the swollen flesh of it.

Gah. This man.

Her head fell back as he rubbed that magical spot and ignited sparks deep inside her core. "Yes," she managed to say, her voice coming out a bit breathless.

He lifted his head and removed his fingers. "Yes, who?"

Words? He wants words? She pushed her pussy toward his mouth. "Yes, *Tristan*."

He smiled wickedly before his head descended. His tongue flicked over her sensitive bud teasingly, fanning the flames of the fire but not giving her enough to tip her over. Like a cat to a mouse, he was toying with her.

More, more, more.

Keeping one hand flat on the counter to support her weight, she sunk her other into his hair and tugged his mouth even closer. "Oh, don't stop. Please."

Submerged between the lips of her pussy, he raised his mouth just enough to mumble, "Yeah, Angel. Ride my face. Use it to make yourself come." His hands moved to her hips and, without warning, he dragged her entire butt off the counter and planted her over his face.

Linking her hands behind his head, she shamelessly ground her pelvis on him. With the precision of a man who knew his woman well, he alternated between licking and nibbling her clit, the mix of pain and pleasure driving her arousal higher and higher. The stubble on his cheeks rubbed roughly on her inner labia and the point of his chin was inside of her, massaging her walls. As if she was the most delicious meal of his life, he grunted as he ate her, the vibration resonating throughout her pussy. The fire inside consumed her. All her muscles clenched in celebration as she reached her peak and exploded in toe-curling contractions.

She slid down his face, coming to rest against his chest. He lifted her into his arms and carried her into the other room, where he deposited her on the couch.

Legs curled under her, she watched her magnificent man undress. His biceps rippled as he whipped his shirt overhead to reveal the smooth golden skin of his chest. She followed his happy trail down, down, down to the bulge behind his jeans. With a snap and a pull of the zipper, he quickly removed his pants and stood before her completely naked, his engorged cock weeping at its tip.

Her mouth watered at the sight. Thank goodness she was now on birth control. She didn't think she could wait one more second to have him inside her.

She tore off her shirt and cupped her breasts as an offering.

He didn't hesitate to accept.

Sitting on the sofa, he tugged her onto his lap and reclined against the back cushion. He lifted her up and slowly fed her his cock, stretching her wide and not stopping until he completely filled her with his length.

In all these months, he'd never allowed her to be on top. She frowned, confused. Wouldn't that mean she was in control?

As if he had read her mind, he winked. "Trust me. I want you to ride my cock, Angel." Hands on her back, he leaned forward and captured a nipple between his teeth.

Pain flared first in her breast before spreading to her core. She moaned, driven to move, to increase the friction she needed to come again. She slid upward along his cock, but the sharpness of his bite kept her from rising as far as she wanted.

Now she understood. Even though she was on top, he remained in control.

Over and over, she lifted herself up and dropped herself down on his length, each time limited by his hold on her nipple. Her thighs trembled as she worked, sweat trickling down her neck.

She needed to go faster. Needed to lift higher and sink lower.

Turning off her mind and thoughts of pain, she let herself take what she needed, riding him almost to the tip before slamming herself down on his shaft. He didn't release his bite. In fact, she'd swear he bit harder. But she didn't care because the sharp pain in her nipple was worth the pleasure of his cock dragging along the sensitive walls of her inner channel.

Faster and faster she moved, creating the sweet friction she craved both inside and against her clit. Her pussy throbbed around him, squeezing him with every thrust as waves of pleasure crashed over her. Only seconds later, he pulsated inside of her, his cock twitching as hot come spurted from his tip, drenching her walls.

He let her nipple go and fell back onto the couch, laying her on top of him. She sighed, totally relaxed, and listened to his racing heart under her ear.

These moments made all the struggles worth it.

A few minutes later, Tristan reached out and swiped an envelope off the coffee table. "Oh yeah. I forgot. A letter came for you from the Lancaster Business School."

Ugh, probably another statement of account. Too comfortable where she was, she didn't bother looking. "Just put it with the rest of the mail."

He sat up, bringing her with him. A smile tugged at his lips. "I think you should open it, Angel."

Frowning, she ripped open the envelope and read its contents. As soon as she saw the word *congratulations*, her heart began to race with excitement. "Oh my God. I got into the business administration program." She stared up at Tristan. "But how? I didn't even apply."

"Professor Weaver recommended you, and the committee unanimously voted to admit you," he said, taking her hands in his. "I'm so proud of you. In almost three years, you'll graduate from the top business program in the state."

It was what she'd wanted. She was thrilled. But at the same time, a lump in the form of unshed tears had lodged in her throat. Admission into the program meant spending three years apart from Tristan.

"We haven't discussed what's going to happen when you leave in June," she said.

In addition to working his magic so that Isabella could remain in school, Dean Lancaster had also saved Tristan's job. Using the argument that she and Tristan had begun their "relationship" before the start of the school year, the dean convinced the disciplinary board that the policy didn't apply in their case. Tristan had merely received a verbal reprimand for his failure to disclose the relationship.

His brows furrowed. "Leave? Where am I going?"

"Back to the city. You have a company to run and grow. There's no possible way you won't get the financing you need now."

He nodded. "That's true. My credit score is up over one hundred points since August, and my loan officer assured me that Ryder and I will have no trouble getting the money for the expansion." He paused. "We decided to forgo the bank loan and took a different direction."

But the loan was the reason he had taken the job here. "What other direction?"

"Dean Lancaster has invested in Novateur in exchange for a third of the shares."

"But I thought you didn't want anyone else telling you how to run your business."

Tristan shrugged. "He's not just anyone. He's family."

She hugged him and kissed his cheek. "I'm so happy for you." And she was. But the thought of not waking up with him every morning or falling asleep in his arms every night brought those tears in her throat to her eyes.

"Are you?" He brushed away a tear with his knuckle. "Then why are you crying?"

"They're happy tears?"

"Happy tears," he said slowly. "So, you're happy that you and I will be separated by seven hundred miles?"

"Yes?"

His mouth screwed up into a grin. "Huh. That's too bad,

because I just signed a three-year contract with the university to teach all the Intro to Business classes."

Her breath caught in her chest. "You're not leaving?"

"Disappointed?"

How could she be disappointed when all her dreams were coming true? She kissed his cheek over and over. "You're not leaving."

The next thing she knew, he had a flat jewelry box in his hand. He must have gotten it from behind the couch cushion.

"There's nothing I wouldn't do for you, Angel," he said, a gleam in his eyes.

What was in that box?

She swallowed, her hands shaking. "I know that."

He cupped her cheeks. "But I didn't accept that contract for you. Coming here to Edison showed me there were things more important than money and success. I'd been wrong. I not only need a family, I already have one. Ryder is as close to me as any brother I could've had, and Isaac...well, he's been more of a father to me than the one on my birth certificate. This town, this university, is a part of my family. I can't walk away from it or the people I love."

He removed the top of the box, but a dark fabric hid the contents underneath. "I could never leave you, Angel. Not for a day. My home is with you, wherever the road takes you. Your fight is my fight. So while you finish your degree, I agreed to teach. And I'm not doing that just for you. I enjoy teaching and giving back a little of what Isaac gave to me."

Her pulse fluttered. "What about Ryder—?"

"He's fine with it. We'll make it work." He lifted the fabric and gently raised the jewelry from the box. "There's something else I'd like to discuss. I realize you're not ready for marriage or children—"

She gasped at the sight of the beautiful silver necklace he held out to her.

"But I'm a possessive bastard. I want my mark on you."

"I have your marks all over my body, you pervert," she said, laughing and crying at the same time.

"No one else can see those marks. A ring is a sign of possession, the circle a symbol of eternity. And as much as I'd love that band on your finger, I decided to go another route. One that is just as precious, just as permanent, if not more so, as a ring."

She tilted her head to the side, confused. "A necklace?"

"A collar," he explained. "My collar. A sign of my ownership of you. Of our commitment to one another. I understand if it's too—"

"It's perfect." She covered the hand holding the necklace with her own. "No one will know it's a collar though. They'll think it's just a necklace."

"I'll know. And if anyone looks closely, they'll see an engraving that says, 'Property of Tristan Kelley. If lost, please return to owner.'"

She grabbed the necklace from his hand and looked for an engraving. "It does not."

"No. But it is engraved." He pointed to the tiny etching.

She could read it herself, but she wanted to hear it from him. "What does it really say?"

"My fight is your fight—Forever, Tristan."

She lifted the hair off her shoulders. "Put it on for me?"

After hooking the silver around her neck, he ran his finger along the skin above the collar, his eyes glistening. "It's even more beautiful than I imagined."

She threw her arms around him and nestled into the crook of his neck. "So now that I'm wearing jewelry as sign that I belong to you, how will we show that you belong to me as well?"

He whispered into her ear. "You know the saying..."

"What?"

"If you like it, better put a ring on it."

This man. This beautiful man. She'd follow him to the ends of the earth and back again, so what made him think she wouldn't say yes if he asked her to marry him?

He was her destiny.

She peered up at him with a smile. "Let's go shopping."

About the Author

A sucker for a happy ending, Shelly Bell writes sensual romance and erotic thrillers. She began writing upon the insistence of her husband, who dragged her to the store and bought her a laptop. When she's not working her day job, taking care of her family, or writing, you'll find her reading the latest romance.

Learn more at:
ShellyBellBooks.com
Twitter @ShellyBell987
Facebook.com/ShellyBellBooks

Don't miss the thrilling, suspenseful
next installment of

Shelly Bell's Forbidden Lovers series—
featuring Ryder!

His to Claim

Available Spring 2018